GATES OF ETERNITY

Kathryn —
Tomorrow it no one
promised to no one—
Make each day count!

Bill
July 2022

Proverbs 27:1

Also by William H. Bishop:

Going Home: A Networking Survival Guide

The Currency of Leadership

Leadership in a Box: Developing a Networking Organization

GATES OF ETERNITY

William H. Bishop

Editing by Inked Stained Editing
Front cover image by Emily McCrea

Printed and bound in the United States of America
First printing June 2022

Published by The Cross and Pen
Virginia Beach, VA 23464

For Brooke and Megan, my twin joys—may you always remain in God's Word.

"Enter through the narrow gate. For wide is the gate and broad is the road that leads to destruction, and many enter through it."

       -     Matthew 7:13 (NIV)

Foreword

The 13th century leader, Francis of Assisi, once wrote a letter to leaders in which he admonished leaders to:

> *Consider and see that the day of death draws nigh. I ask you, therefore, with such reverence as I can, not to forget the Lord on account of the cares and solicitudes of this world and not to turn aside from His commandments, for all those who forget Him and decline from His commandments are cursed, and they shall be forgotten by Him. And when the day of death comes, all that which they think they have shall be taken away from them. And the wiser and more powerful they may have been in this world, so much the greater torments shall they endure in hell.*[1]

There is great wisdom in the admonition of this medicant prophet. The remembrance of death as a way to cultivate wisdom (*Memento Mori*) is well attested in the Sacred Scriptures. The Hebrew deliverer Moses prayed to the Lord to *"teach us to number our days that we may get a heart of wisdom"* (Psalm 90:12, ESV). Contemplating our mortality is

---

[1] (Robinson 1905) pp. 125-126.

a time-tested discipline of spiritual practice that desperately needs renewal in our fragmented world.

But what happens at the end? Jesus of Nazareth, towards the end of his earthly life, taught a parable in which he declared:

> *"When the Son of Man comes in his glory, and all the angels with him, then he will sit on his glorious throne. Before him will be gathered all the nations, and he will separate people one from another as a shepherd separates the sheep from the goats. And he will place the sheep on his right, but the goats on the left. Then the King will say to those on his right, 'Come, you who are blessed by my Father, inherit the kingdom prepared for you from the foundation of the world... Then he will say to those on his left, 'Depart from me, you cursed, into the eternal fire prepared for the devil and his angels... And these will go away into eternal punishment, but the righteous into eternal life." – Matthew 25:31-34, 41, 46, ESV*

A careful reading of this pericope unpacks four great truths:

1. Human history will come to an end.

2. Christ will return and judge the living and the dead in holiness.
3. Those who have followed His commandments will enter into eternal life with God.
4. The cursed will be sent away into everlasting punishment.

Dr. Bishop's riveting book invites us to consider these confronting realities and consider our place and fate in the final unveiling of history. Is it possible, at the end of time, that we will be able to join our voices to the question of Abraham, the Father of faith, *"shall not the Judge of all the earth do what is just?"* (Genesis 18:25, ESV). May we also find ourselves at that time dependent on His grace, overwhelmed by His mercy and love? Perhaps we will also be surprised by *"who's there, who's not there, and that I'm there."*[2] But what is certain is that we will know that *"salvation and glory and power belong to our God, for his judgments are true and just"* (Revelation 19:1-2, ESV).

May this provocative book serve as a remembrance of the certainty of our death and the final judgment

---

[2] John Newton, author of the hymn "Amazing Grace," as paraphrased by Dr. Craig L. Blomberg, (Blomberg 2020), p. 32.

and lead us to the wisdom of surrendering to the Lordship of Jesus Christ. Dr. Bishop invites us on a journey to consider the ultimate truth of our existence. May our ears, eyes, and hearts be open to these truths.

Corné J. Bekker, D. Litt. et Phil.
Dean
School of Divinity
Regent University

Sources:
Blomberg, Craig L. *Can we believe in God: Answering ten contemporary challenges to Christianity.* Grand Rapids: Brazos Press, 2020.

Robinson, Paschal. *The Writings of St. Francis of Assisi.* Public Domain, 1905.

Preface

Many years ago, my father said, "Something's going to kill you." It was part of a conversation regarding his health and life in general. For most of his life, he enjoyed good health. Except for high blood pressure, he was healthy and fit well into his seventies. One day while playing golf, he got out of breath walking up a hill to the green. He was later diagnosed with scar tissue on his lungs, most likely due to having been a smoker for much of his adult life. Fortunately, he quit when he was in his forties. As time passed, he ended up on oxygen. His illness progressed over time, and years later led to complications that ended his life. A man of tremendous faith, he was confident about what lay beyond this world and where he would spend eternity. He was also very accepting of the fact that his life would indeed end one day. Younger at the time, I didn't truly appreciate his perspective. Now, in my fifties, I have a profound respect and admiration for his insight. This life is fleeting. It passes by day by day, year by year, until the spring of our youth has become the winter of old age.

As the father of twin daughters, I have the privilege to experience the joy of a child's love times two. My definition of love changed the day I first held my daughters. Knowing that what some refer to as *agape* love means to love others more than yourself, and believing the Bible to be the complete, inerrant Word of God, I wanted to tell a story that would convict readers, including my daughters, and provide the incentive to seek God. So, with that in mind, I chose to tell this story from a teenager's perspective and identify fatal flaws in youthful thinking in order that my children, as well as adult readers, would be persuaded by the graphic descriptions that follow and accept Jesus as their Lord and Savior.

When I recalled my father's words and the peace he knew as he prepared to depart this world, I considered just how close eternity is for all of us — believers and non-believers alike. The choices we make in this life determine where we spend eternity. As the following story depicts, sometimes it is the choices of others that determines our fate. Isaiah said, "Seek the LORD while he may be found; call on him while he is near" (55:6, NIV). The purpose of this story is to impress upon the reader the imminence of eternity — Heaven and Hell — and to encourage all to call on the name of the Lord while there is time.

William H. Bishop
Virginia Beach
2022

Acknowledgements

This book was four years in the making. None of this would have been possible without God's grace and faithfulness. He truly is the Alpha and Omega, the Lord of lords, and King of kings. All glory goes to Him!

I'm eternally grateful to my wife, Barbara, for her unwavering love and support. I love you very, very, very MUCH—forever and a day!!!

To my father, you were the wisest man I ever knew! I am grateful for your spiritual example and wisdom.

And to Dr. James M. Boice, my unofficial mentor and inspiration. Your life inspired me, your sermons motivated me, and your presence is still with me. Thank you for your example. I'll see you on the flipside!

A very special thanks to Emily McCrea for revamping the cover at the last minute. Your talent and ability are unsurpassed and greatly appreciated!

Introduction

The Bible does not provide much detail on Hell, but it makes the point that it does exist and is very real. More importantly, it states non-believers will spend eternity there. This story is not intended to represent theological doctrine in terms of how Hell functions, its location, or what people experience. Nor is it intended to depict Heaven accurately. I am not a theologian and make no such claims. This work is intended to impress the imminence of eternity on the reader and the consequences of decisions made in this life. It was written with the purpose of sharing the Gospel and continuing Christ's work as he commanded in The Great Commission. I have taken creative liberty in interpreting biblical teaching and concepts to present a Christian perspective to the reader that I hope is persuasive and motivational.

1

"Move out of the way, Janel," Timothy Jones shouted to his fifteen-year-old sister while waving his hand back and forth to get her to move. Two years senior to him, she stood in front of the high-definition television, blocking his view.

Spreading her arms for dramatic effect, she paused and said, "Hello! It's a commercial!" With raised brows, she added insult to injury. "Duh."

Dropping her arms, she shook her head as she rolled her eyes, stepped out of the way, and fell backwards into an overstuffed, brown, microfiber chair adjacent to a matching sofa. The once plush arms were worn from excessive use, but it was still comfortable. With long her legs draped over the sides, she occupied herself with her smartphone. No longer a prepubescent teen, Janel was well on her way to becoming a young woman.

"Whatever," Timothy mumbled to himself, with a frustrated shake of his head. Sitting back on the sofa, he continued snacking on Cap'n Crunch. Out of school for the summer, he spent his days lounging in front of the television, playing with his friends, and watching sports. This morning he was catching up on baseball highlights on ESPN. It was the middle of baseball season, and he loved baseball.

When he was five years old, his now-deceased grandfather had taken him to a Yankees game at Yankee Stadium. The players appeared like giants atop the diamond and outfield. Wide-eyed, he had marveled at their skill and grace. His body had tingled with excitement the first time he heard the familiar crack of a wooden bat making contact with a baseball. Leaning forward in his seat, the roar of the crowd had been electrifying. In an instant, he was hooked. Beginning with tee-ball, he progressed to Little League baseball and was now the starting shortstop for his middle school team. Lean and agile, his wiry frame was well suited for the position.

"What are you doing today?" Janel asked, not taking her eyes off her phone.

"Nothing much," he replied, puffing his chest out as he crossed his lean, athletic legs with purposeful exaggeration and placed them on the coffee table. "Just chillin'. Maybe play some ball with the guys later—if it's not too hot. Gotta work on my game, ya know?"

"You got that right," she jibed at him.

Though the two got along for the most part, sibling rivalry was not lost between them. She seized every opportunity to give her baby brother a hard time.

He chuckled. "You know what I mean."

Janel laughed too. The oldest child, she had the honor — if it could be called that — of serving as a role model for her younger brother and substitute mother when the occasion demanded. When Timothy was younger, her maternal instinct kicked in and she took to mothering her baby brother. Now a teenager standing on the precipice of womanhood, she lorded over him but viewed it as more of a chore than a responsibility.

"Will you play at the park?" she asked, turning her head to face him.

Shifting his gaze from the television to Janel, he replied, "Probably. Why?" A puzzled expression wrinkled his face.

With pursed lips, she gave her head a shake. "No reason. Just curious." Lifting her head, she angled it in the direction of the kitchen and gestured with it. "I'm sure Mom will want me to keep an eye on you," she said in a low voice.

He shook his head, looking down as he did. Sitting up, he leaned toward her and spoke in a whisper. "I'm thirteen now. I don't need a babysitter."

"I know, I know," she said, acknowledging his protest. "You know how she is, though."

Timothy's eyes darted toward the kitchen and then back to Janel's. "I know. It's just…" A frown creased his youthful face as he shrugged, unable to find the words to express his exasperation.

In the kitchen, Thelma Jones finished tidying up and preparing her lunch. The television echoed in the background along with the voices of her children. A single mom nearing middle age, she juggled two jobs in order to make ends meet and provide for her children. Janel and Timothy's father had been in the picture only long enough to conceive them. While she regretted the rashness and foolishness of her youth, she never regretted having either of her children. "You're God's little blessings," she had told them when they were babies. And they were.

"Timmy?" she called.

"Yes, Mom?" Timothy answered.

Approaching the doorway, Thelma said, "If you go out, make sure your sister knows where you are, okay?"

"Uh-huh," he replied, an air of dismissiveness in his voice. His eyes never left the television.

"Excuse me?" Thelma said, stepping into the family room and piercing him with her eyes. Her voice possessed a slight lilt, the one often attributed to a superior who senses a lack of respect and sincerity from a subordinate in order to correct it.

Sitting up, Timothy looked at her, his eyes locked on hers as though in a tractor beam. "Yes, ma'am."

She nodded her approval, stared at him for a brief moment, and then returned to the kitchen. Verifying the contents of her lunch bag, she zipped the insulated container shut. In a louder tone, she spoke over her shoulder to Janel. "I'm going to put the Crock Pot on low, J. Just keep an eye on it."

"Okay, Mom," Janel replied.

Walking into the family room, Thelma said to both of them, "Don't forget I have Bible study tonight." Turning to Timothy, she added with a heart-warming smile, "I'll see Mr. Ennis there and pick up the baseball tickets."

Elation washed over Timothy's face and he bolted forward. "That's dope, Mom. Do you know where we're sitting?"

"No, I don't," she shook her head. "I got one for you too, J."

Janel produced an artificial smile. Timothy was the athlete in the family, not her. "Gee, thanks," she managed with raised brows and disingenuous gratitude.

"Oh, stop," Thelma said, throwing her a half wave. "You'll have a good time." Pivoting, she headed back toward the kitchen then stopped. With a quick glance over her shoulder, she added, "Your friends from youth group will be there." She disappeared through the doorway.

Timothy and Janel looked at each other and exchanged expressions of desperation. Janel rolled her eyes upward in a silent plea for help, shook her head, and mouthed, "Whatever." Fearing her mother's comments might be the impetus for another lecture about the perils of youthful folly, Heaven, Hell, and judgment from the Almighty above, Janel hopped up and announced, "I'll be in my room." As though fleeing the scene of a crime, she bounded up the steps to the sanctuary of her bedroom. Janel was at a tender age that revolved around her social life, boys—and avoiding her mother's fire and brimstone lectures. Church and the youth group weren't part of her agenda. With her mother's good looks, she was a teenage diva who was consumed with the wiles of the world.

Family room to himself, Timothy shifted his focus back to Sports Center. Hypnotized by the illuminated screen, he stared ahead as the faint scent of onions, garlic, and rosemary drifted into the modest family room.

"Did the Yankees win last night?" Thelma queried from the other room, disrupting his trance.

"Sure did! Six to one. I wish I could have seen it," he added. With only a basic cable package, Timothy was limited to regional games and those selected for primetime viewing. Due to their location in the south, the Atlanta Braves received more airtime than the Yankees.

Entering the family room, Thelma sat in the chair previously occupied by her daughter. She watched Sports Center for a moment in silence. Turning toward Timothy, a somber expression covered her face. "I know how much you enjoy watching baseball." She paused for a moment, and then, by way of apology, said, "There are more important things in this world than television and baseball."

Sunk into the deep cushion of the sofa, Timothy turned his head and met his mother's eyes. "I know, Mom. I just like to watch the games. We don't get too many Yankees games down here." His voice had a tinge of disappointment in it.

"I don't know where you get that from, son. We're in Braves' country down here!"

His face took on an exasperated expression. "Bunch of bandwagoners," he replied waving his arm dismissively. "The Braves are a bunch of hotdogs."

"Is that what your coach thinks?" she asked, to get his goad up.

"Nah," he said furrowing his brow. "He loves them, just like everyone down here. They just don't know any better." He laughed. Not long after Timothy was born, his and Janel's father abandoned them. Thelma's father, a widower, was only too happy to have them and allowed them to move in with him in upstate New York, where they had lived until he died of a massive coronary six years ago. An only child, Thelma was left with the burden of settling her father's estate, which consisted mostly of debt. The little equity he had had in his house and his modest savings went to pay his creditors. Thelma's inheritance amounted to a few family heirlooms and used furniture. Unable to afford the cost of living in the northeast, Thelma packed up her belongings and two children and headed south. Landing a job as medical assistant, she settled in Georgia, a stark contrast to her northern roots.

"Well, you know how it goes. Most people root for the home team. You're just an anomaly, I suppose," she said.

"Yeah, I guess I'm the black sheep of the family." He smirked at the racial reality of his proclamation.

Thelma laughed at his comment and stared at him. His boyish good looks were already beginning to fade. In their place were the handsome features of a young man.

"What?" he asked.

Snapping out of her momentary trance, she replied, "Nothing. You're just growing up so fast."

"Not fast enough," he insisted.

This forced a wry smile that dissipated as quickly as it had appeared. It seemed like just yesterday she and Timothy's father were bringing him home from the hospital. At the time, the future was bright, and happiness abounded. Glancing at the paneled walls in the family room, she was surrounded by pictures of Timothy, Janel, family members, and friends. Baby photos of Janel and Timothy along with the yearly school portraits and pictures with Santa covered the paneling. They were tangible reminders of accomplishments, festive occasions, and an historical record of times gone by. Turning her attention back to Timothy, she said, "Too fast for me. Don't be in a rush to grow up. You'll miss your youth soon enough."

Timothy remained silent, unsure how to respond to his mother's admonishment.

"I'm proud of you, Timmy," Thelma said, her voice sincere and genuine. "Life hasn't always been easy, but you haven't let it stop you from becoming an upstanding young man. I thank God for you and your sister every day."

"Thanks, Mom," he said, focusing all his attention on her. "And thanks for getting the tickets to the ballgame."

She smiled. "You're very welcome. Perhaps seeing your friends from youth group will inspire you to join them in the fall when Sunday school resumes."

He thought about this for a moment. "Maybe," he said by way of appeasement.

This brought a smile to Thelma's face. "Well," she announced as she stood, "I better finish getting ready for work."

"Okay," he said.

Bending forward, she leaned down, took his face in both of her hands, and kissed him on the forehead. "I love you, Timmy," she said, looking directly in his eyes.

"I love you too, Mom."

Touching his cheek, she said, "I pray for you every day."

Timothy just smiled. The topic of religion and God made him uncomfortable, mostly because none of his friends from school went to church, read the Bible, or prayed. He recalled one Sunday not so long ago, one of Timothy's friends knocked on the door to see if he wanted to play. Opening the door in his Sunday best, embarrassed, he explained, "I can't play right now." Pausing, he threw a rapid glance in the direction of the family room and then back to the open door. In a lower voice, he said, "I'll come find you after lunch," and pushed the door shut.

When Janel turned thirteen, she abandoned the youth group and abstained from church and church activities. When Timothy asked why she didn't want to go to church anymore, she explained, "I'm just not interested in God and church. I mean, I get why Mom's into it — single mom with friends at church — but I'm a teenager. I have my whole life ahead of me. Who wants to hear about death and consequences every week? Not me." She shook her head. Her comments stuck with him and in time swayed him. A few years later he began forming his own values and beliefs. He recalled his words to his mother.

"Mom, you said when I was old enough to decide for myself, I could. Well, I'm old enough, and I've decided. Besides," he added, "you let Janel make her own decision."

With great reluctance, Thelma relented. But she kept her word. She wasn't going to force her children to go to church or brow beat them with the Bible. That wasn't the way to salvation, and she knew it.

In the kitchen, Thelma double-checked the Crock Pot and put her dishes in the dishwasher. She liked a tidy kitchen, and a tidy house, for that matter.

As baseball scores flashed across the bottom of the screen, Timothy sat back and stretched his long, athletic legs out across the coffee table and watched the highlights. Watching an acrobatic double play involving the Yankees' star shortstop, Timothy cheered, "Yes, Didi! That's what I'm talkin' about!"

Thelma smiled at her son's enthusiasm as she zipped her lunch box closed and prepared to head out to work. "What did Didi do now?" She was all too familiar with the Yankees' starting shortstop, whose pictures adorned the walls of her son's room.

"Double play—but it wasn't just a double play, Mom. He fielded a one-hop grounder, tagged the bag, spun around, and threw the ball to first while in mid-air. It was awesome!"

"That sounds pretty awesome," Thelma agreed, as she smiled at her son's unwavering enthusiasm.

The highlight reel moved on to another team, and Timothy's attention was permanently glued to the sofa's cushions in preparation for a lazy morning. Reaching for a handful of cereal, he was distracted by the sudden interruption of shouting voices outside. As he was about to turn and investigate their source, the room went black.

2

Confused and bewildered, Timothy felt like he was being sucked through a narrow vacuum tube.

"What's going on?" he wondered as he tried to figure out where he was and what was happening. Brilliant white light surrounded him, blinding him, as he floated along the invisible pipeline. Having been freed from his body, he was weightless. Unable to move, he was trapped inside the vortex like a butterfly in a cocoon. As though a switch had been thrown, the light was gone. Snuffed out like a candle, complete and total darkness overwhelmed him.

"Hello?" he screamed.

The solitary response was unequivocal isolation. More than just being alone, for the first time he experienced the absence of something—love, perhaps—as though he had been abandoned and forsaken and had no value.

In the solitude of the darkness, his spirit began descending like an elevator in freefall. Though he had no reference, he was aware he was falling and at a high rate of speed, as though he were a lead weight sinking to the bottom of the ocean. Without warning, he felt heat, tremendous heat unlike anything he'd ever experienced. Perpetual and growing in intensity, the heat stifled and suffocated. Amid the swelter, a booming echo crept up and surrounded him. Like a bass drum, its tone was low and forceful, vibrating through his soul like ripples on a pond. Deciphering the sound, he realized it was a laugh—a sinister, evil laugh—the laugh of someone, or something, that takes pleasure in the misery and suffering of others. The predominant sound in the din of darkness, the laugh was deafening and consumed him. Raw fear began to well up inside of him. It was the fear of impending doom from which there was no escape; he was trapped in the void and unable to move or even tremble.

Still descending, his speed increased exponentially. Moving ever faster, a putrid stench overcame him. "What is that smell?" he asked himself. There was no air, yet he sensed a rancid odor—the smell of extinguished coals and decay and…death. But not in the way a rotting corpse assaults the olfactory sense. That would have been pleasant by comparison. This was different in a way he couldn't comprehend or articulate.

A red glow illuminated below him like a hot coal on a dark night. It intensified in brightness as he free fell toward it. Without warning, he came to a complete and sudden stop as he hit something solid — the ground perhaps? Feeling as though he had landed in a frying pan, his spirit seared, enveloped by the intense heat. Diaphanous strands of dim, red light intermittently broke the darkness, providing more shadow than illumination. Disoriented, he looked around and tried to ascertain his whereabouts. *Was this a dream?* he wondered.

Standing, he looked around. Entangled in the faint, red light was a multitude of silhouettes. Traces of red speckled them, highlighting bits and pieces of what appeared to be an infinite number of shadows. Not human, they resembled humans but in a grotesque manner, like images in Fun House mirrors. Twisted, maligned, and contorted, they were all hideous and grotesque in their individual disfigurement. Enveloped by heat, they occupied the crowded space and stared at the new arrival.

Turning to his left, Timothy saw a large figure emerge from the group. "Got another one," he grunted, looking down. His voice was laced with a deep, southern drawl. To Timothy, he looked like a hillbilly and reminded him of a county bumpkin of sorts. Corn Fed was the term that came to mind.

"Where am I?" Timothy gasped. Although there was no air, he felt short of breath.

Corn Fed stared at him with a blank expression.

From behind Timothy, a shrill voice that reminded him of an angry old lady said, "Waiting."

"Huh?" Timothy asked.

Like nails on a chalkboard, the voice repeated, "Waiting. That's where you are, what this place is." Turning around, Timothy saw a decrepit, hideous figure of what used to be a woman. Old, wrinkled, ashen, and covered in scabs and decay, she reminded him of a drowning victim. He thought of her as Grandma.

"Waiting for what?" he asked.

Grandma pointed a crooked finger.

Following her finger, Timothy stared at towering, twin doors in the distance. Menacingly tall and formidable, they reminded him of doors that would lead to a dungeon. The only source of light, they glowed red like molten lava and seemed to burn brighter the longer he stared at them. Intense, smoldering heat radiated from their direction.

"What's that?"

"You'll find out," she spat. "We all will." Her voice echoed with a tinge of finality that was filled with hopelessness.

"I don't understand," he said, frustrated. "What—"

Suddenly the massive doors burst open, and what he could only identify as a creature emerged. Frozen with panic, Timothy stared at the creature in horror and watched as it waded forward. With each step, it trailed hot coals, molten rock, brimstone, and a consuming surge of heat that seared what used to be Timothy's skin. As it did, a fetid odor enveloped him and saturated his soul.

"What is that smell?" Timothy asked, his voice trembling.

"Dying souls," Grandma provided.

Dying souls? he repeated to himself, not understanding. The smell was beyond feculent. Had he been able, he most surely would have vomited. Nevertheless, the stench was nauseating.

Staring in the direction of the creature, Timothy asked, "What is that?"

Corn Fed spoke up. "We call him the Beast."

Almost prehistoric in appearance, the Beast was clad in scaled, black, reptilian skin. Its face was wrinkled and disfigured with a permanent expression of intense malevolence. Gruesome and sinister, it was the face of pure evil. Large, fanged teeth jutted up from its bottom jaw, resting on either side of a primitive snout from which smoke and fire spewed with each exhalation. Curved horns protruded upward from each side of its head, their points sharp and menacing. The Beast was mammoth. Towering above the souls, it dwarfed them. With large, muscular arms and a barreled chest, it possessed enormous strength. The entire waiting area shook with each step, its clawed feet striking the ground with thunderous purpose. Most frightening of all, it had red, piercing, lifeless eyes.

"What is the Beast?" Timothy asked.

No one answered.

With the molten doors open, Timothy detected a faint, high-pitched sound that reminded him of static. It had a subtle metallic tone similar to buzzing bees in the distance. Feeling the screech in his soul, it radiated outward, resonating the very essence of his being, and crawled all over him like a swarm of fire ants.

In a whisper, Timothy leaned toward Grandma and asked, "What is that sound?"

After a brief hesitation, she turned and stared at him. A somber expression covered her disfigurement, and she said, "It's the screams of the damned." There was no emotion in her voice, only recognition and defeated acceptance.

He held her gaze and stared in disbelief. Looking back at the open doors, Timothy shuddered at what he saw. The area beyond the massive doors was consumed by fire. Erupting from the ground, it shot up in all directions and consumed the entire space like a giant incinerator.

As the Beast approached the waiting area, Timothy froze in fear.

Studying the group of disfigured souls with his beady eyes, the Beast raised its prehistoric hand and in single, swift motion snatched a spirit from the waiting area. Satisfied, it pivoted and strode back to the intense furnace. The spirit screamed and wailed with the piercing shrill of absolute fear — fear of the inescapable reality and permanency of unending and unbearable suffering. For a moment, it struggled in a vain attempt but to no avail. It was useless. There was no escape!

When the doors shut, Timothy turned to Grandma. His voice shook as he asked, "What is this place? What's going on? I– I don't understand."

"You will," Corn Fed said. "You will. When you have your re-live."

"My what?" Timothy asked.

"Your re-live. Your final moments alive. It'll explain how you got here."

Timothy shook his head. "What are you talking about? What is…"

His thoughts were interrupted. In an instant, his final moments flashed before him. As if watching a movie in his mind, he saw his neighbor across the street, Mr. Cavanaugh, in a scuffle with a man he didn't recognize. Mr. Cavanaugh was an Army veteran and retired. He spent the mornings sitting out front reading the paper and having his coffee. This morning, a deranged man thought he would make easy prey and attempted to rob him. He was wrong.

As much as Timothy strained, he could not hear their voices. Instead, they were muffled and garbled. When the man produced a gun, Mr. Cavanaugh's Ranger training kicked in. He sprang into action and began to wrestle with gunman. The two men were locked together in a combative dance. Timothy watched as their arms moved upward in unison and then dropped. Pivoting, their arms straight out, the sudden report of the firearm discharging startled Timothy and he jumped. "I never heard that," he said to no one.

His view shifted, and he followed the wayward nine-millimeter projectile. He heard the sound of the bullet as it penetrated the double-paned glass of his family room's bay window. It made a crackling sound, the kind an ice cube makes when being crushed before bursting. He stared in disbelief as the spinning copper jacket entered the back of his skull; the bullet's kinetic energy propelled his head forward with the violent force of a baseball bat. Death was instantaneous. His body went limp before slumping over and falling face-first on the carpeted floor.

"Timmy, what's all that commotion in there?"

He stared straight ahead, not seeing anything except the image in his mind's eye. He heard his mother's voice and watched her enter the living room. Rushing to his side, his body was laying facedown, a pool of blood oozing from a large divot in the back of his head. Kneeling next to his lifeless body, she screamed, "Timmy!" Looking up, she cried, "Oh, Jesus, no! Please, no!"

Janel ran into the room. Seeing her mother on the floor next to her lifeless brother, she brought her hands to her mouth and screamed, "Oh, my God! What happened?"

"Dial 911," her mother barked, never taking her attention away from Timothy, whom she was now cradling.

Janel hesitated at first, frozen in panic. Thelma looked up at her. Staring into her daughter's eyes, Thelma screamed, "Do it!"

Panning right, Timothy saw Mr. Cavanaugh. Straddling the would-be burglar, who was pinned to the ground, his wife stood in the doorway with a phone pressed to her ear. The handgun responsible for ending Timothy's life lay well out of reach on the porch.

The movie screen in his mind went blank. He blinked; his new reality came back into focus. Still in disbelief, he brought his right hand to the back of his head. He probed the area and felt a dry, gaping hole. Surveying his current situation, he asked, "I'm dead?"

"Yup," Corn Fed said.

"We're all dead," Grandma added.

He shook his head in the violent manner of someone receiving unpleasant news. "I can't be dead. I can't! Not me. I was sitting on my sofa watching TV. I'm going to a baseball game with my mom," he protested.

"That's what we all said," Grandma replied. Corn Fed just stared at him, a somber expression covering his face.

"You don't understand," he pleaded. "I'm just a kid."

Corn Fed spat a laugh. It was a solitary exhalation. "Age ain't got nothing to do with it, Youngin'," he said. "Here we're all equally worthless."

Confused, Timothy asked, "What is this place?"

In a voice overflowing with sadness and despair, Grandma answered, "This is the waiting."

"Waiting? Waiting for what?" Timothy questioned.

She didn't reply. Instead, her gaze shifted to the twin molten doors that loomed the distance.

3

"Hello, fall," freshman Lauren Moore said to herself in the brisk morning air as she trekked across the rural college campus a few hours after dawn. Its lush foliage and isolation were two of the reasons she had chosen it. Wearing a university hoodie, jeans, and with a backpack over her shoulders, she was just one of many in the collegiate army of meandering students. Located on the coast of Maine, it was remote and served as a substitute for the Tennessee country town in which she had grown up. A self-contained city in the middle of nowhere, it was free of the hustle and bustle that epitomized many universities. Although held in high regard for its academic programs, and with a nationally ranked athletic program, it remained quaint and inviting.

Just ahead of her on the concrete path, she caught to up Jenny, whose blonde ponytail was swaying back and forth underneath a white university baseball cap. A fellow country girl from Kentucky, the two had met during student orientation over the summer. She was a familiar face in a new environment.

"Hey, Jenny," Lauren said, matching her stride and nudging her with her elbow.

27

"Hi," Jenny replied, turning toward her with a warm smile and nudging her back. "Ready for two hours of lecture?" she asked with a wry grin. Her comment was in reference to the History of Ancient Civilizations, a core requirement for freshmen.

Lauren rolled her eyes and shook her head for dramatic effect as she considered the question. "Ugh! Not really," she grumbled. "Are you?"

"Definitely not! I'll be lucky to stay awake," she said.

"Yeah, me too," Lauren echoed her sentiment.

The two fell into silence, each lost in their own thoughts. Lauren pondered the newest chapter in her life—college. On the distant horizon, orange streams of sunlight burst through slits in the gray clouds of dawn as a new day came to life. The fall air was cool, crisp, and refreshing and had the unmistakable scent of the country, something she missed during her first time away from her family.

Amid the morning air, the slight almost imperceptible scent of a distant fire competed for recognition. Lauren tilted her head backward slightly and took a deep inhalation. "This weather reminds me of Tennessee," she announced. "Football and bonfires." Memories of her not-so-distant past brought a smile to her face.

"Tell me about it," Jenny concurred. "Every Friday night in the fall my family had a bonfire on the farm. My friends from high school would come over after the game, and we'd hang out all night. Willie, my younger brother, and the starting running back, would break out his guitar, and we'd all sing campfire songs. It was the best." She paused, a sudden wave of melancholy washing over her. "Gee, I miss that." A tinge of sadness filled her voice at the realization her youth had dissipated like the morning fog.

Lauren nodded. "I hear ya. We used to cook hot dogs on a stick right over the fire." Thinking about it for a minute, she said, "I could really go for a hot dog cooked over a fire."

Jenny laughed. "For breakfast?"

Lauren smirked, her brown eyes twinkling as the morning sun reflected in them. "Well, maybe not for breakfast...but lunch? Oh, yes!" She paused. "And a big side of potato salad."

"They have hot dogs in the cafeteria," Jenny offered.

"Eew," Lauren replied. "They're gross. Cooked on that roller. Yuck!" Her face screwed into a brief grimace. "Thanks. I'll pass."

"Hey, just trying to help."

As they strode along, Lauren marveled at the collage of colors the fallen leaves provided — red, yellow, orange, and brown. Not releasing their grip, many still clung to the tree branches overhead. Soon they would join the others littered about on the ground and path. Just ahead, a mammoth stone structure loomed — Sutton Hall — their destination. Built in the late 1800s, its interior had been renovated several times to keep up with student demands, modernization, and technical requirements. Its exterior, though, remained unchanged. Twin concrete spires loomed above a large, oval plate-glass window that sat atop oversized wooden doors. Clad in hand cut stone, the building was a tribute to masonry skill and prowess. The architectural behemoth was where several freshman classes were held. Replete with classrooms, several lecture halls, and hallways littered with faculty offices, it was one of the main buildings on the expansive campus.

"The food isn't bad here," Jenny observed, continuing on the subject, "but it's nothing like home. We raise our own chickens. My mom makes the best fried chicken," she said. "Serves it with her 'secret recipe,'" — she made air quotes — "mac and cheese. It's to die for."

"What makes it so secret?" Lauren probed.

With a laugh, Jenny said, "Nothing really. I mean, we all know the recipe, which is nothing more than seven cheeses, heavy cream, and butter, but she acts like she's the only one who does."

"That's funny," Lauren smirked. "It sounds really good."

"Yeah, it is. Baked until a golden-brown crust forms on top," she explained. "Even though it's very filling, there are never any leftovers." Jenny paused, thinking about her mother and home. It still didn't seem real to her — college, moving away, starting a new chapter of her life. As she matured, her mother had become her best friend and confidant, a role model, who wanted her daughter to have a good life.

A wisp of wind tickled Jenny's face, bringing her back to reality. With thoughts of her mother fresh in her mind, she added, "You'd like my mom. She's a hoot."

"She sounds it," Lauren agreed. "My mom cooks too. More baking than cooking, though. I asked her to send me some cookies and banana bread. Of course, I'll share."

Jenny smiled. "I look forward to it."

Approaching the monolith, Lauren and Jenny climbed the twin rows of stone steps designed to enhance its austerity and entered through a large, dark, wooden door that looked like it belonged on a medieval church. The school took great pride in its history and architecture.

"I could use a hot cup of coffee," Jenny said.

"Me too," Lauren agreed.

Inside the oversized vestibule, the familiar aroma of coffee greeted them. They both turned right in unison and headed to a modest snack shop tucked away in the corner. Beverages, pastries, and premade breakfast sandwiches were among the offerings, along with an assortment of chips, cookies, and candy. Apples, bananas, and oranges were available while they lasted.

Three rows of students, faculty, and staff members moved forward and to the side as waiting baristas routinely accepted their orders. Cards were inserted, chips read, PINs entered, and transactions completed as the morning melee continued to its own rhythm.

Standing in the middle line, Lauren remarked, "I can't wait until fall break. It seems like I haven't been home in forever."

Jenny nodded. "Me too. I miss my family, especially Puggles," she said. "When I FaceTime, my mom holds the phone up to him. I talk to him, he looks around, but he doesn't know where I am. Dogs are funny."

Lauren smiled. "Yeah, I miss my family too. Even my little sister," she said with a laugh. "This will be the first year I won't be there for hunting season."

"Yeah, me too," Jenny said. "Dad mentioned it the other day."

"My dad promised to get a deer for me," Lauren said and they moved forward in line.

"Aw. That's cool. Venison in time for the holidays," Jenny said.

"Definitely! My mom makes stew with it, gets the meat really tender. We gobble it up," Lauren said. "I'd offer to bring some back after break, but there won't be any left."

"I bet. We cut ours into steaks and grind some up for burgers."

"Really? I never thought about making burgers with it."

Reaching the counter, they ordered their coffees, and Jenny paid.

"Thanks. I'll get it next time," Lauren said.

"Oh, no problem. It's only a coffee," Jenny said, flashing her country girl smile.

Standing at the end of the counter, they continued discussing hunting and all things country.

"Yeah, one year, my dad on a whim, added some of it to the ground beef while my mom was making burgers. Makes a fifty-fifty mixture. It's a different taste, but if you like venison, it's good."

"Huh. I'll have to mention that to my dad," Lauren said.

"Try it. It's really good. Everyone looks forward to them, especially on game nights."

"Back in Tennessee, the biggest game of the year was homecoming," Lauren explained. "The night before, my high school would hold a pep rally and have a huge bonfire afterward. The cheerleaders, including yours truly,"—she gave a slight curtsey—"cheered and the marching band played. It was awesome." Her face glowed with exuberance. "We'd go to someone's house afterward, sit outside around the fire and have a few beers."

"Our homecoming wasn't quite as elaborate," Jenny said. "I went to a private Christian school, so they didn't get too crazy. We had a pep rally in the gym followed by refreshments and snacks."

"No bonfire?" Lauren asked with genuine surprise.

"Not officially, no. We had one afterward on my farm."

34

"Hmm," she observed as they picked up their steaming cups of java at the end of the counter.

Paper cups in hand, they proceeded down a long corridor toward the lecture hall. Paved in alternating brown and tan Linoleum tile, the hallway's checkered pattern reminded Lauren of a game board. Turning to her right, Lauren leaned into the door and pushed it open with her shoulder as Jenny followed behind.

Several good mornings were exchanged as students seated at the front table looked up in acknowledgement.

"Hey, Steve," Lauren said, passing an athletic young man standing just inside the door.

"What's up, Lauren? Hey, Jenny," he acknowledged with a grin.

"Hi, Stevo," Jenny smiled.

Leaning into her, Lauren said, "He likes you!"

"Stop," Jenny protested, embarrassed, as they made their way behind a row of cushioned chairs.

"What? He's cute."

"He is, but I have a boyfriend back home."

"Oh, c'mon. It's college," Lauren prodded.

"I know, but we've been together for two years."

Lauren's brow raised in disbelief. "High school sweethearts?" she asked, her voice raising an octave as she did.

"Yup," Jenny nodded.

"Oh, please. In this day and age? You're a college woman now. You can get serious after you graduate. It's time to have fun and hook-up."

"I may be a 'college woman,' but hooking up isn't for me," Jenny insisted. "I'm saving myself for marriage."

"Whatever," Lauren said, her face wrinkled with a perplexed expression. "You're the one missing out."

The room was a miniature lecture hall comprised of five ascending levels, each lined with curved tables complete with electrical outlets. Lauren and Jenny always sat in the front row, believing that doing so conferred a measure of confidence as well as offering a modicum of favor.

Slinging their backpacks onto the table, the two took their seats. Retrieving her laptop from her backpack, Lauren fired it up while waiting for class to begin.

Sipping her coffee, she said, "I hope class goes fast today."

"Me too," Jenny said.

"Today is a nice day for a run."

"Yeah. It sure is. Perfect weather. Let me know what time you're going, and I'll go with ya."

"You got it," Lauren said.

With ten minutes before class was scheduled to begin, Lauren stretched and yawned as she glanced around the room. It was half full but would fill quickly in the next few minutes. Her fellow students preferred to cut it closer than she did. The professor, who was known for his punctuality, always arrived right on time and did had ill regard for tardiness.

"Don't yawn," Jenny admonished as she yawned herself.

"Sorry," Lauren said. "Can't help it," she added, fighting back a second one. "I was up late finishing the reading for today's lecture."

"I just skimmed it," Jenny confessed.

As Lauren's computer completed the power-on booting process, the screen's transformation from a black screen to one of her family caught her eye. Standing in front of a red tractor, she and her younger brother were flanked by her mother and father. Shifting her attention, she clicked an icon and was on the Internet courtesy of the university's Wi-Fi in seconds. Logging into her email, she clicked on one from her mother and began reading.

Her reading was abruptly interrupted.

"What the—" Lauren exclaimed, as the room fell silent. In the hallway, a succession of sharp reports rang out followed by screams and shouts. Like firecrackers popping, they pierced the normal cacophony of students roaming the hallway. Startled, her eyes jumped to the door as it burst open, and a young Asian man with short hair, wielding a large silver handgun, entered the room.

"Dara?" she murmured.

Catching a crazed look in his eye, Lauren froze. Frightened. Scared. Terrified. Students screamed, pleaded, hurled expletives, begged for mercy, shouted instructions, and cried out for help as they sought cover in the confined space.

Aiming without deliberation, he discharged the weapon at random targets as they scattered.

"No!" Jenny shouted.

Pop, pop, pop. Students dove for cover behind the expansive tables and chairs. They were no match for the barrage of bullets that easily penetrated the cushioned material and particleboard. Those hit fell to the ground and dropped where they were. Lauren was just about to dive for cover when Jenny slumped forward. As her head turned toward her, it made a dull thud on the table. With a surprised look on her face, her lifeless eyes stared through Lauren as blood began to trickle from her mouth.

That was the last thing Lauren ever saw.

4

Staring at the molten doors, Timothy pondered what lay beyond them. As he stared at them, the initial fear he had sensed upon arrival paled in comparison to what he felt now. It had intensified to a level he had never experienced or thought possible. This place was indescribable. Scorching, dank, putrid, and devoid of life, it was far worse than any nightmare or horror movie.

"What's in there?" he asked, almost to himself.

"Eternal misery, gnashing of teething, the lake of fire, brimstone, and burning sulfur," a screeching voice announced. It belonged to a tall, thin, stick-figure of a soul. His steely voice reminded Timothy of nails slowly being dragged across a chalkboard. From his time in Sunday school, Timothy recalled the terms he used and what they described.

"You mean..." his voice trailed off in disbelief.

"Hell," Sticks deadpanned. "The Devil's playground. The prison where the damned are incarcerated forever without the possibility of parole." He paused. Then, in a whisper, he added, "Our fate."

His explanation was too much for Timothy to comprehend. He shook his head in defiance and denial.

"No!" he shouted. "No." He shifted his gaze toward Sticks. "This can't be real," he pleaded. "It just can't. This is some kind of nightmare."

"It's real, I'm afraid. All too real," Sticks lamented.

"Hell is an eternal nightmare," Grandma said. It was a statement, not an opinion or hyperbole.

Timothy just stared at her in disbelief. More to himself than Sticks, he said, "I didn't think Hell really existed."

During one of the last sermons he had endured before opting out of church, he vividly remembered his pastor's passionate message.

"Whatever one can imagine and construe as pain and torment based on earthly experience is a far cry from Hell," the pastor had said. "It is the ultimate in unabated misery." His fist thumped the pulpit. "Perhaps due to a lack of God's presence, the flaming palace of the damned provides complete and total suffering—forever! In Hell's inferno, hope is non-existent. Only abysmal finality exists. Unending torture and suffering awaits the nonbelievers." He manned the pulpit like a captain on the bridge of ship. "The murderers, rapists, sexually immoral, and the wicked all have reservations at the fiery resort of the ungodly. There will be no mercy, no pardon, or commuting of one's sentence. Non-believers will spend eternity paying for their sins. None are innocent." Quoting Paul, he concluded, "All have sinned and fallen short of God's glory."

Shrugging off his pastor's words, Timothy said, "No, I can't be going to Hell. I can't! I'm only a kid."

Corn Fed, Grandma, and Sticks just stared at him in abject silence for a moment.

"Hell does not discriminate," Grandma said at last.

In a moment of brief cognition, Timothy announced, "You said this was the waiting area. Maybe we're not all waiting for the same thing."

Grandma managed a slight smirk. "No, I'm afraid we are all waiting for the inevitable." Her voice came out flat and hollow.

Timothy's reasoning was a feeble attempt to deny the obvious, one the others had made upon their arrival to no avail. With great reluctance and extreme regret, they had accepted the full import of their situation. He would too.

As Timothy opened his mouth to continue his objection, several new spirits arrived in rapid succession, crowding an already crowded area. Lauren was one of them. Timothy observed her and noticed a gaping in hole in what had been her forehead. Although disfigured, he could tell she was young, though not as young as him. Glancing around, Timothy noted there weren't many young spirits in the waiting area. As the only one close to him in age, he felt a connection to Lauren, like a little brother to his big sister. As he studied her, the doubt and disbelief began to vanish, and Timothy started to accept the finality of this horrible, evil place.

With a quizzical, confused expression, she surveyed her new surroundings. She recognized several of her former classmates, including Steve. She didn't see Jenny. Disoriented, she began asking questions. "Where am I?"

No one was in a rush to answer. Timothy nudged her. "Waiting," he said, providing the same answer he had been given. Though there was no protocol, per se, he reasoned he might as well give the same answer he received.

"Waiting? Waiting for what?" she asked.

"You'll see soon enough, dear," Grandma answered.

"What do you mean?" she protested. "Where am I? Tell me!"

"Just give it a few, young lady," Corn Fed said. "You'll understand before too long."

"I don't want to wait. I want to know now," Lauren demanded. "This must…"

Her voice trailed off, and she froze. Images of her final moments flashed before her eyes. In rapid succession, she relived the slaughter that had sentenced her to a life of eternal damnation. She saw her fellow classmate brandish a weapon and open fire in the hallway before entering the classroom. In slow motion, her eyes followed the projectiles as they hit their targets, including her. As quickly as it had begun, her re-live ended. When it was over, she shuddered at the terror.

"What was that? Did that really happen?" she wanted to know. "Is this some kind of a dream?"

"No, dear," Grandma said. "It's not a dream. This is a real as it gets, I'm afraid."

Disbelief consumed her. Lauren turned to Timothy. Horrified, she began her protest. "No! No, there's no way," she exclaimed. "I can't be…" She struggled to say the word. "Dead," she managed at last, her voice barely a whisper. "I can't be. I can't. I have my whole life ahead of me. I worked so hard to get into college. I have a solid GPA and killer standardized test scores. Do you know how many short lists I'm on?"

Her diatribe fell on deaf ears. In Hell, there was no one to reason with, no one with whom to share one's story, no one to listen to a plea. Though all would gladly bargain if they could, that option did not exist. The Beast did not bargain, nor did he hear confessions. Confessions belonged to the Ruler of Light. Bargaining is been done in life — bargaining for fame, fortune, status, knowledge, and pleasure. All that existed here was misery and finality. There was nothing for which to bargain and trade away one's soul.

Rejection and the refusal to accept one's fate were part of the process. Lauren looked at Timothy. Young like her, she searched his face for reassurance or a shred of hope but found none. He just stared at her and shook his head.

"No," she said to no one in particular. "No. This isn't fair!" She couldn't believe that such a horrendous act could have occurred at a college, *her* college. "How could this happen?"

Grandma snickered. "We've all asked ourselves that, dear. How, indeed?"

Bewildered, Lauren asked, "How did you get here?"

"Old age, my dear. Old age." If she could have laughed at the irony she would have, but laughter did not exist. "Ironically, I lived a long life. Died of natural causes."

Lauren tried to comprehend her words. "So what did you do to end up here?"

"What did you do, dear?" Grandma shot back at her. "Tell me, what did you do to end up here?"

"Nothing," Lauren retorted, shaking her head. "I didn't do anything."

"Neither did I," Grandma said, her voice steely cold. "Neither did I."

"Me either," Timothy added. "I was just sitting on my sofa, minding my own business."

Lauren shifted her gaze to Corn Fed and Sticks, who both nodded their heads in agreement.

In utter denial, she shook her head from side to side. "This is some kind of dream or hallucination," she reasoned. Reflecting on her choice of universities, she thought back to the exhaustive pre-college process she had endured with her mother and father. After touring almost a dozen universities strewn across the northeast and mid-Atlantic region, she had made her decision with ease. From her first moment on campus, the picturesque landscape felt like home. It was quiet and low-key, just like her.

Shifting her gaze from Timothy to Grandma and back to Timothy, she pleaded, "No! Please, no!" She paused. "Why? Why me? I didn't do anything wrong. I don't deserve to be here."

"I don't deserve it either," Timothy said reluctantly. He then recalled his time in Sunday school and church, the many activities with his youth group, and his mother's involvement in the church. "I mean, I don't think I do."

"You might think you don't, but I *know* I don't! I didn't do *anything* to deserve this," Lauren protested, anger singeing her voice.

In the middle of her interrogation, a familiar spirit materialized. It belonged to the young man who had unleashed the carnage in the classroom — the one who ended her life, as well as the others', and sentenced her and them to a fiery eternity. Bewildered and confused as someone roused from deep sleep, he struggled to take in his surroundings. His eyes settled on Lauren, his face frozen in shock.

"Lauren?" he asked.

Unable to cope with the deluge of reality, Lauren stared at her assailant for a moment in stunned silence. Words escaping her, she simply questioned, "Why?"

There was no time for a response. The great doors burst open, releasing a scorching surge of heat that enveloped them. Like a soldier, the Beast marched forward. Trailing behind him, the wail of the damned was piercing. Their number was so great that individual voices could not be distinguished. Rising from the surface of the Lake of Fire, they melded together in a high-pitch screech. The Beast strode forward with precision in the direction of the newly arrived spirit. Surrounding the Beast was the fetid odor of death and decay.

Covered in fear, Lauren did not move. Her eyes were glued to the Beast. Moving her lips as little as possible, she asked, "Wha- what- What is that?"

"The Beast," Timothy supplied.

Approaching the fresh soul, the Beast plucked the shooter's spirit from the waiting area. Pivoting, he turned and began to wade back to his fiery abode. His grip on the soul was an iron vice from which there was no escape. The flailing was of no use. With each giant step, eternal misery grew closer. Timothy stood next Lauren and watched in awe until the massive doors slammed shut.

"Dara?" Lauren said.

"Who's Dara?" Timothy asked.

Lauren's gaze remained fixed on the twin doors for a moment. Slowly she turned toward Timothy. "He's the one the Beast, as you called him, dragged in there." She paused. "He's the one who killed me."

Timothy stared at Lauren, a surprised look on this face as he considered her revelation. Returning his attention to the molten doors, he thought, *Apparently those who sentence others to Hell take precedence.*

5

The paramedics arrived on scene at mid-afternoon within minutes of receiving the desperate call. Bloxom County Fire Department was headquartered in the remote farm area of northern Virginia, only a few miles away from the crash on Lankford Highway, better known as Route 13. Serving as a main corridor along the east coast, the highway was replete with speed changes based on state, principality, and proximity to business districts.

The rural area allowed traffic to surge along at over sixty miles per hour but required slowing to thirty-five for brief periods in congested areas. Shopping districts and urban areas dotted the landscape at infrequent intervals. With the Atlantic Ocean to the east and the Chesapeake Bay on the west, Virginia's eastern border served as a dividing line between the two. Dangling just below Maryland, the narrow peninsula was home to farmland and businesses alike.

Steve Johansen was a veteran paramedic and first responder with over ten years' experience. A Texas native, he was outsized in every way and epitomized the stereotype. Good-natured, boisterous, and daring, he was a testament to his profession. Today was his turn to drive, which was no easy task because all southbound lanes were stopped.

"What the...?" Steve said, his voice filled with frustration at the bottleneck of traffic blocking the road.

"Shoulder, shoulder," Dale Griggs, his partner, shouted, pointing to the right. Dale was younger and less-experienced than his partner, but he was a solid paramedic. Born and raised in the small town, he was all too familiar with Route 13 — or The Strip, as he called it — and the score of drivers who exceeded its speed limit on a regular basis. *Everyone is always in a hurry to die,* he thought.

"Yup, yup. Got it," Steve said, jerking the wheel hard to the right onto the narrow strip of asphalt.

He edged along the shoulder, lights flashing, and siren blaring. Moving with caution, he leaned out his window and studied the vehicles and passengers, quickly assessing damage and injury.

"Anything?" Dale asked, looking over his shoulder.

"Good so far," Steve responded as they made their way to the source of the pileup. "Just some fender-bender action. Nothing too serious."

Reaching the origin of the stopped traffic, they observed numerous vehicles that were mangled, smashed into one another, perpendicular to their lanes, and a few that were smoking. Having burst free from cracked radiators, the stale odor of coolant filled their nostrils.

Staring at the source of the pileup, Dale muttered, "Holy cow!" A northbound driver had crossed the double yellow line and crashed head-on into oncoming traffic at what appeared to be full speed.

Braking the rescue vehicle and throwing it in park, Steve took in the situation from his window. "Oh, my," he said. "What. A. Mess."

In a brief exchange, the two shot each other a knowing expression.

"This is gonna be a bad one," Dale said. He was all business. There was no time for emotion.

"Uh-huh," Steve agreed, nodding his head.

Multiple vehicles were involved, which meant multiple injuries. Behind Steve and Dale, fire engines, police, ambulances, and more emergency responders snaked their way through the melee to the primary crash, the initiating crash, as it was known. There were several secondary crashes, and the occupants of those vehicles appeared unharmed.

"Let's go," Dale commanded.

Steve jumped from the driver's seat of the bright red emergency vehicle. Adrenaline pumping, he slapped on his yellow, insulated firefighting helmet, opened a metal door on the side, and retrieved his medical bag. Dale donned his helmet, retrieved a similar bag, and fell in step as they hurriedly made their way. Moving with practiced speed, he spotted a tan SUV facing the wrong direction.

"I'll take the SUV, Steve," Dale barked.

"Got it. I'm on the blue compact." Steve continued ahead.

"Rog."

No strangers to vehicular carnage, they were all too familiar with wreckage, injuries, and the loss of human life. Years of viewing ghastly sights numbed them to such atrocities. It was all just part of the job.

Dale approached the oversized SUV, the initiating vehicle. He did a quick assessment. Its front end was smashed against and on top of the blue compact. The engine wasn't running, which was good. It meant the fuel pump was off. There was less chance of fire.

Peering inside, he observed a young Caucasian female. Rather than break the window, he tried the door, which didn't appear to be damaged.

Damage to the frame, which could seal it tight, wouldn't be visible. Pulling on the handle, he mumbled to himself, "C'mon, baby. Open for Dale." Yanking the handle, he was somewhat surprised when the door gave way and opened.

"That's what I'm talkin' 'bout," he exclaimed to no one.

The driver, who appeared to be in her early thirties, sat unconscious behind the steering wheel. The instant inflation of the airbag had saved her life, although it knocked her out in the process. From years of training, Dale placed two fingers on the woman's neck. Craning his head out the door, he shouted to Steve, "Got a pulse. Doesn't appear to be critical."

"Gotcha," Steve replied from a distance.

Removing a hooked cutter from the nylon pouch on his belt, he quickly sliced through the seatbelt, releasing the young woman. She slumped forward into the steering wheel and grunted. With a groan, she started to regain consciousness. Easing her back in the seat, Dale donned a pair of blue latex gloves, removed a thin flashlight from his pouch, and checked for pupil response. She had a small contusion on her forehead from the impact. Dale made a standard assessment to himself and concluded she probably had a mild concussion.

Her eyes blinked several times in rapid succession, and she started to turn her head.

"Easy, darlin'," Dale said in his southern drawl. His voice was calm and soothing. "You're gonna be okay. Don't move around. Okay?"

As her mind began to clear, she asked, "Where am I?"

"You were in an accident. Do you remember it?"

With the disorientation of someone emerging from deep slumber, she questioned his explanation. "Accident? What accident? Who are you?"

"My name is Dale. I'm a paramedic. I'm going to take care of you. What's your name?"

From his many years of service, he assessed her condition. In good shape, young, looked like an athlete, or had been one. With a slight, painful shake of her head, she cleared as much of the fog as she was going to for now. "Kate."

"Nice to meet you, Kate. Can you tell me if anything hurts?"

She touched her head where she had made a brief but forceful impact with the airbag that saved her life. "My head."

"Anything else?"

"No."

"Okay. I'm going to examine you for broken bones by gently squeezing your arms and legs, okay? You tell me if anything hurts. Okay?"

She nodded. "Uh-huh."

As Dale began with her leg, he noticed a cellphone on the passenger floorboard. The screen was still illuminated. Throughout the course of the accident, the connection remained intact. Dale finished his examination for broken bones. Retrieving the phone from the floor, he stared at an image of young woman who was rambling on frantically about something. *FaceTime*, he concluded, as he shook his head in disgust.

"Unbelievable," he muttered.

Moments prior, the phone had been in Kate's hand. FaceTiming with her girlfriend regarding her romantic life had been the center of her attention and distracted her from the road. With her eyes fixed on the tiny screen, she sped along the four-lane highway at close to seventy miles per hour in the far-left hand lane, believing the SUV provided a degree of invincibility.

Noticing Dale holding her cellphone, Kate asked, "Is that Brittany?" Her voice was weak.

With a quizzical glance, Dale asked, "Is that who you were FaceTiming before the accident?"

Nodding, she said, "Yeah."

57

He handed her the phone. "I guess that's her," he said, his voice devoid of emotion.

She accepted the phone and stared at Brittany's familiar face. Although her mouth was moving, there was no sound. Touching the red circle, Kate ended the call. She dropped the phone in the passenger seat.

Then she burst into tears and began sobbing as the full weight of the situation settled on her.

Dale studied her for a minute and then offered consolation. "Hey, hey, it's okay. You're gonna be okay. We're gonna get you out of there in a few minutes. You'll be fine. Just try and relax."

"I didn't know…" she sobbed.

Kate had been distracted by her phone and had been unaware that her vehicle had begun drifting across the double yellow line that divided the four-lane thoroughfare. Enraged by conversation, her foot pressed on the accelerator, topping her speed at more than ten miles per hour over the limit.

"I'm so over him, Brit. Done," she had been shouting at the tiny screen. "After what he did, he can go to Hell!"

Glancing up, it was too late. Her front wheels were too far across the dividing line. Directly ahead, a small blue car stared at her. She stomped on the brake in a panicked reflex, but it was too late. She was too close. Seconds later, she came to a complete, sudden stop. The blue compact traveling in the opposite direction absorbed the full force of her SUV's inertia, stopping it instantly. Its own inertia in the opposite direction served as a counter force for the oversized vehicle. Glass shattered, metal crumpled, and tires screeched. In a split second, the smooth routine motion of the highway came to an abrupt halt.

Fortunately for Kate, the massive vehicle sat high off the ground. With large tires and elevated bumper, it was designed for the rugged demands of off-road terrain. The damage to it and her was minimal compared to the blue compact, which had been crushed like a tin can upon impact. She would live.

Kate sat, weeping. Dale stepped away and left her to feel sorry herself. Checking on Steve, he inquired, "What do ya have?"

Inside the miniature car, the driver's head slumped forward, practically lifeless. He was unconscious. His legs were pinned under the crumpled dashboard, and the steering wheel was lodged against his chest, in essence pinning him inside. Mechanical extraction that involved cutting the car apart with hydraulic shears would be necessary.

"Faint pulse, probably massive internal bleeding." Steve paused, studying the distorted metal that just moments ago had been a motor vehicle. Shaking his head in disappointment, he said, "He's not going to make it." His voice was emotional but controlled. It was a simple statement, one he'd uttered hundreds of times during the course of his career, but one he never got used to saying. Pausing for a moment, he looked at the unconscious driver and whispered an apology before moving on to the next vehicle in the successive pileup.

6

"So what's this place called?" Lauren asked.

Before Timothy could answer, Grandma spoke up. "Waiting, dear. Waiting."

Puzzled, Lauren asked, "You said that before. That's its name?"

Corn Fed, Sticks, and Grandma all nodded in unison.

Lauren's voice took on a tone of uncertainty. "I don't understand. What are we waiting *for*?"

After a long pause, Sticks responded, "Our due."

"What does that mean?" Lauren demanded.

"I wish I knew," Timothy chimed in.

"Punishment," Sticks supplied. "Eternal punishment for our sins." Looking from Lauren to Timothy, he added, "That's our due."

"Then why are we waiting?" Timothy asked.

Grandma answered, "As near as we can figure, most who end up here wait before being dragged inside." She motioned with her crooked finger to the twin glowing doors. "Some, as you have seen, are taken without delay." She paused. "Really, there's no rhyme or reason to it."

Timothy followed her finger and stared at the foreboding twin doors.

"Waiting allows everyone to reflect on their misdeeds, no matter how big or small," Sticks said. "Most of all..." his voice trailed off as his focus also shifted to the molten doors, "it adds to the torment."

Corn Fed spoke up, his eyes on Timothy. "As one of the youngest members, Youngin', I expect you'll be waitin' a while." He paused and considered his words, and then with a smirk added, "Oh, you'll be joinin' all of us for eternity, have no doubt about that. But you're at the back of the line, so to speak. And that there line that keeps a growin' too. But your membership is guar-an-teed." He drew out the syllables to reinforce their permanency. "Ain't no doubt about that. No, siree. But you might have a good, long wait." After reflecting on his words, he snorted. "Then again, you might not. Never can tell what that Beast is gonna do."

Timothy stood next to Lauren as the full import of their words washed over him. The realization that he would be dragged inside at some point crashed over him in a tidal wave of finality and fear. He shook as though shivering. Like a dot on an exclamation point, he had been found guilty and sentenced, even though there had not been a trial.

"How do you know all of this?" Timothy asked.

"The longer you wait, the more you understand, dear," Grandma explained. "Part of the process."

"That, and what you bring with you," Sticks added.

"So, that's it? Because someone shot me, my fate is sealed?"

No one was in a hurry to answer him.

Turning to Corn Fed, Timothy asked, "How can you just accept your fate like that?"

Corn Fed shrugged. "Because it's deserved and impossible to reject, I s'pose."

"Why do you believe it's deserved?" Lauren asked. "What did you do to deserve this?"

Corn Fed looked at her for a long moment before responding. "I killed a man. Killed 'im for no good reason really."

Everyone stared at Corn Fed. His personality was amiable. It was difficult to believe he was a murderer. Timothy mulled over what Corn Fed had shared. Then he thought about the man who had ended his life. *I wonder if he will end up here?*

"What happened?" Timothy asked.

"Me and this good ole boy got into a scuffle — a bar fight, or brawl rather. I'd had one too many." He paused. "Well, more like a few too many, I guess I should say. We was playin' pool, and he missed an easy shot. I mean he plum missed it. Only thing the cue ball hit was the rail. I asked him if had grease on his stick or was just cross-eyed. I didn't mean nothin' by it. Was the beer talkin', ya know? That was enough to get his goad up, and he missed another easy shot. Half a mug of beer added to the mix and me bein' me, I made another joke." He paused again, the recollection filling his mind.

"What did he do?" Timothy asked, eager to hear the rest of the story.

"He dropped his cue, walked over to me and pushed me off my bar stool. Drunk, I fell on the ground. Everyone laughed. He pointed at me and tol' me to keep my mouth shut. Wish that I coulda, but beer had a way of making my mouth move, know what I mean?" Shaking his head, Corn Fed continued, "I didn't like that none, so as he walked away I grabbed a beer bottle. Cracked him right over the head with it. He dropped like a stone. It was lights out."

For a time, they all remained silent in the putrid heat. His story, though shocking, held little significance in comparison to the horror of their surroundings. There was no comfort to be found in their shared misery.

"How did you get here?" Lauren asked in soft, restrained voice.

"Got shot going over the prison wall," Corn Fed deadpanned.

"Prison wall?" Timothy asked.

"Yup. They threw me in jail for killin' that fella. What they call involuntary manslaughter. I wasn't havin' any of that. Couldn't stand to be cooped up like an animal. Made a run for it as soon as I could. Managed to hatch a plan with a few other inmates. I was the first—and only, now that I think about it—one to climb up our makeshift ladder. Almost made it over the top. But I caught a bullet in the back, right through my heart. Dead before I hit the ground," he said without emotion. Considering his words, his eyes darted to Sticks for a second, and then he added," I reckon that's justice for ya."

"Maybe," Timothy said. "But still..." His eyes shifted, taking in the dark, hopeless void. "The waiting...that isn't justice. It's..."

"Torture," Grandma supplied.

"Yeah," Timothy agreed. Then, holding her gaze, he asked, "What about you?"

"What do you mean?"

"I mean, how do you accept this? The waiting, being dragged inside, all of it," Timothy said.

"What choice do I have? Can you reject the reality of this place?" she motioned with her decrepit hand. "There's nothing more real than the finality of death and eternal damnation."

Timothy looked around. Other than dim splotches of red light amid the darkness and silhouetted souls, there was nothing to see except the twin fiery doors in the distance. The air, if that's what it was, was thin and insufficient. Breathing was laborious and required deliberate effort and came in tiny, forced gulps. He shook his head. "I guess not."

As he stood waiting with the others, Timothy observed the arrival of new spirits, some young, some old, and many in between. Each arrived with the same look of confusion and disbelief on his or her disfigured face and asked similar questions of those around them. Finality set in with extreme rapidity, especially after the re-live. Then the waiting began.

That was the case with Jacob Barnes. Without warning, his bald, rotund soul appeared next to Timothy. Confused like everyone who arrived in Hell's vestibule, he surveyed his surroundings in a feeble attempt to understand his circumstance. This place was beyond understanding. All one could do is accept it. Still, he asked similar questions like Lauren had.

"Where am I?" he demanded, looking back and forth from Timothy to Lauren to Corn Fed.

Timothy was about to answer him, but before he could respond, Jacob's facial expression froze as he relived his final moments on the highway. He saw himself behind the wheel of his vehicle listening to Led Zeppelin's *Stairway to Heaven*. Tapping his fingers to the beat on the steering wheel, he smiled as he considered his day. Today had been a good day. Just a few months since the April deadline to file taxes, he had received notification of a pending bonus due to his clever, and quite legal, interpretation of tax laws. To celebrate his success he looked forward to going home and watching a favorite movie after dinner before going to bed. Staring into the distance, the scenery was a blur as he sped along the highway. Then, in the blink of an eye, it was over. At twenty-eight years old, he sat unconscious and bleeding to death behind the collapsed steering wheel of his vehicle.

"No," he whispered to himself, as he stared at the retreating images. "No," he screamed. "No! This can't be real." He turned to Lauren and Timothy. "I... I can't be dead. I can't!" Pleading, he shouted, "Don't you see...?" They stared back at him, blank looks covering their disfigured faces. He looked back and forth, from one to the other. "I'm a successful accountant!" he shouted to no avail. "I...

I..." his voice trailed off as he surveyed the dim scene. The sweltering darkness embraced him. In short order, the reality and finality of his situation began to settle in. In a whisper of surrender, he asked almost to himself, "How can I be dead?"

"That's what I wanted to know," Timothy said.

"Me too," Lauren added. "So what's your story?"

Snapping out of his bewilderment, Jacob answered her. "I worked for an accounting firm. Went to University of Maryland and was recruited right out of college," he lamented. Although his voice was sad, it was filled with regret more than anything. Continuing, he added, "Been with the firm for six years. Six years."

"I meant, how did you get here?" Lauren clarified.

Jacob considered her question for a moment. With a slight snicker, he recalled how he had been a miser since childhood. After college, he purchased a small vehicle because it was fuel efficient and inexpensive to maintain. Saving money was important to Jacob, but acquiring it was even more so. His father had been frugal to say the least and taught him the value of a dollar at a young age.

Shaking his head at the memory, he stated, "Car accident." He turned to Timothy. "Everything I worked so hard for is gone. It's all gone!" he bellowed, as the grim recognition of eternal death crashed over him.

Timothy had no response. Jacob's reaction was part of the agonizing, final process of acceptance during which all traces of hope vanished. He turned and studied the disfigured faces of those around him, searching for an explanation.

Grandma spoke up. "It's all gone," she confirmed, "for all of us. Everything we ever had." She paused for moment, then added, "My Victorian home. Belonged to my parents. Gone."

"This just can't be," he mumbled, as he considered his all too brief and frugal life.

"Trust me, it is," Corn Fed blurted. "All things we wasted time and money on are long gone."

Jacob laughed, not in a humorous way, because such laughter is associated with joy. And there was no joy in this place. No, he laughed in disgust.

"I didn't waste money on frivolous indulgences," he explained. "For most of my life, I purchased my clothes at thrift stores. Never really spent money on anything. It was only when I graduated college that I splurged a little, more of an investment, I guess you could say, in suits, jackets, and ties, all of which I bought on sale." Pausing for a moment, he regretted that he had never truly enjoyed the fruits of his labor. "I never paid full price for anything. Nope, money was for saving, for the future, for retirement, for or so I thought." Old age would never come now. His life of simplicity, money hoarding, and modest contentment was over. He would spend eternity in Hell.

Bewildered upon his arrival, he had begun to accept the permanency of his situation. Filled with regret, Jacob realized the foolishness of how he had lived.

"What a fool I was," he said to no one. His voice was filled with disdain. His remorse had nothing to do with his current predicament.

"What do you mean?" Timothy asked.

Staring at him, Jacob said, "I wasted my life hoarding money. What an incredible waste of time money is!"

"What do you mean?" Lauren asked.

"I never took the time to enjoy my life. I spent my life making money and saving it. Saving it…" With a wry laugh, he continued, "My savings and investments will live on without me."

They were useless here. In the fiery isolation of Hell, everyone was equal. There were no rich or poor, no privileged or disadvantaged. No one had any status except the Beast — the master and ruler of Hell. Like a warden, he presided over Hell's confines, subjugating its occupants to his torment.

Noticing the glowing red doors, Jacob asked, "What's in there?"

Timothy and Lauren looked at each other and exchanged a glance as they considered who should answer. Before either one could speak up, Grandma said, "The Beast."

"The Beast?" Jacob asked.

"Yes. The Beast."

"Who's the Beast?"

"You'll see soon enough," Timothy said. "He's a creature of sorts. No one except the Beast emerges from the fiery gates."

"When does he come out? " Jacob inquired.

"There's no pattern to his arrival," Sticks supplied. "Sometimes he makes several trips in succession; other times he emerges and is not be seen for a while."

"He scares me," Timothy said. "I mean, scares me in a way I've never been scared before."

"The Beast is pure evil," Sticks rasped. "Evil in a way that is not experienced or understood outside the confines of this place."

"Exactly what lies behind the great doors is unknown, but whatever awaits those of us waiting is something to be feared," Grandma added.

Jacob studied the doors for a moment as he pondered the explanation. His gaze remained focused as Sticks expounded on the others' comments. "What lies behind the doors represents the finality of all life—the death of the soul and the permanency of suffering."

Unable to articulate the full meaning of Hell's permanence, what was more terrifying than the agony Hell provided was the absence of God's presence. In all of creation, his presence was evident so that no one was without excuse, everywhere—except in this place. God did not exist in this raging inferno where unrepentant sinners received their due. Even the very thought of God was absent because to consider God meant hope, and there was no hope for the damned. The heat was intense and unwavering. It almost seemed to get hotter when new occupants were dragged inside.

Perhaps their souls were what fueled the flames of Hell, Timothy thought.

7

Cocking her left wrist toward her and checking her watch, Jerri Randeski announced, "It's getting late, y'all. I need to get Lexi home to bed." Alexiss Kimberly, her six-month old daughter, stared up wide-eyed at her aunt Theresa, who was cuddling her. Theresa was Jerri's sister. She and her husband, David, had Jerri and Lexi over every Sunday for dinner. The standing invitation always including the option of attending church with them in the morning. But Jerri never accepted. Having an infant provided her with a litany of excuses.

"Nonsense!" Theresa exclaimed. "You just got here."

"I've been here since three," Jerri replied.

"Oh, that's only a few hours," Theresa said by way of dismissal.

"We haven't even had dessert yet," David announced from the kitchen. The two lived in a modest two-bedroom townhouse. Situated just off the kitchen, the living room pulled double duty and served as a family room.

"I don't think I have room for it," Jerri said, patting her flat stomach. The younger of the two, Jerri was also the thinnest.

"Everyone has room for ice cream and cake," Theresa proclaimed. Born with a sweet tooth, Theresa carried a few extra pounds as a teen that had transformed into several more as an adult. Not fat per se, her penchant for treats of the chocolate variety made her a full-figured woman. *Her gym membership exists simply to maintain equilibrium,* Jerri mused to herself. The hours of spin class each week were no match for the brownies, cookies, cakes, and ice cream she consumed on a weekly basis.

"You always did," Jerri poked at her, laughing. "Mom couldn't keep cookies in the house with you around."

"G-i-r-l...was nothing like her chocolate chip cookies fresh out of the oven. Mmm mmm," Theresa proclaimed as she recalled the memory.

"Oh, I remember," Jerri acknowledged with a slight giggle. "I still remember you burning your mouth on melted chocolate chips and guzzling milk from the carton! Mom had a fit."

Laughing, Theresa said, "Remember she grabbed the wooden spoon and yelled at me to put the carton down?"

"Oh, her and that spoon. You got it more than I did," Jerri announced with an air of pride.

"You always were a Goody Two-Shoes," Theresa jibed.

Just then David entered from the kitchen and stood in front of them like an expectant host. A muscular man with broad shoulders, his clean-shaven face was handsome and had gentle features that radiated kindness. "Ladies," he said in preparation to take their dessert orders, "what kind of ice cream would you like with your cake? We have vanilla, chocolate, and strawberry."

Before Jerri could protest, Theresa said, "I'll have all three, Baby! And a glass of milk to go with my cake." Turning on the sofa toward her sister, she asked, "What about you, Sis?"

"Oh, I'm fine. Really," Jerri said.

"C'mon," she objected. "Bring her a thin piece — and a scoop of vanilla."

"T..." Jerri began.

"Have a little cake and ice cream! It won't kill you." She turned to look down at Lexi, who was laying in her arms, as peaceful as an angel. "Besides, it will give me more time with my niece." She smiled down at Lexi and hugged her. "Right, sweet baby?"

"Fine," Jerri gave in. Turning to David, she held up her hand, thumb and index finger practically touching and said, "Just a *thin* piece, please," she emphasized, "And a tiny scoop of ice cream."

"You got it," David said. In almost an about-face movement, he darted into the kitchen. A few moments later he returned. In each hand he held a small, white ceramic plate. The one in his right hand contained a triangular wedge of yellow cake with chocolate frosting over an inch thick. Atop the sloping angle, three half-moons of ice cream — one vanilla, one chocolate, and one strawberry — sat in a row. Extending his hand, he said, "Here ya go, Babe."

"Thanks, Sweetie," Theresa said. "Just put it on the table, please."

"Sure," he said in compliance.

In his left hand, he held an identical plate, only this one had a much smaller slice of cake and only one scoop of ice cream — vanilla. "For you," he said, as he handed Jerri her dessert and retreated to the kitchen.

"Thanks, D. I don't know if I have room for it after that dinner."

"Sure you do," Theresa encouraged, as she shifted Alexiss to her left arm. Snatching her fork, she chopped off a hunk of cake and dollop of ice cream.

Looking over at her sister, Jerri said, "I can hold Lexi while you eat, T."

"I can manage. I can manage just fine, Sis."
She beamed down at Lexi. "You eat up," she added,
never taking her eyes off of her niece. "Mm. That's
good cake. Nice and moist. Don't you think so, J?"

Jerri took a much smaller bite of her cake and
ice cream. "Yes, it is good. Rich, though."

Theresa rolled her eyes. "Rich in goodness,"
she laughed to herself as she leaned forward for
another bite.

David returned and joined them, sitting
adjacent to his wife. He had passed on dessert,
opting instead for a cup of coffee. A former athlete
and soldier, he wasn't one to indulge, preferring
instead to maintain a healthy diet.

Leaning forward, he reached for his niece.
"You're hogging our niece. Let me hold he while
you finish your dessert."

With feigned reluctance, Theresa agreed.
"Just for a minute."

"Hey, there," he said to Lexi in a soft voice.
"I bet you'd like cake and ice cream, huh?" She
stared up at him, a trace of a smile on her face, or so
he thought.

Jerri studied her brother-in-law. He was a
good man and would make a great father one day,
if that day ever came. For the past four years, he and
Theresa had tried to have children with no success.

When nature's process didn't work as intended, they had resorted to the expensive option of artificial insemination. Teresa became pregnant, and the two were hopeful. Their hopes were shattered when she miscarried a month later. With finances running thin, the two were back to doing things the old fashioned way. Theresa's gynecologist urged her to relax and just 'let it happen.' That was easier said than done.

Shifting gears, David and Theresa decided to give it a break for a while and focus their efforts elsewhere, thereby removing some of the pressure. The two were preparing for a mission trip with their church to Rwanda. There they would help build shelters, dig irrigation trenches, and plant food. The ten-day trip was something they looked forward to because they'd get to be around children.

Thinking about this, Jerri asked, "How long is your flight to Africa?"

Theresa turned to David for a moment, as she began to answer, then back to her sister. "What did Pastor Jeff say? Twenty-three hours?"

David shifted his attention. "Yeah. Twenty-three hours and change. And that's if our connecting flights are on time."

Jerri shook her head. "That's a lot of traveling."

"It won't be too bad," David reassured. "I did more traveling than that in Army," he said, and caught himself. He had served in the Army with Roman, Jerri's husband. The two had been Rangers and served together in Afghanistan. Two years ago, Roman had stayed with David and Teresa while on leave. It was during his visit that David introduced them.

"Yeah. I remember those days," Jerri said through a forced smile.

"Sorry," David offered. "I didn't…"

"No, you're fine," she said, shaking her head. "It's part of who you are. You can't walk on eggshells forever. Besides," she said nodding down at the bundle of joy in his lap, "I fully intend to tell my daughter all about her father one day."

Placing her hand on Jerri's forearm, Theresa looked into her sister's eyes and said, "Roman was a good man." She paused, blinking back tears. "I miss him, and I know you do too."

A painful smile crossed Jerri's face as a tear rolled down her cheek. With extreme clarity, she recalled the day Roman Randeski walked into her life. It was a Sunday, and as usual she arrived at her sister's in the afternoon.

"Hi," he said, answering the door and taking her hand. "I'm Roman. Dave and I serve together," he explained. "I'm staying here for a little while."

"Oh," she said at the unexpected visitor. "I'm Jerri."

"I know. What I mean," he backpedaled, "is that's what I thought. Dave said you'd be coming over for dinner."

Her hand still in his, she smiled at him. With rugged good looks, square jaw, and inviting smile, it was love at first sight. At dinner, the two monopolized the conversation, discussing everything from their childhood to favorite books, what movies they liked and hated, and places they'd love to visit. Over the next two weeks, their romance blossomed. Jerri was heartbroken when Roman had to return to his command.

During the course of the following months, the two spoke every day. Then one day Roman asked, "Why don't you take Friday and Monday off? Come down to North Carolina and see me for a long weekend? The weather's great, and there's lots to do. What do you say?"

"That sounds like a plan," Jerri said without hesitation.

The following Friday, Roman picked Jerri up at the airport. The weekend was a lovers' delight and flew by like a dream. On the last night, after dinner at an upscale restaurant, Roman reached across the table and took Jerri's hand.

"Jerri," he began. "I think you are the most amazing woman I ever met. I can't believe the weekend went by so fast."

"Me too," Jerri agreed.

Reaching in his pocket with his free hand, Roman produced a small, square, velvet box. Jerri's eyes darted down at it. Before she could say anything, Roman was on one knee next to her. Staring up at her, he said, "I love you, Jerri. I have since the day I answered that door. Will you marry me?"

With tears of joy streaming down her face, she nodded and said, "Yes. Yes, I'll marry you!" As she leaned forward and hugged him, onlookers and restaurant staff clapped.

Blinking reality back into focus, she smiled at the memory. "He was a great man," she said to more to herself. Turning toward her sister, she added, "And I miss him every day."

Feeling guilty at the turn of the conversation, David attempted to divert everyone's focus by talking to Lexi. "Hey, sweetheart. You're just a happy girl, aren't you?"

Jerri forced a smile. Lexi was all Jerri had now, a living testament to her husband. A few months after Roman proposed, the two got married in a small chapel not far from the base. Her sister was her matron of honor, and David was the best man.

"Roman was always so handsome in his uniform," Jerri commented as a memories bubbled to the surface.

"He was indeed," Theresa agreed. "Dress uniform is always better than a tux."

Having decided to leave the Army, Jerri's wedding was the last time David intended to wear his dress uniform. With the ink barely dry on their marriage license, their honeymoon was short-lived when Roman's unit received orders to Afghanistan. Devastated, Jerri took the news hard. But over time she became inculcated in all things Army and played her role as the dutiful wife. A dependent of the Army, as she saw it, base housing was where she served.

Roman's unit was slated for a twelve-month tour, after which he would out-process and be discharged. The days became weeks, and the weeks became months. Just when Jerri was getting used being on her own, a knock on the front door changed everything.

"Oh, my God," she screamed at the sight of her husband. "What are you doing here?" she exclaimed as she hugged him.

"I'm home on leave," he said. "I wanted to surprise you."

"Well, you did!" she said, as tears of joy sprang from her eyes.

For the next ten days the two were inseparable. They ventured out now and then, mostly to eat. Viewing their time as a mini vacation, Jerri opted not to cook for the duration. On their last night together, however, she chose to stay home in a futile attempt to prolong their time together and delay Roman's pending departure.

The next morning, Jerri and Roman said goodbye at the airport. In the quiet confines of the military air terminal, they held each other, embraced by silent sadness. When it was time to board, Roman kissed Jerri one last time with the passion experienced by young lovers, pulled away and said, "I love you, J. Never forget that."

"I love you too," Jerri replied. She wiped away the tears that had become streams down her face.

He turned and headed down the ramp. Pausing, he turned back and held up three fingers.

She did the same. That was their code for "I love you."

That was the last image Jerri had of her husband. Two weeks later the Casualty Assistance Calling Officer, or CACO, arrived at her door and delivered the news of Roman's death.

Staring at Lexi and recalling the story, the irony was not lost. Had it not been for his surprise visit, Lexi would not have been conceived. Absence had indeed made their hearts, and their desire, grow fonder.

Snapping back to reality, Jerri took a second and final bite of cake and ice cream before placing her plate on the table. "That's it for me," she announced. "I'm full."

Theresa stared at the half-eaten piece of cake in disbelief and said, "I'll finish it. Don't you worry about   that."

"Oh, I won't, sis," she said with a laugh as she stood. Throwing the diaper bag over one shoulder and purse in hand, she led the way to her car. Theresa carried Lexi and strapped her in the car seat.

"Go out the front way," Theresa said.

With the window rolled down, Jerri replied, "I never go that way. The back way is shorter."

"Too many winding roads," her sister admonished. The townhouse development was a small maze with openings to the main thoroughfares on opposite ends. The front way, as Theresa put it, required navigating the bulk of the neighborhood and its ample supply of traffic lights. The back way was circuitous and desolate, but there were no traffic lights to contend with.

"I go that way all the time," Jerri said. "I'll talk to you later." She depressed the button and raised the window and pulled out of the driveway, waving.

Two left turns later, and she was on a dim, winding road that bordered a marsh, now filled by Mother Nature's abundance of rain. Reflections of light danced on the scattered mirrors of water. Once swampland, developers planted neighborhoods in the remote area in the name of spreading urbanization. To her right, remnants of the dense foliage sat motionless silhouetted by a waxing moon. On her left, rows of transplanted trees stood watch in the darkness like soldiers. Guarding their inhabitants, they served as a barrier between the access road and development.

Slowing to take a hairpin turn, Jerri yanked the steering wheel of her vehicle hard to the right to avoid a car that had strayed over the double yellow line. Her vehicle swerved like a roller coaster hitting a tight turn, and she fought to control it. In an attempt to recover and steer back onto the road, she hand-over-handed the wheel in the opposite direction. It was no use. Her rate of speed and sudden change of direction transformed her vehicle into a death trap. The sedan careened off the road and plunged headfirst into the closest of the many ponds that littered the marsh.

"Oh, my God!" she shouted.

Weighed down by the engine, the car tilted forward and began to sink. Water raced up the hood and covered the windshield. Seeping in through the firewall, the car began to fill with water.

"Oh, no. No, no, no," she screamed as fear began to overwhelm her.

In a full panic, Frantically Jerri tried to open the door, but the water pressure held it firmly in place. "Oh, my God. Please! No, no, no!" She pounded her shoulder against the sealed door. It was no use. Turing around, she climbed in the back seat, where Lexi was crying. Quickly unbuckling her, she scooped her up and held her as she stared at the windshield. She watched in horror as the water line raced upward and her vehicle plunged beneath the darkness.

In less than a minute, her car had sunk to the bottom of the twelve-foot swamp. Water continued to gush into the main cabin and was nearly at chest level. With Lexi in her hands, she held her above the rising water. A million images raced through her mind. With less than a foot of air, she recalled the one time she had attended church with her sister. And then she prayed.

"Please, Jesus, save me. Please save my daughter. I know I haven't been a good person, but I believe in you. Please, Jesus, forgive me and save us! Ple..." Her final word was muffled as the force of the water displaced the remaining air.

8

The confines of the waiting area were crowded. Like commuters on a packed train stuck in a dark tunnel, souls bumped into one another haphazardly in the darkness. With little room and new arrivals inundating the confined area, its discomfort added to the misery. Lauren pressed against Timothy's right arm. Jacob was stacked at her back. Corn Fed, Sticks, and Grandma covered his left flank.

Engulfed by the radiating heat and the cramped surroundings, for the first time Timothy was thirsty. He swallowed, but his throat was completely dry. No longer confined by human flesh, his mouth contained no saliva, no shred of moisture. "I'm thirsty," he said to the group, as he swallowed with extreme effort. It was a futile attempt to coax even just a drop of saliva out of hiding and quench his thirst.

His words struck Lauren, and she echoed his sentiment. "So am I. Really thirsty." She mimicked his gesture and swallowed with equal difficulty. The heat was dry and intense. If liquid of any kind existed in the fiery dungeon, it would evaporate in an instant.

"We're all thirsty," Grandma said.

"Just wait," Sticks interjected. "It will get worse."

"Indeed it will," Grandma concurred in a whisper.

"There ain't no water here," Corn Fed chimed in. "It just don't exist."

"It's all part of the suffering," Sticks explained, ever the patriarch of their group.

"Suffering?" Jacob asked to no one in particular.

"Yes," Sticks supplied. "But it's only a small part of it. It will get worse—much, much worse."

In recognition of his own thirst, Jacob, in a failed attempt to swallow, asked, "How can this get any worse?"

They all stared at him; a shared look of disbelief covered their faces. As the newest member of their lot, Jacob had not experienced the full measure of complete despair that characterized the interlude between life and eternal misery. Nor had he experienced the Beast.

"Oh," Sticks began, pausing for effect as he slowly and deliberately turned his head toward the two towering embers in the distance, "it gets worse." He locked eyes with Jacob. "*Much worse.*"

As if on cue, the fiery doors burst open, releasing a deluge of heat that seared their dry skin like a blow torch. The air became saturated with the choking stench of decay, rot, and sulfur. Filling their lifeless lungs, it increased the difficulty of the already laborious process of breathing. The red glow was blinding in contrast to the pitch-blackness that had a moment ago filled the area. Their eyes stung but did not water. Flowing from the gateway to the Lake of Fire, the shrill screams of the damned pierced their ears. Reverberating like a single, high-pitch tone, its cacophony was a mélange of individual wails. Wading forward, the Beast huffed and grunted with tremendous force with each step. His lifeless red eyes scanned the throng of waiting souls as though expecting someone.

"What is that?" Jacob asked, his voice trembling.

"The Beast," Timothy said.

"The *what*?" Jacob asked. His question originated more out of fear than confusion.

"The Beast," Sticks reiterated. "The ruler of this dark abode."

Just the sight of the Beast was enough to paralyze Jacob. He was frozen with fear, horrified by the prehistoric and monstrous appearance of the Beast. This was his first time seeing the gruesome creature. He hoped it would be his last.

Jacob's eyes remained fixed on the grotesque monster as it plodded through the cramped area. With an apoplectic grimace plastered on his face, the Beast peered at the horde of souls jam-packed into the tiny space.

Jacob now understood Sticks's previous pronouncement and muttered, "Worse." His body trembled uncontrollably as absolute fear enveloped him—fear due to the realization that he was helpless.

In the distance, Timothy observed the Beast. "What's he looking for?" he asked.

"Don't know," Corn Fed said.

"I think he's coming this way," Lauren whispered under her breath.

As the Beast made his way in toward them, Lauren attempted to press closer to Timothy. It was no use. There was no extra space, no place to hide from his preying eyes or menacing grip.

Pivoting, the Beast turned without warning to his left and scanned the shadows. Like sardines in a tin, the souls gazed back at him with lifeless eyes as he studied them. Not seeing what he was looking for, he snapped his primeval head to the right.

"He's looking for his next soul," Corn Fed declared in a whisper. His voice was hollow and devoid of emotion, as though what he was observing wasn't real to him. For now, it wasn't. But in time it would be real for all of them.

"Why is he looking?" Jacob asked, turning his face toward Corn Fed and then back to the Beast. "There are certainly plenty of us to choose from."

Corn Fed shrugged. "True 'nough. But there's no explaining the Beast."

"From what I've gathered," Grandma offered, "it seems there's an order to it that only he knows."

"I haven't seen any order," Timothy said.

"You haven't been here long, my dear," she said. "You will."

Timothy didn't look forward to understanding more about this abysmal place. Not knowing what to say, he held her gaze and nodded slowly.

"Waiting is all part of the process," Sticks said. "Might even say it *is* the process."

"It doesn't make sense," Jacob observed, never taking his eyes off the Beast in the distance. "If everyone is going inside there," he shifted his eyes from the Beast to the twin, blazing doors, then back, "why wait?"

"All part of the misery," Sticks said. "It gives everyone time to ponder."

"Ponder what?" Jacob asked.

After a long silence, Sticks said, "Everything." His voice was flat and hollow and teeming with regret. "Here," he motioned with his eyes, "we get to ruminate."

Timothy raised his brows. "What?"

"Think about," Lauren explained.

"Oh," Timothy said.

"Think about what?" Jacob asked. "Our mistakes? What we did wrong?"

"No," Sticks said. "Missed opportunities."

"Missed opportunities for what?" Jacob asked.

Sticks remained silent on purpose. At last, he said, "Opportunities to avoid this place."

With a shudder Timothy stared at Sticks. The meaning of his words was not lost on him. Had he listened to his mother, he might have avoided this place and — he turned his head forward — the Beast.

Curling his right claw into a fist, the Beast emitted a thunderous roar as he raised it above his head and shook it violently. Like an extended clap of thunder, its deafening echo filled the chamber, shaking the unseen walls and floor. Resonating deeply in the souls of the damned, its tone filled them with dread, and they shook violently. Fire spewed from his barbaric snout as he released his umbrage upward.

Unable to control his fear, Timothy stammered, "What's he doing?"

"He's angry," Grandma said.

"He's always angry," Timothy observed.

"No, dear. He's always full of hate. This is different." She paused. "This… this is anger. Believe it or not, it's worse."

"What would make him angry?" Timothy asked.

She shook her head. "I have no idea. But he gets this way now and then. Seen it before."

"How long does it last?" Timothy asked.

"Long enough," she said.

Arching his back, he fired another salvo upward, this time pointing his hooked finger at something only he perceived. Again, the confines of the waiting area trembled, as he roared in his beastly language, shaking his head from side to side. He paused for a moment and was still. In a single, sweeping, violent gesture, he snatched up three random souls in his great mitt. His pointed nails were razor sharp and sliced into them, causing intense pain and suffering. Wailing, they struggled to break the Beast's grip as he turned and stormed back into his blazing labyrinth.

A moment later the doors slammed shut and the surge of heat dissipated. They did seem to confine the blistering heat of Hell's inferno. Like a thermocline, they served as a dividing line between the overwhelming heat of the waiting area and the tormenting incinerator that awaited them all. Silent darkness returned to the void.

"I'm glad that's over," Timothy said. There was no relief in his voice, though, only acknowledgment.

"Me too," Lauren added.

"This place doesn't make sense," Jacob said.

"What do you mean?" Grandma asked.

He stared into her decrepit disfigurement. "This place is packed. We're all going in at some point, right? So what does he have to get angry about?"

Timothy thought about the question as Grandma studied him. He recalled his days in Mrs. Shaw's Sunday school class. On one particular Sunday, she had discussed Revelation and the Book of Life. She quoted, "If anyone's name was not found written in the Book of Life, he was thrown into the lake of fire." *That's why we're here*, he thought.

Sticks interrupted his thoughts. "Perhaps someone side-stepped."

"Side-stepped?" Jacob asked, confused.

"Yeah. Maybe somebody managed to avoid this place."

"How is that possible?" Lauren interjected. "Tell me! I want to know!" Her voice was not filled with hope. Hope did not exist; acceptance and finality took its place. Instead her voice was laced with bitterness and anger...and envy.

"I'm not really sure," Sticks said. "In fact, I don't know if it's even possible. But" he paused, "that might be something that would get that Beast all riled up—if it were possible."

"What makes you think it's possible?" Lauren demanded.

"Well," he began, choosing his words, "how I happened to be here."

"Oh?" Timothy said. "What happened?"

"The short answer is I fell. I fell off a mountain," he explained. "My buddy and I went rock climbing—free climbing, as it's known—no safety ropes." He shook his head at the recollection.

The group remained silent and waited for him to continue.

"He was the better climber, so he led. We were a little over a hundred feet up a steep pitch of mostly flat rock—little to grab hold of, but we were determined. At any rate, he slipped and slid right down the face. His arm caught me when he passed me. That was enough to loosen what little perch I had. We hit the ground within a few feet of each other. Didn't last long after a fall like that. But..."

"But what?" Lauren prompted.

Sticks shot her a glance. "But before everything went black, I heard him cry out. A prayer, really. Don't if it worked, but I ended up here. Never seen him. Kinda thought I would have by now."

Jacob listened intently but did not say anything. He considered Sticks' idea for a moment. "Well, I guess it really doesn't matter, does it? If someone did side-step, as you called it, we'll never know about it. And it won't do us any good if he or she did."

Timothy wanted to share his memory but realized it wouldn't do any good. All too real, their fate was sealed. No amount of speculation, no recollection, and no insight could change that. Not knowing what to say, he simply said, "We're all doomed."

Corn Fed sized him up. "Yup, we are."

9

In the backseat of her flooded vehicle, Jerri Randeski held her last breath and fought the overwhelming urge to inhale. Cradling Lexi in one arm, she groped for the door handle in the murky water in a frantic attempt to escape. Her heart racing, she grabbed at the armrest in a desperate search to release the door and escape. Unable to feel the latch, panic enveloped her like a spider's web. Combined with the rapid rise in carbon dioxide, her lungs burned, screaming for oxygen.

No, she thought. *No, it's not going to end like this. It can't...*

Unable to resist her body's craving any longer, her diaphragm flexed involuntarily, and she spat her final breath into the water. In the underwater darkness, a small cluster of bubbles rose to the roof and skirted forward in a zigzag pattern before becoming lodged against the doorframe.

Jerri's final inhalation filled her lungs with the cold water of death. The sponge-like tissue, whose tiny catacombs were normally filled with air, saturated with cold, swamp water. Reflexively, her body attempted to cough and expel the foreign liquid but failed. After a slight spasm, her body became still and motionless. She floated in her watery grave. Though her eyes were open, she did not see. Her lifeless body settled on the back seat as her soul exited and began to drift away.

From a distance, Jerri could see her body inside the flooded vehicle. Almost tranquil, she thought she looked peaceful, as though she were resting after a long journey. The distance began to increase quickly, and her spirit soared through the blackness and began to ascend. The darkness and isolation of death vanished, replaced by a brilliant white light, many times brighter than the sun. Surrounding her completely, the light wrapped its arms around her and embraced her.

The light was inviting, she thought, familiar in a way, as though it were more than a light. An extremely loving presence perhaps? she considered. As she continued to ascend with the light, joy filled her soul and a smile stretched across her face. An imperceptible sound echoed in the distance. It was pleasant and soothing. Voices, she concluded, singing in perfect harmony. Their chorus comforted her, and she experienced complete and perfect peace.

Coming to a gentle halt, the choir's tune became clearer, and the blinding brilliance of the light faded, allowing her to see beyond it.

"Welcome, my child," a kind voice said to her.

Standing directly in front of her, the source of the light smiled. He had rugged yet gentle features. A confident warrior, his smile was brilliant and welcoming. His eyes were a deep blue, unlike anything she had ever seen, and contrasted against his snow-white robe. They twinkled and conveyed an immeasurable bounty of love. Around his waist, he wore a deep purple sash that sparkled.

"Jesus," Jerri said, smiling, unable to mistake him. She dropped to her knees and bowed before her king.

"Arise," he commanded, touching her shoulders lightly. "Your sins are forgiven."

"Thank you," she said, standing. She hugged him , her Lord and Savior, the way a daughter hugs her father after receiving grace. Then pulling away, she asked, "Why am I here?"

"What do you mean?" he asked.

"I'm a sinner. I don't belong here," she protested.

"My child, Heaven is full of sinners — all of whom have been forgiven."

Releasing him, Jerri stepped back and surveyed the scene. She was in awe. Behind Jesus stood two large pearlescent gates that glistened. On either side of the gleaming gates were cherubim. With human faces and bodies like lions, they were indeed formidable-looking. They wielded flaming swords and guarded the entrance. Heaven's foyer was spacious but empty, she observed. Though the area was lush and enticing, no one waited to enter Heaven.

Placing his arm around her shoulder and smiling, Jesus prompted, "Come with me."

They turned and walked toward the gates. A man greeted her as he held the gate open. "Welcome," he said, his smile beaming.

"Thank you, Peter," Jerri responded. Coming to an abrupt stop, a quizzical expression crossed her face and she turned to Jesus. "How do I know his name?"

With a slight laugh, he explained, "This is Heaven. Here we are all part of one body. Therefore, everyone knows each other."

"Oh," Jerri said. "That makes sense."

Stepping through the gate, they entered and stood on the main path and paused. A fragrant bouquet washed over her like a tidal wave. Pleasing like flowers, it was more intense and satisfying. Inhaling, she found the air to be dewy sweet, and a multitude of scents competed for recognition. Lilac, honeysuckle, roses, to name a few—a full complement of unique and distinguishable scents. Each was enchanting and delightful yet separate and distinct. The voices heard in the distance were now clear and distinguished as their refrain echoed, "Glory to God in the highest." Accompanying them was the faint chirping of birds — flocks of them — that all whistled in harmony. She was able to decipher hundreds of different and differentiated tones.

She marveled at the new experience. "There's so many birds."

"Yes," Jesus replied. "All of them."

Marveling the sheer magnitude of what she was seeing, she smiled. "I've never seen so many different birds!"

"Indeed, many were extinct long before your time on earth," he explained.

Scanning from left to right, Jerri studied the expansive landscape. Majestic, it stretched as far as she could see. A thick layer of grass carpeted the ground like a sea of emeralds. "It's beautiful," she said.

Jesus beamed at her.

Scattered about, throngs of people stood huddled together in groups of various sizes. Clad in white robes, they dotted the sea of green. Free from mourning and sadness, they smiled and laughed together, existing in total peace.

"Come," Jesus said. "This way." He started down the golden path.

"Where are we going?" Jerri asked.

Turning to her, a smile broke out on his face. "To see my Father."

"Your father?" Hesitation filled her voice.

Touching her arm, he gave a reassuring smile. "Yes, he's waiting to see you."

"Me? Why is he waiting to see me?"

"He welcomes each one of his children to Heaven personally."

"Oh."

Walking together, Jerri was in awe at the kaleidoscope of colors that inundated her. More numerous and brilliant than those on earth, Heaven's landscape was riddled with a palette beyond description. Flowers lined the street of gold. Their rainbow of colors dazzled her. Trees dotted the lush, green foliage that seemed to extend forever.

"This is so wonderful," she remarked as they made their way in the direction of the choral serenade.

Her head turned left and right as they walked. Shifting her eyes upward, she studied the sky. Layered with multiple shades of blue, it appeared as though she could almost touch it. She considered this for a moment, then thought better of it. Swiveling her head, she searched for the sun, or some source of light, but found none. Yet the sky was clear and bright in all directions.

"The color are just— I've never seen anything like it," she observed with child-like amazement.

By way of explanation, Jesus said, "Sin marred creation."

As they moved along the path, everyone smiled. Some waved, others nodded, but like an expected visitor, all were happy to see her. *There's so much love here,* she observed. The barrage of faces caused a litany of names to flood her mind, some of which gave her pause. One in particular was Noah. Though she didn't know him, per se, she knew the man who smiled and nodded at her was Noah. *I can't believe I saw Noah*, she thought, as she threw him a quick wave. Recalling the familiar Bible story, she laughed to herself as she mused, *Where else would he be?*

Intermingled with the mass of disciples were animals—hundreds of thousands of them. Deer, giraffes, elephants, zebras, monkeys, rabbits, squirrels, and dogs, just to name a few, filled the plush panorama. They darted across the landscape, frolicking and playing together in the pristine habitat of Heaven. Rising from the ground were trees of every variety. Great in size, their branches stretched over the inhabitants below, yet there was no shade.

Cocking her head, she looked upward.

Knowing what she was searching for, Jesus explained, "My father and his glory are the source of light in Heaven."

Jerri gave a smile of acknowledgement as they continued. She noticed there were no leaves or twigs on the ground. "Not a single fallen leaf."

"There is no death of any kind here," Jesus said.

She nodded.

At the end of the path was an immense throne. Sitting atop a series of wide, marble steps, it was made of pure gold. A host of cherubim flanked either side of it. Their voices rang out in praise. To Jerri's amazement, littering the ground around it was a sea of crowns of every kind: gold, silver, some studded with gemstones, others with diamonds.

Jesus gave a casual gesture with his hand, and Jerri approached the throne and knelt. A great, massive book was opened by him who sat upon it— *The Book of Life*. Pages crackled as they were turned to the appropriate location. At last her name was read.

"Jerri Marie Randeski," the voice boomed. "My child, you have been granted salvation, sealed by the blood of the Lamb."

Jerri turned toward Jesus for a moment, for it was with his blood that her salvation had been secured. Turning back, she looked up into the light and saw the face of her Creator.

"In him is all life," the voice continued. "His resurrection is your resurrection. Through him you receive eternal life."

Jerri rose and turned. Meeting Jesus, they descended the steps. At the bottom, a familiar face approached her. Recognition was instantaneous, and Jerri wanted to cry, but there were no tears in Heaven. Tears, even those associated with joy, had their origin in sadness in some way.

The joy experienced in Heaven had no earthly comparison. It was euphoric, yes, but its euphoria was perfect and pure, beyond anything a human could ever experience. Of eternal duration, its elation did not fade or dissipate. A lasting moment of pure bliss, its intensity never wavered. At a loss for words, Jerri reached out and pulled her grown daughter toward her and hugged her.

"Hi, Mom," Lexi said.

"My baby," Jerri exclaimed. Releasing her, she stepped back. "Let me look at you," she said, studying her grown-up features in her heavenly body.

Then, as though seeking an explanation, Jerri turned to Jesus, who stood behind her smiling.

"Infants are not able to make the choice to believe," he said. "They are all God's children."

Jerri smiled in acknowledgment.

There was no time in Heaven. No one aged. Having cast off their flesh, all were youthful and radiant in their heavenly bodies. Mother and daughter were reunited for eternity.

10

The afternoon sun blossomed overhead in a clear sky, smothering the handful of faded, wooden tables, umbrellas, and benches beneath in a warm sea of golden yellow. Scattered at random, they occupied a worn, grassy area between Barkin' Dogs hotdog stand and the adjacent parking lot. Gray from years of drenching ultraviolet rays, inches of rain, and tropical wind, the wooden picnic furniture stood at the ready for eager patrons. A local favorite, the small take-out only shack served hotdogs, coleslaw, potato salad, lemonade, and iced tea — sweetened, of course. Bottled water had been added in recent years. No soft drinks!

Dogs were sliced down the middle and fried on a grill. Coaxed out by the heat, their juice bubbled and splattered in a sizzling symphony. Rising from the well-used steely surface, the combination of searing beef and spices permeated the air. On most days, Zeke, one of the co-owners, manned the grill. Of African American descent, he and his partner, Obadiah, founded the trailer-sized stand more than thirty years ago. These days, Obadiah battled arthritis. Refraining from involvement in the day-to-day activities, he always worked on Fridays, the stand's busiest day. Regulars greeted him and Zeke by name.

"The usual?" Obadiah asked Officer Danny Ragan matter-of-factly. With a faded smile and raspy voice, Obadiah leaned through the small sliding window. Donning a white ball cap depicting a hotdog with a dog's face at one end, mouth agape to represent barking, he squinted as the afternoon sun snuck under the thin aluminum awning. Although graceful in his old age, his eyes still contained the sparkle of youth.

"Yup," he said. "Two with chili, cheese, and slaw, Obi. Oh, and a sweet tea."

"Got it," Obi acknowledged. He cocked his head to the right and repeated the order to Zeke, who occupied the grill area. With a long, metal fork in his right hand and a white paper garrison cap on his head, he stood poised like a soldier ready to wage battle against a platoon of frankfurters covering the grill.

"And for you?" Obadiah queried Danny's partner, who stood studying the menu of toppings available on the establishment's only offering.

With a final, decisive glance at the menu, the young officer shifted his eyes and said, "Two Texas Tommies, potato salad, and a lemonade."

Obadiah nodded confirmation and fired the order to Zeke.

"Two Texans," Zeke responded, more to himself than to Obadiah.

Nick Fantini, a full-blooded Italian man with thick, jet-black hair, stood next his partner and waited for his lunch. "Who puts coleslaw on a hotdog?" he asked.

"I thought it was weird too, until I tried it," the senior officer explained. "I think it started in Georgia. Wherever it started, I like it."

The dispatcher interrupted their discussion. "Attention all units, attention all units. Armed man reported at the Central Mall. Potential hostage situation. All units respond," the flat female voice announced.

Gripping the microphone clipped to the left lapel of his uniform, Danny turned his head, squeezed the transmit button, and acknowledged, "Unit twelve responding."

On cue the two officers ran to their squad car and climbed in. A moment later, with lights flashing and siren blaring, they sped away. The mall was less than a mile from their location. Running red lights and maneuvering at breakneck speed, the two were the first to arrive on scene. Dispatch reported the suspect was on the lower level, near the Gap, possibly inside the store.

At the east entrance, the closest to the suspect's location, Ragan slammed on the brakes of his vehicle and threw it into park. Jumping from the car, he and Nick each retrieved their sidearms while sprinting toward the mall entrance.

"Keep your head on a swivel," Danny said. "We don't know where this guy is for sure."

"Got it."

A deluge of people flooded past them. They were screaming and shouting and paid no attention to the two officers as they threaded their way through the crowd and made their way inside the building.

Inside the glassed-in vestibule, Danny performed a rapid scan in all directions, clung to the wall on his left, and said, "I'll take point."

"Right behind you, boss," Nick replied, as the two began inching forward.

Outside, additional squad cars and emergency responders arrived and setup perimeters at each entrance. Within minutes, the mall was surrounded, and a police helicopter was circling overhead. The tactical team, better known as SWAT, gathered around a van and armed itself for the siege. News vans and reporters staged behind the police line. Onlookers gathered off in the distance, observing. Many stood, cellphones to their ears, informing loved ones of the event and their safety. Others conversed with one another about what had happened, who saw what, who was where when the rampage began, and replayed the sequence of events.

The mall emptied in a series of panicked bursts and was now deserted. With Danny in the lead, the two proceeded with deliberate and practiced and caution through the large corridor, scanning left, right, left, right. Making their way through a passage lined with stores, they pointed their weapons from side to side as they cleared each store. They emerged at the main body of the mall, an expansive space that served as a gateway to stores and kiosks. Its open expanse provided a full view of the second level. With a ceiling structure that incorporated an array of skylights in order to save energy, natural light poured in and flooded the lower level.

Ten feet ahead to the right, next to one of the many marble support columns, lay the body of a middle-aged woman. Bordering on consciousness, a pool of blood oozed out from under the area where she fell after sustaining a slashing wound to her right shoulder. Shopping bags were scattered across the floor, their contents spewed about. Behind her, a large circular marble fountain that occupied the center of the main entrance continued its preprogrammed aqueous choreography. Silence filled the mall, broken only by the intermittent cascading water.

"Command, this is unit twelve. Inside the east entrance, one victim, female, mid-forties, what appears to be a knife wound. Stand by."

"Copy, unit twelve. Standing by," came the flat reply.

With his weapon trained in front of him, Danny glanced over his right shoulder. Pointing at Nick, he brought his index and middle fingers to his eyes, and then pointed at himself.

Nick nodded, indicating he would cover him.

Danny turned, scanned the area quickly, and ran to the column where the woman lay bleeding. Peering around the marble column, Danny caught a glimpse of a man inside the Gap. Taking cover behind a hoodie display, he was holding what appeared to be a samurai sword against the throat of young female employee. He surveyed the area, pressing the sword's edge against the neck of the young woman hard enough to draw a slight crease of blood.

114

Danny turned to Nick, whose eyes were locked on his partner. Motioning to the woman, he held up his hand, fingers splayed. Then he made a fist and extended his index finger, followed by his middle finger, ring finger, and pinky. When he extended his thumb, Danny pivoted around the column and sprinted. He took cover opposite the store's opening. Telescoping his head forward, he peered inside and made eye contact with man wielding the sword. Meanwhile, Nick dashed to the victim, grabbed her by the waist, and dragged her to the safety of the corridor. Fighting to remain conscious, the sudden movement caused the older woman to emit a protesting moan.

Once Nick and the victim were safe, he radioed for medical support.

From behind the scant safety of the marble column, Danny took a slow but deliberate step, exited from his hiding place, and faced the man. Danny lowered his pistol and shouted, "Hey, the building is surrounded. You're not going to make it out of here alive unless you release the hostage and surrender."

"You don't know nothin'," the man shouted. "I'll get out of here my own terms."

"Listen," Danny tried to reason with him, "I've been in combat. Spent eight years in the Corps with tours in Iraq and Afghanistan. I've seen a lot of senseless death. Whatever you're going through, it can be worked out. You don't need to hurt anyone and leave here in a body bag."

There was a long pause. Danny heard the chatter in his earpiece and made a quick decision.

"My name is Danny. What's yours?"

"Calvin," the shooter said. "Calvin Dobbs. Everybody calls me Cal."

"Okay, Cal. Let's talk for a minute. Can we do that?" Danny inquired as he took several steps toward the store's entrance. As he did, he holstered his weapon and raised his hands.

"I suppose."

"Great. Now, why don't you let the girl go?"

"Why, so you can shoot me?

Shaking his head in protest, Danny stated, "No, Cal. Let her go, and I'll be your hostage, okay?"

As he inched forward, Danny sized Calvin up. He was about five feet ten inches tall, one hundred and seventy pounds, long gray hair with matching beard, and had the appearance of a homeless man. Danny estimated that he was probably in his fifties, though his appearance made him seem older.

"Cal, this is what I'm going to do. I'm going to lay my weapon on the ground, okay?" he said, as he bent down and placed his pistol on the floor. Eyes focused on Cal the entire time, he took three steps forward until he was within striking distance of the razor-sharp sword. Behind him, Danny could feel Nick's presence. Though Danny couldn't see him, he knew Nick was there, ready to return fire should it be necessary.

"Cal, I just want to talk, okay? You can see my hands." Danny stood motionless, awaiting a response.

"Fine. I see ya."

"Okay, great," Danny said. "Now let her go," he pleaded, eyes darting to the frightened woman in his grasp. "She hasn't done anything to you."

Danny locked his eyes on Cal's. He could tell Cal studied him in return, trying to decide if this was just a ploy to draw him out or an attempt to distract him. Staring at Danny with the intensity of someone experienced in violence, Cal decided he was sincere in his offer.

"Fine," he spat, "but no tricks."

"You have my word," Danny replied. Cal lowered the sword. After taking a few hesitant steps, the young store employee threw a quick glance over her shoulder and ran.

Cal raised the shiny blade, its tip just inches from Danny's throat.

"Well, it looks like you're my hostage now." Cal grinned. His teeth were straight and white, Danny noticed.

"I guess I am," Danny said without objection. For a moment, the two men stood in silence. Then Danny asked, "So what happened, Cal? What made you come here today and do this?"

Cal shrugged. "Life."

"What do you mean?" Danny probed.

Using the Japanese weapon as a pointer, he motioned at Danny. "You know what I mean. Life gets ya down. Only so much a man can take. Know what I mean?"

"I do, Cal. I do," Danny concurred. "There's help out there. Do you have family?"

Cal snickered. "Family? Now that's funny. Ain't got no family. Never did either. Been on my own my entire life – since before you were born."

"There must be someone, Cal," Danny reasoned. His earwig crackled to life.

"All units, this is TAC leader. In position." The voice was robotic and devoid of emotion.

With a wry laugh and a slight shake of his head, Cal said, "Nope. No one will miss me."

"It doesn't have to be that way," Danny said. "We can work this out."

"Work it out?" he sneered. "Are you crazy? I killed someone. They'll give me the chair! Better a body bag than all that voltage."

Hearing his words, Danny became aware this man wanted to commit suicide by cop. Being placed in such a grave circumstance was part of the job and was accepted by those sworn to uphold the law. However, living with the consequences was a daunting challenge.

Considering the implications of Cal's words, Danny said, "Better the chair and a chance to save your soul than spending eternity in Hell."

On the second floor, a sniper lay in the prone position facing the suspect. Sword extended, Cal's figure remained fixed in his crosshairs.

"TAC lead, TAC-1. On your go."

"Rog, TAC-1. Stand by."

Ragan monitored the communication on his radio. Time was running out.

"Listen, Cal. SWAT is in the building. They're going to take you out if you don't surrender. If they do, I promise you'll spend eternity in Hell."

"Hell?" Cal roared in disbelief. "This is Hell." He motioned back and forth with the sword. "My whole life is a living Hell!"

"Your life might be bad, but it's nothing compared to what you'll endure if they take you out. I'm begging you, Cal, don't do it. Put the sword down and we'll talk," Danny pleaded, leaning ever so slightly forward.

"Stop," Cal shouted.

Danny stared into Cal's listless eyes. They were a pale blue, faded from years of heartache and disappointment—the eyes of someone who had experienced a difficult life. The eyes were the gateway to the soul and bore the truth of an individual. Cal's pleaded for help and understanding. With no place to duck for cover, Cal was exposed. "I'll slice you good. I mean it."

Hands still raised, Danny said, "I believe you, Cal."

Laughing at him, Cal said, "You must be outta your mind, trade your life for another's."

"'No greater love,'" Danny quoted.

"Huh?"

"It's from the Gospel of John. Jesus said there is no greater love than to lay one's life down for his friends."

"Friends? That girl ain't your friend!

With a slight smile creasing his face, Danny said, "Perhaps not in the traditional sense, no. But she is a fellow human being who deserves to live."

120

Cal shook his head, perplexed. "I think you're the crazy one."

"Maybe I am. But I know where I'm going when I die. I'm not afraid."

"You should be."

"No, Cal. *You* should be afraid. Hell is real. You don't want to spend eternity there."

"That's where you're going," he said, poking at Danny with the sword, its tanto tip almost touching his throat.

"There's still time," Danny urged. "Pray with me."

"Pray with you?" Cal questioned, his voice filled with disbelief. "You're the one who needs to pray."

"My soul is secure," Danny responded. "I've accepted Jesus as my Lord and Savior. I bear witness to Him as long as there is breath in my body." Danny took a step toward him.

"You're a fool, Danny" Cal said, quickly drawing the sword back in a practiced arch. As he did, a single shot broke the mall's deafening silence. Cal's body recoiled, bounced off the display rack, and dropped to the ground. Danny knelt next to him. He had been shot in the chest, close to the heart. His gray t-shirt began turning a deep crimson. The life began draining from his pale eyes. Cal stared up at Danny.

The color was fading from his face, his rosy cheeks turning white. Danny knew he wasn't going to survive. "Stay with me," he commanded, cradling his body. "Stay with me."

"I guess I'm the fool," he mumbled, blood sputtering from his mouth.

"No, you're not. Pray with me," he said slapping his face several times in rapid succession. "Pray with me. There's still time. Jesus will forgive you if you ask him. Just pray with me."

Cal nodded.

As Danny prayed with him, Cal struggled to repeat his prayer. "Jesus, please forgive me. I accept you as Lord and Savior." Then he took his last breath.

11

Timothy glanced around the cramped confines of the waiting area. The heat was repressive and suffocating. The intense glow from the menacing doors provided the only light. Like the unpredictable flicker of a campfire's flame, it intermittently illuminated row upon row of dark shadows cramped in the vestibule of the damned. Uniquely heinous and wretched, they were assembled in a haphazard formation, each waiting his or her turn to be snatched up in the great claw of the Beast.

Studying the cramped quarters, Timothy observed conversations were diminished to incoherent murmurs, muffled by the distant but unrelenting metallic pulse contained within the confines that lay beyond the twin formidable doors. The screams of the damned were too numerous to count or distinguish and blended together in a torturous harmony. Except for the unmistakable shrill pitch of agony, the sound could have passed for a bee farm.

"There are so many people here," Timothy observed. "It doesn't seem real."

"Yeah, I know what you mean," Lauren agreed as she studied the shadows.

"Never a shortage of the damned," Grandma deadpanned.

Timothy tried to move, to shift his weight, but he did not have the strength. "I'm having difficulty moving," he said. "What's happening?"

"All part of the process," Sticks explained. "There is no light here, as you can tell. Only darkness. Strength is found in light, whereas the darkness has little to none. What little it possesses," he paused, "is fleeting and insignificant in comparison to that found in the light."

Light, Timothy thought, attempting to recall a faded memory from long ago. He was unable to summon an image or idea of what light was or had been. The only thing that existed now was complete and total darkness that was interrupted by the pulsing orange glow of the molten doors.

Listening to him and Sticks, Lauren and Jacob both attempted to twist around and shift position. Each found the task cumbersome and completely taxing. The simple motion was beyond difficult.

"I can barely move," Lauren said.

"Same here," Jacob added.

"Just wait," Grandma said. "Soon all of your strength will be gone like mine." For the first time, they realized she and the others stood poised like statues attached to the ground. Her movements were strained and infrequent. "The fear you feel now will get worse."

"Worse?" Timothy said in disbelief. "How can it get any worse?"

"Because you'll be even more helpless than you are now," Corn Fed chimed in. "Y'all feel pretty much helpless now, which is its own kind of anguish, I reckon'. But it's different from actually being helpless. Adds to the torment, I s'pose."

With his mouth agape and his brow beetled, Timothy remained silent in disbelief as he pondered Corn Fed's words. Until now, he had never really felt helpless, except once, as a child. Recalling the incident, Janel was supposed to meet him after school and walk home with him. She forgot, and he didn't know what to do. That was nothing compared to what he felt now. He was hopelessly damned for eternity

The last in their group to arrive, Jacob stared down in disbelief at his disfigured body. He fought to turn his shoulders and lift his arms. They were non-responsive and dangled next to his torso like foreign objects. The absence of light and consuming presence of the darkness had in short order depleted what little strength his soul possessed.

Staring at Grandma, Jacob said, "You're right. This is worse." The fear that had consumed him upon arrival intensified a hundred-fold. Beyond the permanency of this place and exceeding the anticipated agony that awaited him beyond the furnace doors, the overwhelming realization of being defenseless and the loss of will provided a level of terror beyond comprehension.

Attempting to lift his right arm, Jacob found the minor level of exertion draining and abandoned the endeavor. Looking from Timothy to Grandma, he said, "I– I can't even lift my arm."

Timothy turned to Grandma for an explanation.

"All effort is a matter of the will," she began. "Here," she glanced around, "individual will does not exist." She paused. "At least it doesn't exist without tremendous effort."

Sticks spoke up. "When we were mortals, we had the luxury of free will. That is, we were free to make decisions and choose. Here, we have no will."

"I don't understand," Jacob said.

"You see, when you had a body made of flesh, you lived in a world that contained light. Light is the source of all life. Only in the light can one's will be realized. Here," her voice trailed off to almost a whisper, "here, there is no life, only death. The will only exists as an abstract concept, with exhausting effort."

Timothy considered her words for a moment. A memory from one of his last coerced forays to church flashed through his mind. Sitting in the pew next to his mother, at the conclusion of the pastoral prayer, the congregation recited the Lord's Prayer. He remembered the words, "...*thy will* be done in earth as it is in heaven."

"*Thy will*," he muttered to himself.

Considering Grandma's words, he never realized the incredible freedom the will provided. Timothy recalled it was something his mother's Sunday school class had studied once. Thinking back, his mother had referenced the class and the concept when she relented and afforded him the same privilege as his sister, to opt out of church and youth group. "You're free to choose," she had said. "God gave man free will. Adam and Eve both had the ability to choose. So do you. But," she had admonished, "choose wisely."

Timothy did not have time to ponder the full import of his mother's words. The nerve-rattling shrill of iron hinges squeaking open pierced his memory. Skittering along his spine, the squeal crescendoed for a moment and ended with an ominous thud that shook the ground and walls.

127

Shifting his eyes toward the cacophony, Timothy stared at the vast gateway to the Lake of Fire. Molten doors cast open, the Beast stood silhouetted in the doorframe. He remained motionless, transfixed against the fiery background. This was unusual for him.

"What's he doing?" Timothy inquired in a whisper.

"Waiting." Sticks broke the silence.

"Waiting for what?" Lauren asked.

"A fresh soul," Grandma answered.

"*Fresh*?" Jacob asked. "What does that mean?"

"Someone who's 'bout to die," Corn Fed supplied.

"How does he know that?" Timothy asked.

For a moment no one spoke. All eyes focused on the flaming orange rectangle that was the door to Hell and the shadow occupying its center. Even silhouetted, the gruesome features of the Beast were evident. Like a primitive creature from a horror movie, he stood poised in Hell's doorway.

"He's the Prince of Darkness and the ruler of death," Grandma said. "The Beast knows his own and waits in anticipation of their arrival."

"What do you mean? He wasn't waiting for me," Timothy inquired.

"My dear," Grandma began, locking eyes with Timothy, "he most certainly waits for all the newly dead. Some, though—" Here she paused and allowed her eyes to shift back to the Beast before continuing. "There are some whose arrival he anticipates more than others. I'm not sure why."

As Timothy thought about this, the Beast took several giant strides forward. Fire spewed out around the door frame behind him, accompanied by a wave of blistering heat. The stench of smoldering ashes and decay engulfed them. It was sour and putrid, like a stale wound that been charred.

"That smell," she exclaimed.

"The stench of the damned," Grandma said.

The Beast stood just feet away from them and waited. No one dared make eye contact with him, lest they capture his attention. While the torment of the waiting area was intolerable, the fury that waited them was far worse and something to be postponed, if only for the time being.

Shifting his massive head from side to side, the Beast suddenly looked up, a quizzical expression on his ghoulish face. Cowering ever so slightly, his reptilian body recoiled, almost as if in pain. He staggered backwards, as though he had been stuck by some invisible force.

Regaining his footing and composure, he flung his arms back, puffed out his chest, and roared upward at something only he could perceive. Fire sprayed out his mouth. The incinerating heat in the waiting area intensified.

"What's happening?" Timothy asked as he experienced a new level of fear.

"He lost one," Grandma explained.

"Lost what?" Timothy wanted to know.

"A soul."

"How do you know that?" Lauren asked.

"Seen it before, dear," Grandma said.

Before Lauren could inquire further, the Beast beat his chest several times and launched a salvo. Roaring and shrieking, he spat a diatribe upward at an unseen presence. Though his language was unintelligible, it was decidedly evil.

Enraged by this loss, the Beast released his umbrage. Reaching back with his prehistoric arm, he motioned it forward and repeated the process with his other arm, bellowing as he did.

Suddenly, the gaping orange doorway turned black.

"Don't look," Grandma said, urgency in her voice.

"What?" Timothy asked.

"Close your eyes, youngin'," Corn Fed blurted.

Timothy did as he was commanded. "Okay, my eyes are closed. What's going on?"

"Demons," Grandma said. "If you look at them, they'll devour your soul and regurgitate it in Hell."

As Timothy was visualizing Grandma's explanation, he was jostled back and forth. Like a commuter on a crowded train, he was bumped on a regular basis, almost violently. A high pitched shrill pierced his ears. Resembling a colony of screeching bats, the demons swarmed over them. Feeding on their helpless souls, they devoured all those who dared make eye contact.

"What's happening?" Timothy screamed.

"Feeding frenzy," Grandma shouted. "Keep your eyes closed until the screeching stops."

Amid the screeching, pushing, shoving, and cries for help, Timothy kept his eyes shut. The torment went on for an indeterminate amount of time. Then suddenly it stopped. It was almost too quiet. The familiar buzz returned to the darkness. After a brief hesitation, Timothy opened his eyes one at a time. For a moment, he stared down, afraid to look up.

Shifting his gaze upward, his eyes locked on Grandma's. "Is it over?"

"For now. They'll be back," she explained, her voice devoid of emotion.

Timothy did a quick scan of the area. It was so dark it was impossible to tell how many souls the demons had devoured. Taking inventory of his immediate surroundings, he noticed Jacob was missing.

"Where's Jacob?" he asked.

No one answered. Explanation wasn't necessary.

Looking at Lauren, he said, "I didn't think this could get any worse." He paused. "I was wrong."

12

As if from a rooftop, Cal stood looking down on his lifeless body. He saw Danny crouched over him, holding his hand. Although at a distance, he noticed tears in his eyes. Danny's lips moved, and Cal heard his words with extreme clarity and precision.

"Thank you, Father, for hearing Cal's prayer, and for being the God of salvation. Amen." He looked up as fellow law enforcement agents entered the store with caution. "He's gone," he announced.

For a moment, Cal was filled with a tinge of sorrow for Danny as he continued to watch the scene unfold. Sensing a presence, Cal realized he was not alone. Turning to his left, he was blinded the most brilliant white light he had ever seen. As he continued to stare at it, the image of a man came into focus. Clad in a snow-white robe with a purple sash wrapped around his waist, Cal observed he was rugged and strong. *A man's man,* he thought. He flashed a welcoming smile at Cal.

Recognition set in, and Cal realized he was standing next to Jesus. For an instant, he froze, unable to move. Then he dropped to his knees, head bowed, and cowered.

"Arise. I've come for you," Jesus said.

"Come to condemn me?" Cal asked, as he rose to his feet, defeated acceptance in his voice.

"No," Jesus replied with a gentle shake of his head. "I've come to take you home."

"You mean—" Cal stopped, perplexed.

"Yes. Come, let's walk together," Jesus said, and motioned with his hand. Cal noticed a wound in the palm of his hand.

Looking back over his right shoulder, the image of Danny was gone, replaced by a resplendent blue sky and lush green grass.

He turned to Jesus. As he opened his mouth to ask a question, Jesus said, "Don't worry about him. He's one of mine. He'll be just fine."

"Oh," was all Cal could manage as he kept pace.

Suddenly, Jesus stopped and turned toward Cal and faced him. "And so are you!" Jesus smiled.

Cal studied Jesus's face. His blue eyes twinkled when he spoke, and his smile was brilliant and inviting.

"I– I don't understand," Cal began. "How?"

With a slight laugh, Jesus turned and continued to walk. Cal joined him. "You accepted me, Cal."

"All I did was say some words," he replied. "I was about to die and knew it."

"Yes, that's true. But you chose to believe — to say those words," Jesus said, glancing at Cal. "You had faith. And that — That is all that is necessary."

"My whole life, I was a wicked person," Cal said.

Throwing Cal a smile of recognition, Jesus said, "I know."

Grabbing Jesus' arm, Cal stopped abruptly. "I killed someone."

Jesus took a step toward Cal. Just inches from his face, he stared at him. A solemn look on his face, he said, "I know."

"Well, of course, you do but —"

Grabbing Cal by the shoulders, Jesus said, "Cal, you have been forgiven."

"Forgiven?" Cal said.

"Yes, my child. You have been forgiven." Jesus smiled at him and placed his arm around his should. "Let us continue. We're almost there."

As they walked, Cal pondered the word *forgiven*. He'd never given it much thought. It was a strange concept, something he had never really experienced either as a giver or receiver.

At last, he asked, "How can you forgive someone like me?"

With a smile, Jesus said, "It's easy. I am the way, the truth, and the life. The only way anyone can come to my Father is through me. I died on the cross to provide salvation for all.

Cal considered his words for a moment. "I see."

Out of the corner of his eye, he noticed Jesus had stopped. "We're here," Jesus announced.

"Where?" Cal asked,

"My Father's house, of course." Jesus beamed.

Eyes wide with wonder, Cal stood in Heaven's foyer. He was overpowered with the fragrant scent of flower—hundreds, thousands of them. On either side of the pearlescent gates stood flaming cherubim. They were formidable and daunting, not to be trifled with. In the distance, a chorus could be heard singing in perfect harmony.

A man stood at the gate. Also in a white robe, he wore an inviting smile. "Welcome, Cal," he said.

Although he wasn't sure how, Cal knew it was Peter. Turning to Jesus, he said, "I can't go in there. I don't belong here. I'm not one of them."

Dismissing Cal's comments with a slight laugh, Jesus said, "Oh, you most certainly do belong here. Come, we must go meet my Father. He will explain everything to you."

Before Cal could protest, Jesus led him by the arm. They entered through the narrow gate and began walking along the golden pathway. Gathered in groups, Cal observed the endless sea of believers, all youthful, clad in white robes. A few caught his eye, smiled, and waved. Cal smiled and waved back.

Noticing all the wild animals roaming about, he commented, "This place looks like a zoo."

Smiling, Jesus said, "We're very fond of animals. Here," he motioned with his arm, "we live in harmony with them."

"I see," Cal commented, as he took in the scenery. Off to his left, he stared as a lion and lamb played together in total harmony.

Veering off the golden pathway, Jesus navigated their way through a throng of people. They called out to him, and, Cal observed, Jesus responded to them by name.

Noticing their change of direction, Cal asked, "Where are we going?"

"There's someone I want you to meet," Jesus said.

"I thought we were going to meet your Father."

"We are," he said. "Just a slight detour."

"Oh."

Standing under a massive oak tree, a small group chatted amongst themselves. When they saw Jesus, they all smiled and greeted him. In no rush, Jesus spoke to them in turn.

Gesturing to a man to his left, Jesus turned to Cal and said, "Cal, I'd like you to meet Robert."

"Welcome," Robert said with a smile.

Cal stood frozen in place, staring into the face of the man he had shot and killed.

*   *   *   *   *   *

At twenty years of age, Robert Kenyon was on his way to success. Just two years away from graduating college and taking over the family business, a gas station and convenience store, he had met a fetching young woman at church. New to the small Ohio town, Melanie Dupree had transferred from the community college.

A day after meeting her, Robert was working the night shift. Usually, he worked at night because his classes were during the day. Although his parents were paying for his education and planning to turn the business over to him, he wasn't getting a free ride.

"Your father started out stocking shelves and sweeping the floor," his mother had told him as a boy. "It was good enough for him; it's good enough for you. Remember," she had admonished, "no one is above doing any job."

It was ten-thirty in the evening. The store was empty. There wouldn't be much traffic, not on a Monday night during football season. Maybe a few stragglers filling up and coming inside for a slushy. In an hour and half, Robert would lock up and head home.

Sitting behind the register, Robert's focus was on his cellphone. Having hit it off right away with Melanie in Sunday school class, and realizing they were attending the same university, they had exchanged numbers.

The unmistakable hum of a car engine interrupted him. Glancing over his shoulder, he peered out the window at a beat-up pickup. An old Dodge covered in more gray primer than black paint sat with its lights on outside the twin glass doors.

Hearing the electronic door chime, Robert placed his cellphone under the counter. Looking in the direction of the chime, he said, "Evening."

A thin man with gray scraggly hair threw him a quick glance and nodded as he headed to the back of the store where the beer refrigerators lined the wall. Wearing a worn olive green, army-style jacket and faded jeans, he looked like a senior citizen, Robert thought.

As he approached the register with a cold six-pack of Bud, Robert studied the man's face. It bore the lines of a hard life and was covered by weathered skin that reminded him of a worn catcher's mitt.

Smiling, Robert greeted him. "How are you this evening, sir?"

"Good," he stated, his voice hollow and empty.

Robert rang up the beer and placed it in a plastic bag. "Is that going to do it for you tonight?" he asked.

For a long moment the man just stared at Robert. At last, he said, "No. Not quite." Withdrawing a revolver from his pocket, he leveled it at Robert. With a nod of his head, he said, "Open the register and put the cash in the bag." Almost as an afterthought, he said, "And don't trying anything."

Hands raised out of fear, Robert said, "Okay, okay. Just don't shoot, okay?"

"C'mon, make it fast," the man said glancing at the door.

Moving as fast as he could, Robert entered his code. The cash drawer was released and sprang out. Removing the bills from their slots, he stuffed them in the bag and stared into the pale blue eyes of the robber.

As he reached for the bag, Robert's cellphone vibrated under the register. Without thinking, his arm flexed for a split second.

In that split second, Cal panicked and fired a single shot, hitting Robert in the chest.

*　　　*　　　*　　　*　　　*　　　*

Eyes fixed on Robert, Cal said, "I thought you were reaching for a gun. I did," he pleaded, as he glanced at Jesus for reassurance. "I didn't mean to kill you. I swear."

"I know, Cal." Robert smiled at him.

"How can you smile at me?"

"Because," Jesus answered for him, "Robert is one of my children. His soul belongs to me."

Reaching out, Robert hugged Cal. "I forgive you, Cal. I forgive you!" Robert took a step back, his hands still on Cal's shoulders.

"How? I took your life," Cal said in disbelief.

"Simple," Jesus answered. "Robert can forgive you because my Father has forgiven him. He alone has the power to forgive sins."

"Oh, I see," Cal said, looking from Jesus to Robert.

Jesus smiled at the two men and said, "Let us continue, Cal. My Father is waiting."

As they made their way back to the golden path, Jesus turned to Cal. "I wanted you to know that, even though Robert died that night, the eternal consequences were not dire."

Cal walked in silence for a moment. "This is a lot to take in, I have to admit."

Throwing his head back in laughter, Jesus said, "Yes, I imagine it is. But it will all make sense very soon."

Approaching a sea of crowns scattered at the base of a golden thrown, Cal listened as the angels sang. Their unison voices were peaceful and comforting. Jesus gestured to Cal. Looking at him for reassurance, Jesus smiled. "I want you to meet my Father."

Cal walked up the steps and knelt, head bowed.

A great voice boomed. "Calvin Dobbs..."

Cal lifted his head and looked up. "Yes, my Lord."

"Rise, my son."

Cal did as he was commanded. The figure upon the throne was adorned in radiant glory — the source of all light in Heaven. To his left, on a smaller throne, sat a man Cal somehow knew was John the Baptist. A matching, but larger throne, sat empty on the right. As he focused on the empty chair, Jesus walked past him and sat in it.

"Calvin," the voice bellowed, gripping his attention. "Yes, my Lord?" he responded, looking up into the complete presence of God.

With a great book flung open on his lap, the voice turned the crinkled pages for a moment then stopped. Sliding his finger down the page, he stopped and looked up. Staring into his eyes, he pronounced, "Calvin, you have received salvation, secured by the blood of the Lamb." His brilliant eyes shifted to Jesus in recognition of his sacrifice. "His death is your death; his resurrection is your resurrection." He paused and closed the massive book with a dull thud. "You are forgiven. Welcome to Heaven!"

13

Mel's Diner sat just off Route 321 in Pigeon Forge, Tennessee. A popular eating establishment with a large, traditional neon sign perched above its stainless steel and fire-engine red exterior, it was a throwback to a bygone era when food was sold from trailers. Offering a traditional menu that included a full array of home-style meals, including meatloaf and chicken and dumplings, it truly was an anachronism.

Entering through the double glass doors, Jonathan Smith stood on the black and white tiled floor and surveyed the dinner crowd. *Not too bad,* he thought, *for a Wednesday evening.* Clad in faded jeans, work boots, and a navy-blue polo shirt with Tennessee Valley Authority emblazoned on the left breast, Jonathan stood just over six feet tall. With his mop of jet-black hair combed straight back and a chiseled jaw, he was fit and rugged.

Reminiscent of the trailers that had once delivered food to patrons, Mel's was a narrow structure with a single aisle lined with booths on either side. Dividing the row of booths opposite the door was a counter lined with blue, round, vinyl stools that swiveled.

As he took a step toward one of the empty stools at the counter, he heard a familiar voice over his left shoulder.

"Johnnie?" the elderly voice queried.

Stopping and turning, Jonathan saw Mrs. Ellen Winters sitting in a booth by herself. With wavy, gray hair and pleasant features, she had aged with extreme grace. Her oval tortoise-rimmed glasses contrasted with her hair and skin tone, reminding Jonathan of a librarian.

Closing the distance, he said, "Hey, Mrs. Winters. How are you?"

"Good, Johnnie. Won't you please join me?" she said, motioning to the empty side of the booth.

"Sure," Jonathan said, as he slid into the booth. "Be happy to."

No sooner had he settled in when a young girl clad in jeans and a bright pink t-shirt emblazoned with the diner's logo arrived to take their order.

"Good evening," she said in a light southern drawl indicative the region. "I'm Gina. Are y'all ready to order, or do y'all need a minute?"

Shifting his gaze across the table and then back to Gina, Mrs. Winters glanced up and responded, "Give us a minute, dear."

"Sure," Gina said and pivoted away.

"How have you been, Johnnie?" I missed you in church last week."

"Good, good. Working, mostly. A lot of OT, with the expansion to plant." He paused. "It's keeping me busy."

"Sounds like it," she said. Ellen Winters leaned against the back of the booth and studied him for a moment. His high school football days behind him, Jonathan was still in shape and possessed boyish good looks.

"How are things at church?" he asked.

"Oh, they're just fine. In fact," she leaned forward, "I'm on my way to Bible Study. Just stopped in for a bite."

"That's right," he said. "It's Wednesday. I lose track of the days sometimes," he said with a laugh. "I'm on my way into work," Jonathan explained with a nod of his head in the direction of the highway in the distance. "Night shift."

She nodded. "I see."

"Didn't feel like cooking," he said.

"Yes, imagine so. I don't cook much either anymore." Her voice trailed off as she focused on something out the window that only she could see.

Jonathan remained silent for a moment. Henry "Hank" Winters, Ellen's husband, had passed away over two decades ago, leaving her with only Stanley, her son. Next door neighbors since childhood, he and Jonathan had been best friends their entire lives.

Shifting her focus back to Jonathan, she said, "You were always so good to Stanley." The brief smiled she managed faded, replaced by a somber expression. "You were a good friend to him — especially when he got sick."

Jonathan didn't know what to say. He felt a lump in his throat. "I miss him," he said at last. "He was my best friend."

For a moment the two sat in silence, oblivious to the familiar din that was the rhythm of the diner. Neither spoke. Instead they stared out the window, each lost in thought.

Turning back, Jonathan said, "He was a fighter."

A weak smile washed over her face and was gone. "He was. He was indeed."

Not long after graduating high school, Stanley Winters fell ill. Unbeknownst to his family and friends, he had not been feeling well for quite some time. He had ignored the symptoms until he lost his balance at work and collapsed. A battery of tests revealed he had leukemia. Doctors were somewhat hopeful for his chances of remission.

Although he fought like a warrior, Stanley succumbed to the disease just over a year ago.

Reaching for a menu that stood vertically at the end of the table behind the napkins, salt, and pepper, Mrs. Winters said with a smile, "He's in a better place, Johnnie. No need for us to be so glum." Her eyes twinkled as she spoke and proffered the menu.

Taking the menu, he joined her, and smiled too. "You're right. He's in heaven."

"Indeed, he is—along with his father! I bet they are having a marvelous time, too," she mused. "A lot of catching up to do, I imagine."

Nodding his head, Jonathan agreed. "I'm sure."

Gina appeared almost out of nowhere. "Y'all ready to order?"

Jonathan placed the menu off to the side without looking at it. "I'm ready, are you?" he said, turning to Mrs. Winters.

"You haven't even looked at the menu," she commented.

With a grin on his face, he said, "Oh, I eat here a lot. I know what I want."

"Oh, alright, then." She turned to Gina, who stood with her pen poised. "I'll have the meatloaf."

"Anything to drink?"

"Sure. Sweet tea, please."

Turning to Jonathan, she asked, "And for you, sir?"

"I'll have the Ottis burger, fries, and a Coke," please.

"You got it," she said, as she scribbled and was gone.

"Meatloaf," Jonathan said. "You used to make the best meatloaf."

"Oh, I still do. But…" she stopped. Catching herself, she recovered, "It's all in the gravy. They do a pretty good job here." She tapped the table. "But not as good as mine." She smiled.

"I remember your gravy," Jonathan said. "Every Monday night during football season." He smiled. "Practically its own food group."

She laughed. "Secret ingredient is all I can say," she said with feigned aplomb.

"You'll have to tell me what that is one of these days," he prodded.

"Never," she said with an air of defiance as she laughed.

Gina arrived and placed their drinks on the table without comment.

"Thank you," Jonathan said.

"Worcestershire," Mrs. Winters said.

"What?" Jonathan asked, confused.

"That's my secret ingredient. I add three drops—only three drops—to the gravy. Gives it its signature flavor."

"Oh, I see," he said. "Well, your secret is safe with me."

Leaning forward, she placed her hand on his arm and whispered. "The real secret is that it isn't even my recipe. I got it from the newspaper's food section years ago." She leaned back and laughed. "Don't tell anyone."

Jonathan couldn't help himself and laughed too. "Mum's the word."

"If the Women's Circle ever found out, I'd be banned," she jested.

"Oh, I'm sure you would be." He patted her arm as he chuckled.

"Could you imagine if they ever found out?" she asked. "Some of them can be quite catty, even for church ladies. Take Beatrice Owen, for example. She still lords her win at last year's bake off over my head!"

He nodded. "I've heard that," he said, taking a sip of his soda. "Mom said that on several occasions."

"How are your folks doing? I miss seeing them every day. Such wonderful neighbors," she said.

"They're doing well. I see Dad at the plant almost every day, although he's getting ready to retire. Our paths usually cross at some point."

"That's so nice," she beamed. "He's a good man. You're very fortunate. And your mother is just the best!"

"Yes, I know," he agreed. "Mom keeps busy too. She took early retirement, but she gardens, cooks, and sews. Plus, she volunteers a lot."

"That's wonderful, Johnnie. I'm still getting used to life on my own." She paused. "It's funny, when Hank and I bought our house, I thought we'd live there forever. You know, raise our kids, grow old together, sit on the swing during the summer and drink lemonade." She took a mouthful of tea. "Funny how life turns out. Now I'm living alone in a senior's community."

"I thought it was a fifty-five and over place?"

"Oh, it is. I'm in the 'over' category!"

He laughed. "It can't be that bad."

"It's not, really. I mean, they always have something to do. And I have church — the Women's Circle and Bible Study — but..." she stopped and gave her head a shake. "It's just not the same." All of a sudden, she looked sad and lonely.

With a slight nod, Jonathan said, "I understand."

152

He wasn't sure what to say. Saved by perfect timing, Gina arrived with their food. They both sat back as she announced each meal as she placed it in front of each of them.

"Can I get y'all anything else?" Gina asked.

"No, thank you," Mrs. Winters said.

"No, thanks," Jonathan said.

"Johnnie, would you ask the blessing, please?" she asked reaching across the table for his hands.

"Of course," he said, taking her hands in his. They bowed their heads. "Heavenly Father, thank you for this meal, for this time to catch up. Please watch over Mrs. Winters, bless her, and strengthen her. Nourish this food to our bodies and help us to be your faithful servants. In your name I pray, amen."

"Amen," she replied.

Jonathan skootched out of the booth and announced, "I'll be right back. I want to wash up before I eat. You go ahead and start without me."

"Okay, dear. I think it will. It smells devine."

Jonathan made his way to end of the center aisle and entered the one-person restroom. In the middle of lathering his hands with soap, he heard a tremendous crash followed by screams and shouts. From the sound of it, it was close. *The parking lot perhaps,* he thought. Rinsing the soap from his hands, he dried them under the hand blower, its cacophony drowning out the muffled din of the diner, and reached for the door. He took two steps and was horrified by what he saw.

The booth where he had just been sitting had been obliterated and replaced with the front of a mangled pickup truck. Patrons had gathered around the melee, still in shock. Jonathan raced to the scene.

"Mrs. Winters," he shouted. "Mrs. Winters?"

"Here…" her voice coughed.

Turning to his left, on the opposite side of the diner, Mrs. Winters lay on the ground, body twisted and contorted.

Jonathan knelt beside her. "Don't try to move," he commanded. "Help is on the way. You're going to be okay."

He studied her for a moment. She didn't appear to be bleeding. That was a good sign, he thought.

"Johnnie," she whispered.

"Yes?" he leaned closer to her, placing his ear near her mouth.

"It's okay, Johnnie. I'm going to be with him…"

Lifting his head, he looked down at her. "With who?"

"Him," she raised her brittle hand and pointed at someone only she could see before it fell to the ground in an act of finality.

Jonathan looked but didn't see anyone. His attention returned to Mrs. Winters. Eyes open and a smile on her face, she was gone.

Jonathan held her hand and wept.

14

Ellen Winters stood across from Jonathan. She watched as he held her hand and spoke to her. "It's okay, Mrs. Winters. It's okay," he mumbled, as tears streamed down his face. "You're in Heaven now. You're all in Heaven now." He gently rubbed the back of her aged hand against his face.

Rescue workers arrived at the scene. Taking a quick assessment, they divided their attention to the driver of the truck and Mrs. Winters. Jonathan stepped back as they knelt beside her, checking her vitals.

"She's gone," he said, almost to himself.

Without acknowledging his comments, they proceeded to check her pulse and respiration — all part of standard procedure. Unable to make a pronouncement of death, they followed protocol and prepared their patient for transport.

With a blank expression on his face, Jonathan watched the scene unfold with the other diners, now all unwitting spectators to the devastation. *Poor boy,* Mrs. Winters thought. *He looks so sad.* She was impressed at the speed with which they had gotten her body on the gurney.

As they wheeled her body away, Ellen was blinded by a brilliant white light. Off in the distance the faint sound of voices, hundreds, perhaps thousands, singing in union began to grow.

Sensing she was not alone, she turned, searching for the unseen presence. Enveloped in overwhelming love, she saw no one.

"Ellen?" a familiar voice said. "I'm here."

In an instant the light dissipated and she looked directly into the face of her savior.

"My Lord," she said, dropping to her knees and bowing her head.

Bending down to meet her, Jesus touched her shoulder and said, "Arise, my child."

They stood together, and she hugged him like a long lost friend.

"Welcome," he said. "You have been a good and faithful servant."

"Thank you," was all she could manage.

"Come," he said, motioning with his hand. "There is much to show you."

Taking his arm, they walked together. "I don't know what to say," she began. "I mean, when I got up today, I never imagined I'd be here, or meeting you…"

He laughed. "Yes, I'm sure. No one knows the hour."

"Not at all," she said, shaking her head. "But it's a wonderful surprise," she added. "Don't get me wrong…I mean…I feel bad for Johnnie…and the women at church. I have a cake in my car for Bible study tonight," she added as an afterthought.

"Well, Johnnie will be just fine," he reassured her and added a knowing smile.

"Oh, sure, sure…yes."

"And so will the women at church," he said, reaching over and patting her arm. "They're all my children."

She smiled up at him. "Of course, they are."

Stopping, he said, "We're here."

Ellen marveled at the simplistic opulence of Heaven's gates. "It's beautiful," she exclaimed.

"Yes. Welcome to Paradise," he said, leading the way.

Passing the cherubim, they paused inside the gate. The singing voices were louder and distinguished. Overcome with emotion, Ellen was speechless. Her senses were inundated with an array of colors, sounds, and scents that transcended anything she had ever experienced or imagined. She felt like a blind person seeing for the first tie.

"This is…fantastic," she said at last. "Just so…incredible."

Jesus responded with a knowing smile.

Unable to completely absorb Heaven's grandiosity, Ellen said, "It just goes on and on and on."

"In my Father's house there are many mansions," he said and began to walk.

So that's what that verse meant, she thought.

Ellen fell in line with him. As they made their way through the throng of believers, Ellen's head turned in every direction in an attempt to survey the splendor of Heaven.

"The flowers," she said. "They're beautiful! And so many trees." Tuning past a large oak tree, a crowd of believers smiled at her and waved. She threw them a wave back, as their names ran through her mind. For a moment, this struck her as odd, but then she dismissed it. As they made their way, a lion approached them, heading in the opposite direction. Jesus stopped, bent down, and petted it.

Looking up at Ellen, he said, "This is Fredderico."

Possessing no fear, Ellen bent down and rubbed his mane. "He's amazing."

They stood and continued in the direction of the voices. "Is this what Eden was like before the fall?" she asked.

He nodded. "Yes."

As his words sank in, she heard a familiar voice off to her right. "Hey, Elle."

In a pristine patch of grass, clad a white robe, stood Hank. Without delay she ran to him.

"Hank," she screamed, bear hugging him.

"Elle," he said. He had never called her by her full name, always dropping the 'n.'

"Hank," she said, studying him, "you're so youthful and young."

"So are you," he said, stepping back and pointing at her.

Pausing, Ellen stretched her arms out and studied them, holding her hands in front of her. A look of astonishment washed over her face.

"I'm young," she said, turning to Jesus.

"Yes. Here," he gestured with his hands, "no one ages."

Turning back, she said, "Oh, Hank! How I've missed you!" She waited for him to respond in kind. When he didn't, she asked, "Didn't you miss me too?"

"Well..." he began.

"To miss someone is a form of grief and associated with sadness. That does not exist here," Jesus supplied.

"Oh. Of course," Ellen assented. "That makes sense."

"We have a lot of catching up to do, Hank," she began.

"Indeed you do," Jesus agreed. "And you have eternity to do it. But first we must see my Father."

Hank gave Ellen a hug. "You go ahead. I've already met him. I'll be right here when you get back."

"Okay," she said, and hugged him one last time.

Returning to the path, Ellen joined Jesus, and they headed in the direction of the voices. "Do you escort everyone to meet your Father?"

"Yes. No one comes to the Father except through me," he quoted with a smile.

She smiled, recalling the familiar Scripture reference. "I remember that verse."

He smiled. "It's true. I am the way, the truth, and the life."

"Indeed you are," Ellen said in acknowledgement of her salvation.

They approached a series of marble steps upon which sat a formidable gold throne. The figure who sat on the throne was adorned in a long, white robe. In a choral arrangement behind him were multiple rows of ascending angels singing in unison, "Glory to God in the highest."

Ellen stood at the foot of the steps, admiring the sheer beauty, and taking in the moment. Reaching out, Jesus took her hand and said, "Right this way."

Ellen followed him up the seven steps carefully, taking care not to tread on any of the crowns that dotted the marble. She could see some were gold, others silver, all were ornate and decorated with gemstones. When they approached the throne, Jesus took his seat at the right hand of his Father, and Ellen knelt, head bowed.

"Ellen, my child," an authoritative, yet familiar, comforting voice said, "arise."

Staring into the face of God, Ellen felt complete and perfect peace. With a loving smile, he picked up a heavy book, inches thick, and placed it on his lap. Ellen read the cover, *The Book of Life*.

Slapping it open, he thumbed the thin pages, as he scanned them. "Ah," he said and stopped. "Ellen Winters," his voice boomed as he looked down at her. "Your sins have been forgiven, and you have been granted eternal life, sealed with the blood of the Lamb." He studied her for a moment, then turned to his right.

Jesus reached to the side of his throne before standing. With a crown made of gold and silver adorned with jewels in his hand, he stood in front of

Ellen and carefully placed it on her head. "Well done, my good and faithful servant," he said.

"Thank you," she replied as she bowed her head.

She turned and together they made their way down the steps. When they reached the bottom, Jesus stopped and turned toward Ellen, who removed her crown, studied it for a moment, and then, recalling what Scripture said about receiving rewards in Heaven, tossed it among the others.

"No need for that," she said, turning as a smile creased her lips.

Jesus just smiled at her. With a dip of his head, he nodded in the direction of Hank, who stood a few feet away, waiting.

Ellen strode over to him. "Hank, my darling, I have so much to tell you."

"Oh, I have quite a bit to tell you too," he replied, eyebrows raised.

"Well, ladies first," she said.

"Fine," he smiled, taking her hand. "Let's walk."

"Okay."

As they departed from the throne area, Ellen stopped, turned, and looked back at Jesus.

With a wave he said, "It's fine. We have all eternity to spend together. Catch up."

"Thank you," she said.

As they walked, Hank served as tour guide. "It's more beautiful than I could have ever imagined, Elle, " he said. Pointing to a peach tree, he said, "The fruit, Elle...incredible! You'll wish you had them for your peach pie."

"I bet!" Her head turned in all directions. "I just can't believe it. Look at all the people...so young and happy. I– I don't recall ever being this happy." she stopped and looked at him.

"You weren't. None of us were. Here," he waved at the landscape with his arm, "there is only happiness."

Ellen considered the term *happiness* for a moment and realized that, absent God and forgiveness, it really does not exist. *Here, in this moment, forgiven, and in my heavenly body I truly know happiness,* she mused to herself.

With a broad smile on her face, she bear-hugged him. "Oh, Hank, it's so good to be here with you."

"You too, Elle," he said.

They continued walking, making their way through a field carpeted with emerald, green grass. Glancing down, Ellen remarked mostly to herself, "Not a brown spot or dead blade of grass to be found." Off in the distance, she saw a small group of men conversing. With a bit of surprise, she recognized the one man.

"That's Paul," she said. "The one on the left."

Laugh, Hank replied, "Yes, I know. I've met him."

"You have?" she asked, disbelief filling her voice.

"Yes. I've been here a while," he added. "Remember, a day with the Lord is like a thousand years."

"Oh..." her voice trailed off. "I guess you have. I forgot."

"Let's go say hi," he encouraged.

"Well, I don't want to interrupt," she protested.

"I don't think he'll mind," Hank said, leading her.

"Hank, I can meet him later," she said. "He's busy talking to people."

"Trust me, Elle. You'll be happy you did."

She was about object, when the man Paul was speaking with turned to her.

"Hi, Mom," Stanley said.

"Stanley! My baby," she said, taking him in her arms.

Stepping back, she said, "Let me look at you."

Stanley stood without a sound, as his mother studied him. He had been just as overwhelmed when he arrived and acted much the same way.

"You're so, so...healthy," she said, a smile beaming on her face.

Stanley smiled in response.

Realizing she had disrupted the group, Ellen said, "Oh, I'm sorry I interrupted."

"That's quite alright," Paul said. "This is an experience quite unlike any other."

"Oh, it is," she said. "I've always wanted to meet you, by the way."

"Really?" he replied, puzzled. "Why?"

"I wanted to ask you what it was like on the road to Damascus when God called out to you."

"Well," he began, "it was quite unsettling. There's no mistaking the voice of God," he explained. "You see, there really is no such thing as a non-believer. Oh, there are plenty of people who don't believe, don't get me wrong." He paused and pointed at himself. "I know, I was one of them. What I mean is that you can't hear the voice of God and deny it's him. We just aren't capable of doing that."

"I see," Ellen said. "I suppose that makes sense. People can pretend God doesn't exist, but, in the end, like you wrote to the Romans, man is without excuse."

"Indeed he is," Paul said. "Indeed he is."

15

Jacob's departure was a stark reminder of the fate that awaited them all. In stunned silence, they each contemplated what lay beyond the enormous gates that glowed molten red and pulsated heat to a rhythm all their own. Until now, Timothy had never thought about pain other than times when he hurt himself. That pain dissipated as his body healed. Here, the pain endured forever; there was no healing process. A memory of burning his hand on his mother's waffle iron as a child jolted him to reality.

With Jacob gone, all eyes were fixed on the gateway to Hell—a one-way entrance that had no exit. Admittance was permanent. Final. The Lake of Fire would burn forever, the souls of the damned provided an eternal source of fuel.

Timothy shifted his eyes to Lauren. Feeling his gaze, her eyes met his. "We're all doomed," she uttered with a shake of her head, brows raised. Her voice was flat and hopeless with an air of finality. Looking back at the twin doors, she shook her head again and said, "I– I don't understand."

"Nothin' to understand," Corn Fed said. "It's just how it is."

Lauren shot him a glance almost in an effort to reprove him.

Timothy's eyes met Corn Fed's then shifted to Lauren. He wanted to say something to console her, but no words came to him. There was no consolation in Hell, no way to ease the pain and torment. Only anguish and misery existed here.

They fell back into silence for a moment. At last Grandma broke it. "Fate," she said to no one in particular. "Just a matter of fate."

With a shocked expression, Timothy stared at her. He wanted to argue, to explain that she was wrong, but he was unable to speak. Puzzled, he tried in earnest to make his mouth move, but it was no use. The words from his Sunday school class resounded in his mind like a gong, yet they remained silent. Eyes bulging, he looked from Sticks to Grandma to Corn Fed to Lauren in desperation. Oh, how he wanted to share his recollection with them, but his tongue was stilled, held firmly in place by an imperceptible force. He wondered if they could tell he was fighting to speak. Their blank expressions were indication enough. They were oblivious.

The full import of the moment sank in as he realized he could not recount his exposure to the Bible. *Here,* he thought, *I can't talk about those things.*

Surrendering to the brutal reality of his situation, he abandoned the idea and said instead, "It's true. Our fate is sealed."

Lauren turned to him and met his eyes with a slight reproach. Unable to convey what he was thinking, Timothy dropped her stare and focused on the menacing gateway in the distance. He was filled with perpetual fear—not the kind of fear that comes from the unknown, which is based on uncertainty and speculation and doubt. No, it was fear of the known, which is much different and uniquely terrifying. Although he didn't know for certain what awaited him, Timothy knew it involved fire and intense heat—and pain—unimaginable, unending pain.

As he was contemplating the moment when the Beast would come for him and drag him into the fiery pit, a shadow appeared next to him. Earl Yeggerton stood in the cramped confines between him and Lauren.

Confused, he asked, "Where am I?" in a deep southern drawl.

Nobody answered right away. Instead they all just stared at him—the newest member of their group.

"Waiting," Sticks replied at last.

"Waitin'?" His voice was raspy. "What in tarnation for?"

"Waitin' for our due," Corn Fed replied, one Southerner to another. Earl's presence seemed welcome by Corn Fed, Timothy observed.

Earl was about to ask a question, when Corn Fed nodded in the direction of the towering, fiery twin doors. Ominous and foreboding, their appearance portended evil and elicited fear.

"What's in there?" Earl asked, bewildered.

"The Beast," Timothy said.

"Beast? What Beast?"

"You'll see soon enough," Grandma said, her voiced filled with certainty.

Unsure what to make of things, Earl's distorted features took on a perplexed expression.

Observing him, Corn Fed advised, "Just wait a bit until your re-live." He paused. "Then it will all make sense."

"My what?" Earl exclaimed and then fell silent.

Timothy stared at Earl. Poised like a statue, his face was blank. *Must be having his re-live,* Timothy thought.

Corn Fed verbalized Timothy's thoughts. "Re-live," he announced, as though it were a command that would magically invoke the process.

Catching Timothy's eye, he mumbled, "Strange right-a passage, I s'pose."

"Yeah," was all Timothy could manage. *Indeed it was,* he thought. Reliving your last moment alive—not your death—was part of the anguish. It was Hell's way of establishing its finality and permanence by reminding you that your earthly life was over. Hope was gone, for that was something that belonged to the living, not the dead. While the moment was brief, Timothy realized, it was enduring and only served to reinforce the abject desolation that was Hell. It was a fitting welcome.

With a shake of his head, Earl's re-live was over. As the realization of his surroundings sank in, he looked around, rapidly scanning left, right, up, down, and back. "This can't be," he said. "Ya gotta be joshin' me, right?" He looked at the others for confirmation but found none.

"No," Grandma replied. "This is all quite real, I'm afraid."

"I was just driving..." his voice trailed off. "On my way to town to get a bite." He shook his head. "That dang 'shine," he said, his voice filled with defiance, as he shook his head. "Always knew it'd a be the death of me."

"What?" Timothy asked, not understanding his reference.

"Moonshine, youngin'," Corn Fed explained. "Booze. Alcohol. Get it?"

"Oh, yeah, yeah. Sure."

"Had too much, I guess," Earl explained.

"What happened?" Corn Fed asked.

"Passed out behind the wheel of my pickup. Crashed into a diner," Earl said shaking his head. "Spilled my bottle of hooch, too. Dang shame."

Pursing his lips, Corn Fed nodded understanding. "Make your own?" he inquired.

"Heck, yeah, I do." Then, considering his situation, he added, "Or at least I did."

Their reverie was interrupted by a blast of singeing heat and a thunderous roar that drowned out the symphony of the damned as the Beast emerged from his flaming chamber.

"What—" Earl began, then fell silent, his voice choked by fear.

Trailing large molten embers that resembled glowing bricks in his wake, the Beast waded into the waiting area with purpose. Standing behind Earl, Timothy watched as his menacing red eyes scanned the throng of waiting souls. Those closest to him cowered and averted their eyes. It was no use, though, because the Beast saw all of them. There was no place to hide, no way to avoid being seen. And there was no escape.

174

Arching his neck back, he emitted a piercing screech. The floor and unseen walls of the waiting area shook. Timothy and the others trembled as he strode toward them. They stared up at him as he swiveled his head back and forth, as though trying to decide who to select.

"What's he doing?" Lauren whispered.

"Don't know," Sticks said.

Suddenly the Beast thrust his massive claw forward. Like a baker squeezing dough, he grabbed a handful of souls, who struggled in his firm grasp. Repeating the action with his other claw, he looked triumphantly upward and shouted to an unseen presence. His speech was unintelligible. Organized screeches comprised the primitive, demonic lexicon that was unique to the Beast.

With an air of satisfaction, the Beast studied the souls trapped in his massive hooks and gave them a squeeze of finality. They flailed and screamed to no avail. Their time had come. Pivoting to his left, the Beast returned to his lair with just a few enormous strides.

Before the gates shut, Timothy watched as the Beast flung the souls from his grip with little effort. Suspended above the lake of fire for a brief interlude, they burst into flames but were not consumed. Like stones, they plunged into the fiery depths below. Their screams of torment joined the others and were indecipherable. Timothy thought about Jacob and how he was now a permanent resident in the Lake of Fire. Soon he would join him. They would all burn for eternity.

"What was that?" Earl asked.

"The Beast," Timothy said.

"What's the Beast?" he asked.

"The ruler of the damned," Grandma supplied.

"Kinda runs things here, if ya know what I mean," Corn Fed added.

Earl nodded his understanding. "Where exactly is 'here'?" he asked. "I mean, I get that I'm dead. Crashing into the diner took care of that. But what is this place?"

Ever the matriarch of their group, Grandma took the lead. "'Here,'" she paused, gesturing with a swivel of her head and swirl of her eyes, "is the waiting area."

"That big feller said that before," he motioned with his head at Corn Fed. "Something about our due, whatever that means. What exactly are we waitin' *fer*?"

"To be dragged in there," Grandma stated, as she turned her head slowly and deliberately in the

176

direction of the twin doors that gave off a faint metallic hum as their orange glow pulsated.

Timothy studied Earl's face as the full import of Grandma's words sank in.

"Hell," he uttered to himself. He shook his head slowly, almost in disbelief. "Always knew I'd end up here. Just didn't imagine it would be like this."

"What do you mean?" Timothy asked.

"I mean, I knew I wasn't a good person. All those years makin' 'shine..." his voice trailed off, lost in his own thoughts for a moment. "I never expected to end up any place good, ya know? Knew I didn't deserve it. But this..." He paused as he rolled his head around in the darkness. "Nobody deserves this."

"They sure don't," Lauren agreed. "Especially me."

Timothy remained silent. He knew better but was incapable of explaining.

Earl studied the molten doors in the distance. Large and foreboding, they radiated scorching heat. "This heat reminds me of summers on the farm, out in the field tillin'. No shade, no way to escape the sun. Feel like a pig on the spit."

The others remained silent except for Corn Fed. "Yup, I hear ya. Ain't nothin' like that summer sun beatin' down on ya." He paused. "Until this. Those summers ain't nothin' compared to this."

"Nope," Earl agreed. Then as an afterthought, he added, "Could sure use a drink."

Again, Timothy tried to swallow, wanted to swallow, but couldn't. Though stripped of his flesh, he still possessed the ability to feel and sense. In his new, distorted form, the desire to quench his thirst was extreme. With concentrated effort, he tried again to swallow with no success. Quickly, he looked to the others, who were oblivious.

"I still can't swallow," he announced to the group.

"No one can, dear," Grandma said.

"There is no comfort of any kind here," Sticks added. "Quenching one's thirst is a luxury."

"I've never been this thirty," Timothy said.

"All part-a the torment," Corn Fed said. "It'll get worse too."

"Worse?" Timothy asked in disbelief.

Listening to the conversation, Lauren tried to swallow with no success. "I can't swallow either."

"The heat is oppressive," Grandma explained. "Combined with the darkness, it robs you of all your energy."

"Is that why I'm so thirsty?" Timothy asked.

"No," Sticks answered. "Your thirst is extreme because it is the thirst for life. Here," he paused, shifting his eyes from side to side, "there is only death."

Sticks' words hung in the air. Timothy recalled a lesson from his Sunday school class about the rich man who died and went to Hell, how he had begged Abraham to allow Lazarus to dip his finger in water to cool his tongue. At the time, such imagery didn't seem real to him. It was just a story, allegory used to frighten people, all part of the fairy tale of Heaven and Hell.

But this is no fairy tale, he thought. This was all too real.

16

The morning sun carved a perfect rectangle of light against the outline of the brown and tan striped window shade. Sneaking inside Shelinda Hill's bedroom, it stretched across the floor and climbed diagonally up the giraffe print comforter, where it found its way to her closed eyes. Irritated by the crude interruption to her slumber, she rolled over and buried her face in the fluffy down pillow.

Outside her window, birds chirped and the leaves rustled, as the world came to life. Pushing its way under the shade, a light breeze danced across the room, filling it with the floral aroma of spring.

Tickling Shelinda's protruding foot, she kicked in an attempt to find refuge under the comforter, which eluded her. With a fatigued moan, she rolled over and propped herself up her elbow. "Guess it's time to get this day started," she said to herself as she yawned.

Flinging her legs over the side of the bed, she sat up and was assaulted by a sliver of piercing sunlight. She averted her eyes, feet fumbling for her tattered slippers. Standing up, she extended her arms outward and stretched, in a vain attempt to ward of the effects of the previous evening's binge.

The nightstand was littered with glasses of varying sizes. Some were empty; others contained various amount of unfinished alcohol—wine, vodka, and Scotch. Scattered across it surface, they surrounded a large photograph in a silver frame.

Shelinda stared at the frame, at the young couple in a wedding dress and tuxedo. A wave of sadness washed over her and she fought back tears.

"Just me now, T," she spoke to her husband, Tyrone. "Just me..." A stream of tears escaped and ran down her cheeks in parallel lines. With the back of her arm, she wiped them away, cleared her throat, and said, "Gotta toughen up, right?" she addressed the photo. "That's what you always said, remember?" She coughed a laugh. "Gotta toughen up," she announced, her voice full of mock sarcasm. "If you only knew, T. If you only knew."

After donning a pink floral robe that was long overdue for a wash, she meandered downstairs. Measuring both the coffee and water haphazardly, she depressed the brew button. While the coffeemaker did its job, she opened the cupboard, found the Ibuprofen, poured several in her hand, and washed them down with a long swig of orange juice right from the carton.

Filling the kitchen with its aroma, the coffee flowed in a steady stream. Slowly, a thin, dark line began to rise in the glass carafe. When the last drip made splashdown, Shelinda filled an oversized mug and took a seat on the sofa in the living room. Legs curled, she sat and sipped, waiting for the relief she hoped the pain medication would bring.

Mahogany wainscoting lined the walls topped with floral print wallpaper. The sofa was tan leather, Italian. Sitting opposite were two matching chairs, between which sat a narrow table. With a wrought iron base topped with chocolate marble, it matched the impressive square coffee table anchored in front of the sofa. The hardwood floor was covered with a golden Bukhara rug, whose pattern of tan and dark brown flecks brought the room together.

The far wall was covered by a brick fireplace that was flanked by matching bookcases. Above it hung their wedding portrait, taken at the Botanical Garden. It was the only picture in the room—the focal point.

"Don't know what I'm gonna do, T," she spoke to the portrait. She sipped her coffee. "Don't know what I'm gonna do." She shook her head. "Haven't paid the mortgage in months." She sneered. "I guess they figured out I wasn't going to pay them 'cause they stopped callin.' That ain't gonna be good." She laughed to herself.

Having cooled a bit, she took a full gulp from her mug. The caffeine and Ibuprofen were beginning to kick in. Her headache started to dissipate as she began to wake up. "My job don't pay much," she said in the direction of the portait, resuming the one-sided conversation. "Barely got enough to keep the lights on and buy food." *Booze, too,* she thought.

She sat in quiet contemplation as she worked on the java. Her new normal was anything but normal. The absence of her husband left her feeling alone and abandoned, a lost sojourner in the world. Their marriage had just begun when it was abruptly and cut short by tragedy.

"Ahh, T. Why'd you have get on that plane?" she asked and burst into tears. Unable to hold back, she sobbed as the dam of emotions burst. She cried; a flood of tears dripped from her face, a few finding their way into her coffee.

With a whimper and several snorts, she pulled herself together. Absent tissues, she used the sleeve of her robe to sop up the shed tears. Taking a long drag from her mug as though its contents would ward off the sadness, she placed the almost empty mug on the table and stood. Walking to the fireplace, she studied the small, wooden box that sat perfectly centered on the mantle. Except for a small brass plate on the front, it was plain and unassuming.

Tyrone Thadius Hill

April 11, 1990 – October 3, 2018

Staring at it, she spoke. "I failed, T. I failed." As her eyes filled with tears, she continued. "I'm sorry, baby. I know how much you believed in me, but I'm not strong like you…" Her voice trailed off as a lump rose in her throat. Swallowing it, she continued her monologue. "I couldn't handle school after you…after you left. You were the smart one. Not me." She pointed at her chest.

With her hands on her hips, she pivoted, consumed by defiance, and paced before returning to the mantle. "I just couldn't do it." She paused, head dropping. Shelinda stared at the floor, almost in shame. Pensive for a moment, she resembled a toy whose battery had died. With a sudden energy, she flung her head up and announced, "I quit." Her bottom lip quivered, and her bloodshot eyes gushed, as her faced contorted. Overcome with grief and remorse, she lamented, "Oh, T. I'm so sorry. I'm sorry. I… I quit, baby. Please don't be disappointed in me. Please…please…" she wailed as she sank to her knees in front of the fireplace, which had now become her personal altar and confessional.

With nothing to do all day, Shelinda remained on the floor until she could no longer feel her legs. The numbness from lack of circulation had escalated to pain. Shifting to her side, she eased her legs out from under her and restored the flow of blood.

Broken and spent, grief had been replaced with self-pity. "I'm just a quitter. Always have been and always will be," she said. Dejected and defeated, she managed to rise, using the corner of the coffee table like a cane.

Not bothering to retrieve her mug, she made her way into the kitchen. The clock on the oven read 10:53. Headache gone and caffeinated enough to function, the morning fog that had enveloped her brain had been lifted. For a moment, she debated on a second cup, but dismissed the idea.

As she was gathering her thoughts and contemplating how she was going to fill her day off from the restaurant, the doorbell rang.

"Leave me alone," she sighed. "I don't have money to buy anything," she muttered, heading to the door. Her slippers dragged on the hardwood floor. Light and shadows spilled in through the twin strips of marbled glass that lined each side of the doorframe.

Peering through the peephole, two men in brown sheriff's uniforms stood waiting.

"And so it begins," she said and opened the door.

"Shelinda Miller?" the closest one asked. The opposite of his partner, he was rotund with a gray mustache and matching sideburns.

"Yes."

"Good morning, ma'am. I'm Deputy Vose and this," he gestured with a quick turn of his head, "is my colleague, Deputy Essington." Younger by twenty years and lighter by as many pounds, he gave a brief nod.

Shelinda forced a faint smile.

Deputy Vose continued. "Mrs. Miller, I'm sorry, but I have an eviction notice." He raised his right hand and presented Shelinda with an oversized manila envelope.

Reluctantly, Shelinda accepted the proffered envelope and stared at it. Her name was displayed in all capital letters along with her address. It was thick and bulky.

"You have two weeks to be out of the house," Vose continued his speech. Although memorized from years of repetition, his voice still possessed a hint of compassion.

"I understand," Shelinda said, her voice flat and devoid of emotion.

"There's information in the envelope — resources, phone numbers, places to contact. There is help available," he said.

Glancing at the envelope like she had never seen one, she nodded before shifting her gaze back to the deputy. "Thank you," she managed, unable to smile.

With a nod, Vose and his partner turned and headed to their squad car parked at the curb. Shelinda stood in the doorway and watched as they drove away. The neighborhood — her neighborhood — was quiet and serene. Oblivious to her magnanimous failure, a squirrel darted across the lawn, stopping, then starting several times before it reached the mighty oak tree that shaded most of the front yard and porch. With practiced ease, it scampered up the trunk and was gone.

Looking down, Shelinda studied the envelope again. For some reason, it now felt heavier, a tangible indication of her failure. Leaning against the door to shut it, she slid to floor. Convulsing in tears, she sobbed as the finality of the moment sank overtook her.

"T..." she called out. "T, I'm done, baby. I'm done. I lost our house. I'm..." she cried, "I'm sorry, T. I'm sorry."

Pressing her feet into the floor, she rose as tears continued to stream down her face. Passing the foyer table, she tossed the eviction notice on top of a collection of unopened past-due notices and letters from debt collectors. Dragging her feet into the kitchen, an open bottle of vodka sat poised on the counter, ready to offer consolation.

With her life in a downward spiral and with no way to extricate herself, alcohol had become a constant companion and friend. Offering temporary relief, it dulled her pain and provided a brief respite on a daily basis. Calling out to her, its promise of intoxicating consolation beckoned.

Shelinda did not refuse. Grabbing the bottle, she skipped a glass, tossed her head back, and downed a mouthful. Wincing from the burn, her eyes blinked in rapid succession. The alcohol was warming. In little time, she felt its euphoric effect wrap its arms around her, enticing her to seek refuge in its embrace.

After another gulp, she began to feel less concerned about her plight, her senses beginning the gradual dulling process that alcohol provided.

Staring at the bottle, she said, "You and me today," and raised the bottle in a toast.

She continued to sip as she wandered throughout the house. Not entering any of the rooms, she moved from room to room and stood in the doorways while she reminisced.

"Remember how long it took to pick out this wallpaper, T?" she asked, outside the dining room. "We argued for months." She laughed, the insincere laugh of those who've imbibed. "Got it hung just in time for Thanksgiving." Her eyes stared into the room, as though looking back in time and reliving the moment.

She continued throughout the house, taking her time as she drained the clear liquid from bottle along the way. At last, she made her way upstairs. The fleeting comfort provided by the vodka had been replaced by depression and despair. Stumbling, she fell against the wall and slid to the floor.

Laughing, she said, "Oops. Never could hold my liquor, T," she said as she took a swig from the bottle.

Pushing herself up from the floor, she stood and staggered into her bedroom. Plopping on the bed, she leaned against the headboard, her mind was numb. She no longer tasted the clear panacea.

From the nightstand, she removed their wedding photo. Pausing, she stared at the red leather Bible next to it that had belong to Tyrone. For a moment she considered picking it up but decided against it. Instead, she was content with image in the silver frame.

"Oh, T. Why did you have to leave me? Why?" she questioned in reference to the plane crash nearly a year ago. "I told you small planes weren't safe." She clutched the frame to her chest. Fully submerged in the sea of depression, she wept.

In an attempt to silence her feelings, she gulped from the bottle to no avail. Her emotions refused to be silenced.

She tossed the picture on the bed and sat up. Placing her hand on the nightstand, she steadied herself. As the room began coming into focus, she held the bottle up to her face. "Hmm," she mused at the scant amount remaining and sat the bottle on the floor.

Shifting her eyes to the nightstand, a small bottle next to the lamp caught her eye. With a smile, she reached for it. *Sleep Well*, the label read. Giving it a shake like dice, the pills rattled around. Popping the lid with her thumb, she poured the entire bottle into her hands and studied the little white pills.

She stared at them for a moment, eyes transfixed. Sobriety nowhere to be found, drunken logic ran rampant. Turning her head, she retrieved the photo. *You were my whole life, T. My whole life,* she thought.

"I miss you, T. So, so much," she said to the picture. "I don't want to live without you. I don't." She wept, tears pouring down her face. "I can't, I'm sorry," she pleaded. "I'm not strong enough." Unable to control her sobbing, she asked, "Why, T? Why me? Why did you have to go? It's not fair. It just isn't!"

Dropping the frame back to the bed, she retrieved the bottle from the floor. Slamming the handful of pills into her mouth, she washed it down with the remainder of the vodka and tossed the empty bottle on the floor.

"That's it, T. Done deal." She sank back on the bed and stretched her legs out. "Yes, sir," she slurred. "I'm on my way. You'll be seeing me soon, T. You'll be seeing me soon. Together again."

Shelinda took a final, bleary look around the room. Her eyes locked on the Bible, which she saw with remarkable clarity for some reason. "Guess I'm gonna find out if you were right," she said.

Her eyes focused on the ceiling. As her breathing began to slow and become more rhythmic, darkness crept into her field of vision. Like day turning into night, it snuffed out the light and wrapped its arms around her as it carried her away to eternity.

17

With no way to measure how long he had been in the waiting area, Timothy forced himself to think about something other than the oppressive heat. He glanced at Earl, who was still somewhat confused about where he was and why. Timothy wondered if he had been the same way upon his arrival. *Finality sets in quickly*, he thought.

"How long do we have to wait?" Earl asked.

Perplexed by the strange question, they all stared at him. None of them had given much thought to how long they would have to wait before it was their turn to be dragged into the blazing inferno. Perhaps it was due to not wanting to accept their fate, or maybe it was the misguided belief that contemplating that moment could somehow bring about their turn, they had not spoken about it.

"Well?" Earl persisted. "How long?"

"Long enough," Grandma answered.

"What's that s'posed to mean?" he asked.

"It means ya wait until it's your turn," Corn Fed said. "And there ain't no way to know when it's your turn until..." his voice trailed off as he shifted his gaze to glowing gates.

Earl thought about that for a moment. "So, like ya said when I got here," he looked at Sticks, "we just wait."

"Exactly," Sticks said.

"It's part of the torment," Timothy said.

"I s'pose it is, young feller," he said. Then, thinking about it for a moment, he asked, "Ain't you a bit young to be in a place like this?"

"Apparently not," Timothy said.

"What you'd do end up here?" Earl probed.

"I don't know."

"Humph," Earl sneered. "Musta been somthin' bad 'cause only bad people end up here."

"I'm not a bad person. I didn't do anything wrong," Lauren spat.

Timothy considered her words. She was angry, he thought, and for good reason. But he knew better. He knew they did, in fact, deserve to be there, but he was unable to speak of such things in this place.

"Well, I know what I did," Corn Fed announced. "Ain't no taking that back either. This is the price I gotta pay." He didn't dispute his fate. For some reason that Timothy could not comprehend, Corn Fed was accepting of this place.

"As I said," Grandma added, "it's simply a matter of fate." She shook her head. "I lived a long

196

life, didn't really do anything wrong, spent a lot of time volunteering too, but I ended up here."

"I know I didn't do anything wrong," Lauren shot. "I was in college with my entire life ahead of me until—"

A shadow landed in their midst. Standing between Sticks and Cornfed, her face was covered in confusion. *Never seems to be a shortage*, Timothy mused to himself.

Uncertain of her surroundings, Shelinda blinked several times in an attempt to clear the darkness.

"Where am I?" she asked, trying to discern the shadows that surrounded her.

"Outside the..." Timothy began, then changed course. "Waiting."

"Waiting? That's the name of this place?" Shelinda quizzed.

"You might say that," Grandma said. "Yes."

"Hmm." Shelinda pondered that answer for a moment. "Waiting, huh? For what?"

Catching her eye, Timothy nodded in the direction of the awaiting furnace. Turning her head, Shelinda stared at the twin orange doors. Unable to look away, finality set it. The consuming heat, putrid smell, and darkness all made sense to her.

"You were right, T," she muttered to herself. She had no doubts about where she was now. It was unmistakable. She was in Hell.

Timothy studied her. For some reason, she wasn't in denial like the others when they arrived. *Strange,* he thought.

Curious, he asked, "Have you had your re-live yet? You know, seen how you got here?"

She studied him for a moment. "I'm well aware of how I got here," she said, then added, "no, I haven't relived the experience yet."

"Oh," he said. "Well, you will. Should be soon. Happens pretty quick."

"Thanks," she replied. "As if arriving at this dreadful place for all eternity weren't bad enough, I'm going to have the displeasure of reliving it."

"We all did," Lauren said.

"I see."

Like a politician running for office, Sticks explained, "It's all part of the torment."

"Something to look forward to," Shelinda said, and then fell silent as she relived her final moments in the flesh.

When it was obvious the moment had passed, Timothy inquired, "How did you get here?"

Shelinda wanted to smile halfheartedly but couldn't make her mouth curve upward. "I guess you could say I chose to come here."

"What do you mean, dear?" Grandma asked.

Shelinda did not answer. Her gaze was fixed on the molten gates in distance.

"Hey," Timothy said.

"What?" Shelinda asked.

"How'd ya get here?" Corn Fed demanded.

"I killed myself."

No one spoke. Her words hung in the air.

"Wha'd ya do a thing like that fer?" Earl asked.

"No good reason," she responded. "No good reason at all."

Timothy didn't know what to say. Looking away, he wanted to feel sorry for her but he couldn't. He couldn't feel anything except fear. That was the solitary emotion that existed. Timothy recalled a story his mother told him about his great uncle committing suicide. He never met him. Now he wondered if he had ended up here.

"What happened?" Lauren asked, prodding.

"I quit," Shelinda deadpanned. "I quit life. I was all by myself, lonely. My husband died in a plane crash," she explained. "One day... I just couldn't take it anymore. Figured dying was better than living." As an afterthought, she added with a shake of her head, "I was wrong. So very, very wrong."

Timothy stared at her. They'd all ended up outside the gates of Hell due to the actions of someone else, accident, or in Grandma's case, old age. But not Shelinda. *You chose this?* Timothy questioned to himself. *Why would anyone kill themselves?* he asked himself. *True, many people didn't believe in the afterlife, but why take the chance and end up here?*

In the middle of considering what drove Shelinda to abandon her life for this place, the enormous gates burst open. Like opening an oven door, heat spewed out and engulfed the waiting area. Amid the inferno, the Beast emerged and plodded in their direction.

"He's coming this way," Timothy said under his breath to Lauren.

"I– I know," Lauren stammered.

He's coming for me, Timothy thought.

Just a few steps away, Timothy observed the Beast's red, lifeless eyes. They were piercing and menacing. Red dots with no pupils that stood out against his black, scaled exterior.

Another step. The intensity of the searing heat increased. *The Beast radiates heat,* Timothy observed, noting the rapid increase in heat as the Beast approached.

One step away. Timothy wanted to vomit. The Beast emitted the stench of death. Timothy was surrounded by the most rancid smell he'd ever encountered. *Smells like pus, garbage, and burnt hair, but much, much worse,* he concluded.

. Paralyzed with fear, he was frozen in place. With a mighty wail, the Beast extended his giant arm and snatched up Corn Fed. Too frightened to scream, Timothy's mouth hung agape in silence as he experienced raw fear for the first time.

No longer requiring the resupply of air breathing demanded, Corn Fed's scream was unending all the way to the blazing pit of Hell, his tail trailing behind him. Timothy and the others watched as the Beast flung his powerful arm and released Corn Fed into the fiery abyss before the great doors slammed shut.

The silent darkness returned broken only by the metallic buzz emitted from the pulsating gates. They didn't speak or look at each other. Instead they all focused their attention to the closed doors in the distance. Corn Fed's departure reinforced the reality of their pending fate.

"He's gone!" Lauren said, breaking the silence.

"Yeah," Timothy said. "Gone."

"He was a murderer," Grandma said as though her pronouncement somehow justified the Beast's actions.

Timothy glanced at her and considered her pronouncement of judgment. He recalled his pastor's word so often used out of context, "Judge not lest ye be judged." *Ironic she's judging him when we all share the same fate,* he thought.

Shelinda did not have to ask who the Beast was. From her time with Tyrone, she knew perfectly well who the Beast was. Shortly before Tyrone died, he had become a Christian. She recalled the event.

*   *   *   *   *   *

Tyrone Hill had worked in construction since he was a teenager, starting out part-time while still in high school. With a job offer in hand, he had planned to go into the business full-time, but his mother insisted he go to college. "You'll never get a good job without a college degree," she had said. Not wanting to disappoint his mother, but also not wanting to turn down a job offer, he compromised and did both.

As a full-time online student with a full-time job that often-required overtime, Tyrone slept little.

When he could, he spent time with Shelinda, his high school sweetheart. Somehow, they even managed to get married along the way. An overnight stay at the local Hilton was all they could afford in the way of a honeymoon, but it sufficed, and they were happy. They lived in the makeshift apartment above his mother's garage while he finished college. Shelinda worked as a server.

When Tyrone graduated, a job was waiting for him at the construction company, but he turned it down. As much as he enjoyed working with his hands, it was time to do something different and put his education to use. He was offered a job as a building inspector and took it. "You have years of valuable experience and a degree in engineering," the hiring manager told him. "You would be a great fit." And he was.

Shortly after he started, he and his supervisor, Terry Dombrowski, traveled over a weekend to an industry seminar scheduled for the upcoming week. Although Tyrone was a college graduate, his training was not over. On Sunday, Terry invited Tyrone to attend church with him.

"Sure," he said, figuring it couldn't do any harm.

"You much of a churchgoer?" Terry asked, when they entered the parking lot of the small, brick building, complete with a steeple and cross on top.

"Not really, no," Tyrone said.

"Well, I've been here before on a previous trip. This is a Baptist church—I'm Baptist, born and raised. Anyway, I traveled here last year and found this little church. They do a nice service. I think you'll like it," Terry explained as they made their way inside.

"Sounds good."

Tyrone found most of the service benign and uneventful—until the sermon. Not quite fire and brimstone, the pastor's sermon discussed the urgency of salvation. "Today is the day of salvation," he repeated as he thumped the pulpit with his fist. His eyes locked on Tyrone's for a brief moment while he spoke.

When the time came to go forward and receive salvation, Tyrone surprised himself and joined a group at the front of the church. There, on his knees, he accepted Jesus as his Lord and Savior.

Eager to share the good news with his wife, he called her. "Shel, the most amazing thing happened to me today."

"What, baby? Tell me."

"I accepted Jesus."

Silent for a moment, she asked, "What do you mean?"

"I went to church with Terry. God really spoke to me, Shel. I mean, that sermon — something really got to me. I went forward and accepted Christ. I can't wait to share it with you. They even gave me a Bible after the service."

*   *   *   *   *   *

The Bible, Shelinda thought. The one that sat on the nightstand, the last thing she remembered seeing before everything went dark. *You tried to tell me, T,* she thought. *Said you were praying for me, quoted verses to me, but I wouldn't have any of it,* she mused to herself. Thought it was all just some kind of fable. *I should have listened, T. I should have listened.*

"In time he'll come for all of us," Grandma broke the silence, snapping Shelinda back to the present. It was a definitive statement, a fait accompli, something they all knew but did not verbalize or discuss. Grandma's words were hollow, devoid of emotion.

"I reckon' you're right," Earl assented. "Now it makes sense."

"What makes sense?" Lauren demanded.

"Waitin'."

205

"How?" she questioned. "How does this make sense?"

"'Cause it's torture," he replied. "It's one thing to know yer gonna die. Eventually it passes, and yer dead. But this," his eyes took in their surroundings, "this is much worse, 'cause yer already dead. Can't die again. Nope." He stopped for a moment, contemplating a way to describe his thoughts. "In there," he motioned with his head, "ya die over and over and over. Never ends. Here," he looked around the waiting area, "all ya can do is think about it, knowing it will never pass."

"You're spot on," Grandma said.

As Shelinda thought about Earl's comment, her mind drifted to Tyrone and the plane crash that had taken his life. She wondered what he was experiencing.

Timothy listened to Earl's analysis and realized he was right. What lay beyond the gates would never pass. The suffering would be absolute, total, and enduring. It would not diminish, fade, or grow weaker over time.

Eternal damnation, Timothy thought.

18

"We're gonna be late, Ray," Betty Davis said to her husband as she rinsed their plates from dinner and placed them in the dishwasher.

"Relax, B," Raymond said. "It's right up the street, and we have—" he checked his watch, "twenty minutes."

"You have twenty minutes," she jabbed. "I have to get ready."

"What's wrong with what you're wearing?" he asked.

"Nothing," she said, flipping the door of the dishwasher shut. "But I need to run a comb through my hair and freshen up. All that wind today in the garden...I look a fright," she explained.

Raymond shook head. After fifty years of marriage, there were some things about his wife that he still didn't understand—or want to understand, for that matter.

"I'll be down in a minute," she announced, as she made her way upstairs.

"I'll be here," he said and laughed. "You better hurry or I'll leave without you."

"Oh, you will not!" she said, scurrying up the steps.

After ensuring the back door was locked, Raymond headed to the foyer to wait. Lining the walls and adorning the tables were a collection of photographs. There were collages, individual portraits, and group photos. Pictures of their two daughters and son along with even more of their seven grandchildren were intermixed with those of various vacations, holidays, and family occasions. A photograph of Raymond taken just after he received his naval commission sat on the foyer table next to one of the newly married bride and groom. Evidence of a well-lived life.

Raymond checked his watch. Ten minutes to six. If they made the light, it would take just under three minutes to get to church.

"Ray, is my Bible down there?" Betty shouted.

Turning toward the bench, it sat next to her purse. "Yes," he affirmed.

"Okay. I'll be right down."

He glanced at his wrist. Eight minutes.

A moment later, Raymond turned and looked up as Betty came down the stairs, shirt changed, hair combed—not that he could really tell—and a fresh coat of makeup, along with a hint of perfume.

In short order, she grabbed her purse and Bible. "Are we good on time?" she asked.

"Yup, we should have a few minutes to spare," he said, holding the front door open for her.

On the way to church, Betty noted the time displayed on the display panel mounted in the dashboard.

"You might be cutting it close, Captain," she said in jest, referring to his final rank in the Navy after twenty-six years. "Early's on time, right?"

"That's true in the Navy, dear. Not in the Presbyterian Church. There, on time is early." They both chuckled as they pulled into the parking lot with a minute to spare.

Inside they joined a small group in what was referred to as "the parlor," a cozy space that resembled a family room, complete with a gas fireplace. A series of sofas and chairs were arranged in a semicircle around the fireplace.

Betty and Ray shook hands and exchanged hugs with the other couples, who were part of the Wednesday night Bible study.

"Evening, John," Ray said.

"Hey, Ray," John said, pumping his hand. He was also retired Navy, a one-star. Despite his small frame and gray hair, he still had the commanding presence of a flag officer.

"John, how are you? Hit the green today?" he asked in reference to his golf game, something that occupied a significant amount of his retirement.

"Hittin' 'em straight and true," he replied, as he mimicked a golf swing. "You need to join me one of these days."

"I will if the admiral ever lets me," he said, with a laugh, poking fun at Betty.

"She give admirals a bad name," John said. "I was never that strict with my captains."

"Must be that Army blood," he said and they both laughed.

Ever the social butterfly, Ray made his way around the room. He shook hands, exchanged hellos, patted a few shoulders, and smiled like a politician working a room.

All retired, they were part of a generation that might well be the last to actually enjoy their twilight years not working. Referring to themselves as the 'Roundabouts' because of the busy schedule they all kept, they were a small but tight group who volunteered in the community, planned and organized day trips, and attended Bible Study each week.

Coffee, tea, and ice water were available, arranged by category on a sideboard that matched the contemporary décor of the room. Ray helped

210

himself to a coffee—black—and took up his normal position in a chair near the fireplace. Betty joined him a minute later, and the others followed.

Once everyone was settled, Ray said, "Let's open with prayer." He paused for a moment, bowed his head, and then asked God's blessing for their study.

"Okay, folks," he began as he opened his Bible, "we're in Romans, chapter three…" his voice trailed off while he found his place, "…beginning in verse twenty-one through verse twenty-six."

"I'll read it," Betty volunteered.

After she finished, Ray posed a series of questions as they deciphered Paul's words. "So, what is his message here?"

"Well," John began, "it's simple. We're all sinners in need of a savior."

"I agree. For all have sinned and fallen short of the glory of God," Betty said, quoting Romans 3:23. "Such powerful words. We're all sinners in need of a savior *and* forgiveness."

Several heads nodded along with a few "Yes," "That's so true," and "Uh-huh."

"Indeed," Ray intoned, "the two go hand-in-hand."

"The role of the savior, Jesus, is to save. In the case of sinners, the only way to save them is to forgive them," John stated.

"Very true," Ray concurred. "Very true. And a what a magnificent savior we have!"

The study concluded with prayer and, after cleaning up the coffee, tea, and water, they all headed out. Roundabouts didn't make it a point to linger outside and socialize. They saw each other enough during the week at various functions and didn't need to catch up.

"I always enjoy Bible study," Betty said on the way home.

"So do I," Ray agreed.

"Oh," Betty said, "before I forget, stop at the store. I want to pick up a few things."

"We're going shopping this weekend, aren't we?" Ray objected.

"Yes, but Tammy and the girls are coming for dinner Friday," she explained referring to their daughter and granddaughters.

"Oh, when did she tell you that?"

"She texted me this afternoon. I thought I told you."

"Must not have heard you," Ray offered his feeble excuse.

"You do that, don't you?" she jested.

"All those years with those big guns," he said.

"Sure," she laughed as they turned into the grocery store parking lot.

"Huh?" Ray asked, cupping a hand to his ear in an effort to bolster his case.

"Just park," Betty commanded.

"Yes, dear." They both laughed.

After returning from the store, they settled in for an evening of television. Taking up their traditional places in the family room, Ray manned the recliner while Betty sat at the end of the sofa.

Clicking on the television, Ray said, "Celtics are playing tonight, I think."

"Sounds good," Betty said, not really paying attention. From a tote bag that had been her grandmother's, she had retrieved a set of knitting needles. Picking up where she had left off, she glanced down from time to time to ensure her stitches were neat and tight.

Fumbling with the remote, Ray scrolled through the channels until he found the game. "There we go," he announced, the oversized flat screen filled with images of players clad in green. "Go Irish," he cheered.

"Oh, don't get started. The game hasn't even begun," Betty said.

Ray laughed. "Never too early to start, B." Sliding his hand down the side, he pulled on the handle and released the footrest. Properly supine, he asked, "How's Tammy?"

"Good," Betty said. "She's got the day off from the hospital and thought she'd stop over in the afternoon. I told her to stay for dinner since Jeremy is deployed."

"Shoulda married a Navy man like her mom," he jabbed.

"You hush. Nothing wrong with the Army," Betty defended her son-in-law. "He's a good man."

"He can have that ground pounding. I'll take being at sea any day over that."

"She says it's not that bad where he is, though she isn't exactly sure *where* he is."

"I bet," Ray said. "We got reassigned all the time."

Betty laughed. "I recall that one deployment...you moved around so many times, your care package arrived two weeks after you returned to port."

"Yeah, I remember that too. Your homemade cookies were nothing but crumbs," he laughed. "But I ate them anyway."

"I'm sure you did," she said. "I'm sure you did."

"Shared them with the wardroom, too," he mused. "They didn't care either. Beats Navy chow."

"Chow?" she rebuked.

"Hey, you can take me out of the Navy, but you can't take the Navy out of me."

"I suppose you're right, *Captain*," she said, emphasizing his title with intended sarcasm.

He laughed despite himself. "Once a sailor, always a sailor," he fired back.

"I think that's *marine*!"

"No, they stole it from us," he laughed, on a roll.

"Oh, did they now?" she asked, brows raised.

"Sure did," he emphasized, as they both laughed.

"Well, we know one thing for sure," Betty said, "we know which branch of the military is full of it!"

"Yeah," Ray blurted, "the Marine Corps!"

They both laughed together at the shared humor.

Laughter subsided; Ray focused on the game while Betty repeated the detailed process of knit one, purl two.

"You'll be nodding off in a few minutes," she said.

"I'm wide awake," he retorted. "Besides, this is a good game."

"We'll see about that," she jested as her hands worked the needles in practiced rhythm. "You fall asleep in that chair every night."

Ray smirked. "Not every night. I'm sure there's been a few I managed to make it to ten."

"Ten?" she paused, eyeing him over the top of her glasses. "That would be a record."

"Oh, hush now, woman," Ray said. "I've made it to eleven a few times."

"Humph," Betty exhaled. "Who was president when that happened?"

They fell into practiced silence. Players ran up and down the parquet floor as Betty created a new row. Now and then she glanced up and took in the action. Not much of a sports fan, she didn't mind. As long as she and Ray were together, she didn't care what they did.

Reaching into her bag for scissors, the familiar sound of deep breathing filled her ears. Looking over at Ray asleep in the chair, she laughed to herself. "Ten, my ear," she said to her sleeping husband. For the next hour, the familiar sounds of the basketball game kept her company.

Betty checked her watch and placed the needles in her bag. She had made as much progress as she was going to make tonight. After picking up the remote and switching the television off, she nudged Ray.

"Let's go, Captain. It's time for taps," she said, referring to the naval custom of turning in for the evening.

"Huh?" he said, in a daze. "Oh," he acknowledged, swinging the recliner closed. "I almost made it."

"Almost doesn't count except in horseshoes," Betty admonished him.

After they finished their nightly routines, they hopped into bed. Window open a few inches and the ceiling fan on, the down comforter provided coziness and warmth.

Holding hands, they took turns praying. When they finished, Betty switched off the light, leaned over, and kissed Ray goodnight. "Night, Ray. I love you."

"Night, B. I love you more," Ray replied, squeezing her hand. For fifty years they went to sleep holding hands. "I'm gonna hold onto you forever, B," Ray had told her on their wedding day. From that day forward, he always held her hand when they went to sleep, unless he was at sea.

*　　*　　*　　*　　*　　*

The morning sun brightened their bedroom like a lamp in a dark room. Inhaling the fresh air of a new day, Betty turned and studied her alarm clock until the blue digital display. Opening her eyes and blinking several times, the bedroom came into focus. Squinting, she double-checked the time — 6:32. Feeling Ray's hand still in hers, she rubbed the back of his hand with her thumb.

"Looks like someone missed reveille," she said, giving his hand a squeeze. When he didn't move, she increased the pressure. "Let's go, Captain. Time to heave out and trice up." Ray didn't budge. Then Betty realized Ray's hand was cold and still. Turning in a panic, she shook him vigorously by his shoulders and shouted his name. "Ray? Ray?"

There was no response. She bolted upright and shook him with disbelieving violence. "Ray!" Betty screamed. "Ray! Wake up!"

Realizing he was gone, she stopped. "No, Ray, no. You can't be gone, my love," she said as a river of tears washed down her face. "You can't," she sobbed. "We were supposed to go together, remember?" Sitting up, she studied him. He looked peaceful and content.

Leaning forward, she hugged him, her head on his chest. The tears streamed down her face. "Oh, Ray," she wept. "Tell Jesus to come for me soon, okay?" Breaking down as the full weight of Ray's demise collapsed on her, Betty mourned.

19

Standing across the room, Ray viewed their quaint bedroom as a spectator, the way one watches a movie. Although familiar, he was removed from it. No longer a participant, he was relegated to the position of a bystander who was only capable of observing as the scene unfolded before him. He watched in silence as Betty mourned and lamented his departure. Although he wanted to reach out to her, comfort her, hold her close, and tell her that everything would be okay, he was unable to intercede. Just before the morning sun woke Betty, Ray had taken his last breath. He slipped peacefully from his body, leaving his human shell behind.

An onlooker no longer bound by flesh, Ray stood in the distance, the sole member of the audience. In a solitary performance, Betty wept, her head pressed against Ray's chest. As he watched, Ray couldn't recall a time that he had ever seen her cry with such ferocity. Theirs was a love that had transcended more than five decades.

For over twenty years of his naval career, Betty had been his rock. Raising three children while he was out at sea, she had done a remarkable job maintaining the household. He recalled her familiar response to his diatribes about the demands and pressure of his job.

"Navy wife—toughest job in the Navy," she'd say. "Don't tell me about how hard your job is!"

Betty sympathized but never felt sorry him. "I may not spend months at a time out to sea, but hustling three children off to dance class, soccer games, and music lessons isn't a picnic," she told him. "Not that I mind. You've got your job, and I've got mine. We're partners, and that's just how it goes."

Ray marveled at and admired her strength and stamina. Unrelenting, he couldn't recall a time when she had ever been discouraged or acknowledged defeat. "Life's tough, but I'm tougher," was her standard retort whenever things didn't go according to plan.

Feeling a presence, Ray turned to his right. Standing next to him in a flowing snow-white robe that was almost blinding was Jesus, smiling.

Placing his hand on Ray's back, he said, "I've come for you, my child."

Overwhelmed by the realization that he had indeed passed from the earthly realm into the heavenly one, Ray remained silent. Glancing back, Betty continued to lay next to his human remains.

Pulling herself together somewhat, Ray heard her familiar voice.

"Oh, dear Jesus, I don't know why you took him, but I pray you will help me to understand," she began as her breathing slowed. "Please, please be with me now." The tears poured through the slits of her closed eyes. "Grant me your peace, Jesus, your perfect peace — please." She took several deep breaths and was still.

Ray wanted to feel sorry for her, but he couldn't. Sadness was not part of his new, eternal world. Looking away, he shifted his attention back to Jesus.

"She will be fine, Ray," he reassured with a smile. "I have heard her prayer. My peace is already upon her. It is peace that passeth all understanding. A peace that heals and provides comfort." His smile beamed and reassured Ray.

Turning his head, he saw Betty was calm, almost tranquil. Ray smiled.

"Come," Jesus said, extending his hand. "Let me show you the splendor of Heaven."

In an instant they were no longer in Ray's bedroom. Replaced with lush green foliage, they walked side by side in a field of green that extended as far as Ray could see.

"So why today?" Ray asked, curiosity filling his voice.

"It was your time."

"But I had so much left to do…with the church, Bible study, my kids…" he protested.

"As long as sin exists, there will always be work to do. And there are many who will do it. You, my child, have served faithfully. It is time for others fill your shoes. Besides," Jesus added, "there is work for you in Heaven, as there is for all my children. You see, there will a new Heaven and Earth. My Father's will is done both here and on Earth."

"I don't understand. If there's so much to do, why not let me stay and do it?" Ray asked, stopping and facing Jesus.

Smiling, Jesus answered, "My child, think of it as," he paused for effect, "a change of command."

Ray stared at him as the import of his words sank in.

"You see," Jesus said, "it is time for others to grow in their journey of faith, the way you grew in yours. You have set an example for many, many whose faith will not grow with you leading them. Now," he gestured toward Ray, "with your departure, others will grow in their service to the kingdom." He smiled. "It was time, and only my father knows the appointed hour."

"Well, that makes sense," Ray conceded.

They continued walking. "We're almost there," Jesus announced.

Ray remained silent. He contemplated Jesus's words; staring down, his bare feet sank into the emerald, green sea of grass beneath his feet. While he had been a believer most of his life, he had never considered himself a strong Christian role model. It hadn't been until his retirement that he had taken an active role in the church. Christianity and the Navy often did not mix well. Many times throughout his career he struggled, as his duty and faith were in conflict.

Permeated by a floral bouquet tidal wave, Ray looked up. Just ahead of them he saw what appeared to be an enormous compound. Not constructed of bricks and mortar, its walls were pearlescent and shimmered. Twinkling in the light, it glistened and sparkled like silver glitter. In the distance, the voices of angels tickled his ears.

Jesus stopped suddenly and turned to Ray. "Let not your heart be troubled, my son," he said. "You filled the role given you."

Realizing Jesus knew his thoughts, he gave a slight laugh. "It's just…I feel like I could have done more."

"It is not for you to understand. You see," he said, heading toward the gate, "many are called, but few are chosen. *You* were chosen."

As they passed through gate, they were greeted by Peter. "Welcome, Ray," he said.

"Thank you."

Inside, they paused. Lined with a multitude of flowers, a golden pathway ribboned out in front of them. The expanse was covered with a sea of grass. Dotting the landscape were the tallest, most magnificent trees Ray had ever seen. Roaming about freely, animals abounded. Horses galloped, monkeys climbed trees, and elephants meandered about. Birds soared through the air. Turning his head left and right, Ray marveled at the sheer beauty.

"This is incredible," Ray observed.

"The splendor of Heaven is beyond comparison," Jesus said.

"Indeed it is," Ray agreed.

"This way," Jesus said, indicating the path ahead. "We must go and meet my father."

"Yes, I supposed so," Ray said. "You know, now that I'm here, I've always wondered something. Why did you cry when Lazarus died? I mean, you knew you'd be bringing him back from the dead. Were you relating to us? I ask because

226

pastors and commentators always related that back to your humanity, but I always felt there was something deeper to it."

Stopping, Jesus faced him. "I wept for Lazarus because death is filled with an unequaled sadness. Man was not created to die; he was created to live," he explained. "Yes, I knew I was going to bring him back to life and that he would die again one day at his appointed time. *But* that does not eliminate the sadness of death. Having been present at creation, I know my Father's plan for man. Death was never part of it." He turned and began walking. "I was incarnate and wept for the same reason others weep."

They continued in silence. As they approached the great throne, the choral voices grew in volume.

"You thought I wept for another reason?" Jesus asked as they reached the bottom.

"No, not really, I guess. I was just curious. It just seemed strange since you knew he'd live again—and soon."

Smiling, Jesus replied, "Many have denied my humanity. I assure you, it was complete and not lacking in any way."

Reflecting on his words, Ray thought of the cross and the pain he must have endured, not to mention the full wrath of God. Like many, Ray focused on his resurrection and looked past the cross. *The cross,* Ray thought, *the cross was everything*!

"Indeed it was," Jesus said with a smile, acknowledging his thought.

Ray stopped and stared at him. Looking down, he studied his hands, where the nails had pierced him. He locked eyes with Jesus. "The cross…" Ray said.

Jesus smiled. "No need to focus on that now. Please," he indicated with an extended arm, "my Father is waiting."

"Yes, of course," Ray said, as they continued to the great throne. Making his way up the marbled steps, Ray was careful not to step on any crowns that littered the steps. At the top, he dropped to his knees.

"Arise, my child," the voice boomed.

Ray did as commanded.

From a heavy volume spread open on his lap, he read, "Raymond Davis. You have been granted salvation, secured by the blood of the Lamb. Your sins are forgiven. Welcome!"

"Thank you, my Lord," Ray bowed.

Standing, Jesus presented Ray with a crown. "You were chosen. Well done, my good and faithful servant," he said, placing it on Ray's head.

"Thank you, Jesus," Ray said.

Accompanying Ray down the steps, Jesus said, "By the way, you'll get to meet Lazarus at some point."

They stopped at the bottom. "I suppose I will," Ray said with a laugh. Without giving it a glance, he tossed his crown among the others. "I have eternity to spend with him."

"Indeed you do! I think you'll find he's quite an interesting character."

"Not to mention the disciples, Mary, Moses, Abraham…"

"Yes," Jesus said, amused, "you'll get to meet everyone."

Catching himself, Ray said, "I guess I'm getting carried away."

"Not at all. What a joy it is for the body to be assembled."

Turning right, they exited the path and made their way to a throng of believers.

"Where are we headed?" Ray asked.

"Oh, I'm going to introduce you to a few people."

"Sounds good," Ray said as they approached a small group.

Introductions weren't really necessary. As part of one body, everyone knew each other.

"Everyone, please welcome Ray," Jesus announced.

They took turns saying hi and exchanging hugs. Ray found it interesting that no one shook hands, but he recalled the practice originated as a means of showing an opponent you were unarmed. *No reason for that here,* he mused to himself.

Turning, Jesus said, "Please excuse me."

"Where are you going?" Ray asked.

"I have to meet someone at the gate," he explained.

"Oh, okay. Well, I will see you later."

"Yes, yes you will," Jesus assured him with a smile and departed.

Ray resumed his conversation with the group of believers. As he did, he studied the splendor of Heaven. The sky was a brilliant blue turquoise with streaks of navy. Birds chirped in all directions, skittering about without a care. Flowers bloomed, filling endless fields. Trees sprang up from the ground and extended into a clear sky. Squirrels raced around tree trunks, and rabbits hopped through the fields of grass. Cats and dogs played together. *Indeed,* Ray thought, recalling Scripture, *the lion lay down with the lamb.* Everything existed in perfect harmony, the way it had been intended.

Gathered together, everyone smiled. There was no sadness, only joy. Filled with God's glory, there was only light—the one, true light that had always existed and would endure forever.

"Ray?" A voice called out.

Turning, Ray saw Jesus making his way toward him, another believer by his side.

Then recognition set in and he began to run. "Betty!" he shouted.

"Ray." She met him and they embraced.

Catching up to them, Jesus said, "You see, Ray, I told you she would be fine."

"I don't understand," Ray said. "I just left."

Laughing fully, Jesus said, "No, I'm afraid that was a little while ago. You see, a day here is like a thousand years on earth, and a thousand years on earth is like a day here."

"Oh, I see," Ray said, recalling the familiar passage and description from 2 Peter. "How long has it been?"

"Not long at all," Betty supplied. "After you left, Ray, my heart was broken." Ray recalled hearing about broken heart syndrome.

Ray turned to Jesus, his words echoing in his mind. "Change of command," he had said. It was time for others to continue in the work as commanded.

"You two can catch up after I take Betty to meet my Father," Jesus said.

"Yes, of course," Ray said.

"I'll come back, Ray," Betty said and gave him a hug.

"I'll be here," Ray said. "I'm not going anywhere. Not anymore."

20

The shrill beeping of the alarm clock startled Li Hung Cho, rousing him from a deep sleep. Rolling over, he swatted and managed to silence it on the second try. Moving onto his back, he lay on the bed and stared at the sliver of light that had snuck through the top of the shade and darted across the ceiling. Except for that and the blue digits on the clock, the room was shrouded in darkness.

It was 5:00 a.m. On any other day he wouldn't be up at such an hour, but today was race day, and races started early. He had never understood the need for races to start at such an hour. *Sure, it makes sense that it's cooler and would inconvenience drivers less, but so would an evening race,* he had reasoned.

While he was contemplating this, his phone vibrated and lit up, filling the room with an explosion of light. Retrieving it from the nightstand, he smiled at the text. May Ling Sanders, his fellow runner and girlfriend.

You up?

Yes, he responded. *Gonna grab a shower and get ready. I'll text you when I leave. Love you!*

K. See you soon☺. Love you more!!!

Flinging the covers off like a matador, he swung his legs over the side and flicked the lamp on. An unwelcome light flooded his sparse bedroom. In the corner, laid out one a wooden chair that looked like it belonged at a dining table, were his race shorts, socks, and tank top. All were laid out with precision and care, as though ready for a military inspection. His bib was adhered via four safety pins – one in each corner. It bore the number 2074. Under the chair were his new shoes—shoes that he had broken in several weeks prior.

For a moment, he studied the paraphernalia common to runners. *I'm a runner now*, he observed, as he considered the magnitude of the race ahead. Standing before the chair as though at the foot of an altar, he smiled, satisfied, at the accouterment.

Making his way to the bathroom, he got the shower running and brushed his teeth while he waited for the water to heat up. He studied himself in the mirror, turning left and right. *I don't look like a runner,* he observed. *But I am!* He smiled at his reflection.

Eyes closed, he buried his face in the showerhead's spray. The needled hot water began its job, washing away the sleep. As the water soaked his hair and ran down his back, he pondered the event that loomed in the distance.

I can't believe I'm going to run thirteen miles today, he marveled. *Thirteen point one,* he corrected himself. *The point one is probably going to be the tough part.* He laughed.

Not bothering with soap because he knew he'd need another shower after the race, he finished rinsing off and turned off the water. After drying, he returned to the bedroom.

With a towel wrapped around his waist, he stood in front of his chest of drawers and picked up a picture of himself. *I can't believe how fat and out of shape I was,* he thought. Taken just over a year ago, he barely recognized the obese figure bearing his pudgy face. A hundred pounds overweight, cholesterol sky high, triglycerides off the chart, and a fasting blood sugar that even made his doctor look twice, Li was on his way to an early grave.

Quickly donning his shorts — runner's shorts with a split up the side — he laughed to himself, never imagining he'd wear something so skimpy one day. But as he had come to realize, such shorts were invaluable. Outfit complete, he ensured he had his sunglasses — an essential element of any running ensemble.

He sent a message to May. *On my way. Be there soon.*

I'll be waiting, she responded.

He grabbed his wallet and keys from the table, pulled the door shut and headed out. May only lived a few minutes away. *There won't be much traffic at this hour. Especially on a Sunday.*

As he exited his neighborhood, he stopped at the corner. Crossing in front of him, a heavyset middle-aged woman clad in tights speed-walked in the cool of the early morning. Oblivious to his presence, she continued on as he turned. *That used to be me. No anymore, though. Not anymore.*

Traffic was light and the few lights he encountered were all green, expediting his travel. Within minutes he turned left across an empty two-lane road and entered May's neighborhood. Two lefts and a right, and he was on her street.

Li pulled up in front of a row of brick townhomes. Constructed in similar fashion and design, each resembled the other with little distinction. Complete with a one-car garage, their small, manicured lawns were neatly trimmed and uniform, giving the upscale neighborhood an institutional appearance.

Sitting on the stoop of the end unit, a young, Chinese woman sprang to her feet. Although somewhat plain looking, her features were attractive. Dressed similarly to Li, her creamy legs were smooth and toned from years of running. Her sunglasses sat atop a lavender visor. With the exception of her shoes, her outfit matched completely. *She could pass for a sports model*, Li observed.

Opening the passenger door, she hopped in.

"Good morning," she said, her voice exuberant and kissed him.

"Good morning," Li said.

Li started to drive off as May fastened her seat belt. Like a child on Christmas morning, May was giddy and chock full of enthusiasm.

"Are you psyched?" she asked, jabbing him in the arm.

"Not as much as you are," he said.

"Ah, c'mon, Li. You got this, man," she persuaded.

"I'll believe that when I cross the finish line," he protested.

"Dude, you ran twelve miles two weeks ago," she reasoned. "What's one more mile?"

"One point one miles," he corrected.

"Whatever," she said with a dismissive wave of her arm.

"You're not worried," he continued, "because you've done this before."

"So?"

"So? So, I haven't." His voice rose an octave.

"Calm down, baby," she said, patting his leg. "You're going to do great."

He shook his head. "We'll see. I have my doubts."

"Why? You did terrific at the training run."

"It took me almost three hours," he said.

"Big deal. You finished, and that's all that matters," she reassured him.

"Maybe, but it wasn't hot that day. It's hotter today," he explained.

"You'll be finished by the time it starts to warm up. You'll see."

"What's this, like your tenth half-marathon?" he asked.

She laughed. "I don't know. Something like that. I don't count them anymore."

"Anymore?" he pounced. "Anymore? You've run so many you've lost track."

"Maybe," she said placing her arm on his shoulders and rubbing his neck, "but someday so will you! I wasn't always a runner."

Li glanced at May. She was smiling. She always smiled. It was that smile that had drawn him to her. *And that changed my life.*

"I suppose you're right," he said, his fears starting to subside a little.

"You've come a long way," she encouraged. "You forget. When you started, you walked one lap around the block and were winded. But," she added, pointing a finger at him, "you worked you way up to a mile and started a walk-to-run program. Now look at you!"

He laughed. "Yeah, now look at me! About to run thirteen miles. I must be crazy to have let you talk me into this," he said.

"All runners are crazy," she replied.

"How so?" he asked.

"I mean, we run for a t-shirt and bragging rights, so yeah, that's crazy."

"It is," he concurred.

"Yeah, but now you're one of us!" she proclaimed, her voice bursting with pride.

"Yes, I am. Yes, I am," he said, turning to smile at her and steal a quick kiss. "Thanks to you, babe, I am indeed!"

"We're happy to have you too," she beamed at him.

Joining the throng of cars all jockeying for position to find a place to park, Li asked, "This starts and ends at the Convention Center, right?"

"Yup." She nodded. "There should be plenty of parking. And we're a little on the early side, too."

In single file, all of the cars made their way to a designated lot under the direction of a volunteer clad in an orange vest. Another volunteer waved him into the next available slot. It reminded Li of the ground crew that guided airplanes on the tarmac. One by one, the cars filled the vacant lot.

Li paid to park and was guided by an elderly man with a large, gray mustache that reminded him of a push broom. After placing his wallet in the glove box, Li depressed the lock button on the key fob and double-checked the car was locked by pulling on the door handle.

"Are you pumped?" May asked with the look of a child at the circus.

"Not yet," he said. "I will be once we get started."

"Pre-race jitters," she said. "Happens. Nothing to worry about."

"Not for you," he jibed. "How much do you think you'll embarrass me by?" he asked as they walked toward the starting line, where a huge crowd occupied the street out front of the convention center.

Looking straight ahead, her face contorted into a mischievous smile. "Oh, I'd say at least an hour."

Li shook his head in disgust. "That's insane."

"Well, I've been doing this for years, remember? You'll get faster. Speed isn't important. Getting out here and just doing it is. Don't forget that!" she lectured. "Besides, if you hadn't started running and eating right, you might not be here now. Running saved your life."

He stopped and looked her in the eyes. "No," he said, his voice emphatic. "You did!"

"Aw," she said, stopping to hug to give him a hug and kiss. "That's so sweet."

"It's true," he said as they rounded a corner and entered what was on every other day a major thoroughfare that had been barricaded on each side to accommodate runners. "You helped me cheat death."

"I might have helped," she countered, "but you did all the work."

"Perhaps, but I wouldn't have done it had it not been for you," he replied.

Continuing on to the end of the barricaded area, they reached the entrance. They took their place in the back of the line, where the slower runners gathered. The people in this part of the pack were in it for the fun, the t-shirt, and free beer at the finish.

"You're gonna stick with me for the first mile, right?" he asked.

"Sure am," she said, smiling from ear to ear. "And I'll be cheering you at the finish line."

"Okay," he said. "I'll be looking for you."

A loudspeaker crackled to life as a race official announced the race would start in two minutes.

"This is it," she said. "I'm proud of you, Li. You should be proud of yourself too. This is a major accomplishment. Tonight we will go out to dinner and celebrate."

"Dinner sounds good," he said. "Let's skip the race and go straight to dinner," he added with a laugh.

Sharing his laugh, she said, "Too late for that now." With extreme exaggeration, she shook her head. "Nope. Gotta earn it, buddy."

With the pre-race announcements finished, the final countdown began, followed by the burst of an air horn. They were off.

Li pulled her in for a kiss, and said, "I love you, May."

"I love you more, Li."

As in all big races, they crept toward the starting line where the herd thinned out and began running as soon as they crossed the two rubber strips that would track their time. Just as they crossed the line and started running, May reached out and grabbed Li's hand. Giving it a firm squeeze, she turned to him and said, "Love you!"

"Love you too," he replied. And with that they were off. Glancing at her, Li studied May. Fit, lean, clever, and funny, he didn't know what he had done to deserve someone as wonderful as her.

He turned his focus to road ahead. Together they meandered their way through the throng of runners, power walkers, and stroller pushers in search of open space so they could find their pace. As they rounded the bend that led to the first leg of the race, the herd thinned enough for Li to ease into his stride. Next to him, May glided along without the slightest effort he wondered if her feet were even touching the ground.

She turned to check on him. "You good?" she asked, not even out of breath.

"Yeah," he said, not taking his eyes off the road ahead. "I feel good."

Running wasn't a social sport by any means, but it was especially not at long distances. Li and May maintained their pace. As necessary, they detoured around slower runners. Li found this encouraging.

Maybe my time won't be so bad, he thought.

With the lead pack too far out in front to see, the remainder of the runners began to settle in and separate. They were an odd mixture comprised of men, women, young, old, some in shorts, others in tights, tank tops, t-shirts, gloves, beanies, hats, long hair, ponytails, bald, headphones, and sunglasses. *Amid all the diversity and variation, we are an eclectic group united by a single goal — cross the finish line,* Li observed. And now he was one of them.

Off to his right, the morning sun was beginning its climb out of the ocean, filling the sky with a pool of orange. Li was too far away to hear the ocean, but its distinctive salty smell permeated the air, providing a faint reminder of its presence — and the finish line!

The minutes that passed were uneventful, as runners all ran their own race. Unlike the starting line and finish line, there weren't many spectators. All the action took place at the finish line. Li focused on the road. Up ahead the two-lane thoroughfare rounded a bend to the right. Just prior to it, a green and white banner stood off to the side. Supported by a plastic pole, it read MILE 1.

As they approached the mile marker, May turned to Li and gave him a quick one-arm hug and said, "I'll see you at the finish, okay? You've got this. I'm so proud of you. Love you."

"Thanks. Love you too," he said.

Li watched as May coasted away from him with ease. He recalled how she wanted to run the entire race with him, but he wouldn't have it. "I don't want to hold you back," he had said. "Just stay with me for the first mile," he had reasoned. May was a seasoned runner, capable of maintaining a seven-minute mile pace that, compared to his, was light speed.

Relenting, she agreed.

The sun began its arc overhead, illuminating and heating the asphalt. Li checked his FitBit. He had run his first mile in 10:33, which wasn't bad for him. He hadn't set a mileage pace, but he was happy with his first mile. *Only twelve to go,* he thought. Having started at 8 a.m., he estimated he would be finished by 11 a.m. at the latest. He decided could live with that, although he hoped it was closer to 10:30.

Mile three included a water and Gatorade station. Following May's advice, Li stopped and walked while he downed the lime-flavored electrolytes. After a hundred feet or so, he discarded the waxed paper cup into a large, black trash bag held open by a young volunteer and began running again.

Picking up the pace, Li did a quick self-assessment. *Feeling pretty good,* he thought. *Legs feel loose.* From a clear blue sky, the sun watched with approval. The cool of the morning had dissipated, replaced by the pending heat of the day. Not one for hot weather, Li groaned to himself, caught in the sun's embrace. So close to the oceanfront, the course offered little shade.

From the race map, he recalled miles five, seven, nine, and eleven all provided water and Gatorade along with port-a-potties, a vital necessity at any race. Shortly after delving into the world of running, Li realized the meaning of the phrase "nothing gets you going like running."

A mile from the halfway and turnaround point, Li saw May heading toward him. *She's gorgeous,* he observed as he studied her form. Giving his watch a quick glance, he saw she was running at just below a seven-minute mile pace. Almost in unison, both runners shifted to their left, straddling the invisible line that separated the two groups of runners. When they passed, Li and May exchanged a high-five and smile. Words required breath, and breath was not wasted during a run.

Less than ten minutes later, Li rounded a lighthouse that served as the official halfway point of the race. He smiled as he muttered to himself, "I'm halfway home." Now he was heading toward the finish line. Although he had more than six miles to go, he was halfway there.

Drenched in sweat thanks to an unabated sun, Li took full advantage of the water stops at miles seven, nine, and eleven. In addition to gulping several cups of Gatorade, he doused himself with a few cups of water. Its cooling effect only provided momentary relief as it dissipated in the morning heat.

With two miles to the finish, Li was battling himself and the sun. Mocking him from a distance, he was an easy target along with the other runners given the lack of shade. *If only this had been an overcast day*, he thought.

At the twelve-mile marker, older man ran next to him, matching his pace. With a quick glance, Li could see the man was much older. *Sixties? Seventies maybe?* he wondered. *Nah, he can't be that old. Can he?* Taking another glance, he noticed the man had gray hair and a matching, well-trimmed beard. A few sparse chest hairs sprang out of his tank top. *Maybe he is in his seventies*, Li concluded. *Nothing like getting beat by a man old enough to be my grandfather*, he lamented.

"I feel like I'm melting," he said, breaking the silence, sweat pouring down his face.

"Yup," came the solitary response.

With the mile twelve marker looming up ahead, the old man muttered, "Good luck," and drifted ahead of him until he was just a dot.

"You too," Li said, more to himself than the old man.

Passing by the marker, a wave of euphoria washed over Li. *This is it,* he thought. *A mile to go. I've got this.* He forced himself not to pick up his pace, a lesson he had learned over the previous Thanksgiving. During the Turkey Trot, he increased his pace too soon and had to slow down to a light jog less than a quarter of a mile to the finish line due to side stitch. Turning left, he crossed one block to the boardwalk that ran for miles along the oceanfront. Made of concrete, it spanned the entire length of the resort area and was the location of the finish line.

Making a quick right turn, Li entered the boardwalk and could see the finish line looming in the distance. *About a half mile away,* he recalled from the race map. Cordoned off by metal barricades, spectators lined each side. *I wonder which side May will be on.*

Adrenaline kicking in, he began to increase his pace. *I can't believe I'm doing this,* he mused. He could hear the people cheering—cheering for him! Eyes scanning, he looked for May but did not see her. Just ahead, a series of orange cones strung together with yellow taped marked the beginning of the chute that led to the finish line.

With just under a quarter of a mile to go, his legs and arms pumped like an Olympic sprinter. The official race clock read 2:34:48. *I'm going to break three hours,* he exclaimed to himself. Increasing his speed with each step, Li bolted toward the finish line. Fifty feet from the finish, he flung his arms upward in victory as he sprinted.

On the other side to left, he saw May. She was smiling and cheering and waving him on to victory. An uncontrollable smile broke out on Li's face. With a final push, he darted across the finish line. Slowing to a walk, he accepted a finisher's medal from a race volunteer with gratitude, as he fought to catch his breath.

"Congratulations," May said, as she made her way to him. Disregarding the sweat, she wrapped her arms around him and bear-hugged him.

"Thank you," Li replied. He held the medal in front of himself and admired it for a moment before placing it over his head. Beaming with pride, he held it away from his body and smiled as though it were an Olympic medal.

As he let go of the medal, he felt it slap against his chest. Locking eyes with May, who stood next to him, he stopped and stood still. A blank expression covered his face. Like erasing a chalkboard, his elation was gone. Taking a misplaced step, his knee buckled, and he wobbled for a few seconds like a top running out of energy before collapsing to the ground.

21

Timothy tried not to think about the torment Corn Fed must be enduring or the unbearable agony that awaited him behind the molten gates. The heat in the waiting areas was searing, but it was nothing compared to the inferno of Hell. Such heat was unimaginable and beyond description. He tried to push the thought of burning for eternity out of his mind, but it was no use. Suffering was his fate, the fate of all non-believers. Though they were all cramped together in the narrow confines of the waiting area, they were very much alone. *Hell is an individual experience,* he reasoned, *not something that is shared.* There was no collective body of the unrepentant, no group or unit or cohesion from which to draw strength or inspiration. Unlike prison, Hell was occupied by individuals who were punished collectively for their individual sins.

Never ceasing or diminishing in intensity, scalding heat washed over them in successive waves. Timothy thought, *Hell is the ultimate in solitary confinement.*

"Your time's coming," Grandma interrupted his thoughts.

Removing his eyes from Hell's doorway, he looked at her. "So is yours," he retorted, somewhat

251

offended by her remark. After a quick glance around, he added, "For all of us, that is."

She nodded. "Indeed. Been here long enough."

Timothy pondered her words. *How long have I been here?* he wondered. There was no way to tell. Time did not exist here. Looking at Grandma, he placated himself by concluding that she had been here when he arrived. *She'll go before I do,* he thought. *But eventually I'll go too. We all will.* Then he considered Corn Fed's words. There was no rhyme or reason to the Beast. Consumed by evil, he acted in irregular, indiscriminate patterns.

"In due time," Sticks added, "we will all be dragged inside." He paused. "There is no escape for any of us," he stated, an air of finality in his voice.

"Don't imagine there would be," Earl chimed in. "If there was, somebody'd a gotten out by now, I 'magine."

Sticks nodded in agreement.

"Not that I'm not for tryin', mind ya," Earl added

"There is no way out," Grandma said. Full of gloom, she continued, "Our fate was sealed the moment we died, bound for all eternity."

With Corn Fed gone, the grim finality of Hell was becoming all too real for Lauren. Refusing to accept her fate, she blurted, "This just isn't fair! I don't belong here," she argued.

Timothy wanted to agree with her, but he knew better. *We all belong here,* he thought.

"And what about you?" she asked Timothy. "I mean, you're younger than me. What did you do to deserve this?"

Before Timothy could respond, Shelinda interjected. "We died," she stated with definitive authority . Her voice was even and flat, devoid of emotion. She stared into the darkness, not looking at any of them.

All eyes trained on her, they remained silent, not sure of her meaning or how to respond. Timothy knew she what she meant. *Spiritual death, not physical,* he concluded. He also knew neither of them would be able to elaborate. At first, it didn't make sense that such things could not be discussed here. But as the certainty of eternal punishment settled in, Timothy realized those things could not be discussed because they were not able to exist here. They were the very antithesis of this horrible, wretched place. Evil, hatred, and fear were all the existed or could exist. Nothing more. Knowing that only added to his misery and torment.

Eyes fixed on Shelinda, Timothy agreed. "We did."

Shifting her focus from the dark to Timothy, they locked eyes. It was a brief moment of recognition in which they both realized their mutual understanding of things not spoken.

"What's that got to do with anything?" Lauren demanded. "I shouldn't have died. I'm too young to be dead."

"My dear, life is precious, the most precious gift we are ever given," Grandma said. "But it is never really ours and can be snuffed out in the blink of an eye."

"We all gotta go sometime," Earl said. "I'm s'prised I made it as long as I did."

"You lived your life," Lauren spat. "I didn't. It was just getting started."

"Life is fleeting," Sticks declared. "Nothing more than a grain of sand on the beach of eternity."

His words took Lauren off guard. Unsure how to respond, she said nothing. Instead she simply stared at him.

"It certainly is," Shelinda agreed. "It certainly is."

Timothy stared at her. Out of their group, she was the only one who had ended up there as the result of her own deliberate action. And based on her previous comments, he knew she had rejected her opportunity to avoid this place much like he had.

You were right, Mom, he thought. *You were right.*

In the middle of his thoughts, a shadow materialized next to Sticks. Surprised, confused, and bewildered, Li Hung Cho joined the waiting area.

"Where am I?" he asked.

Everyone asks the same question, Timothy thought.

"Waiting," Sticks said.

Sticks and Li completed what had become a somewhat standard exchange, in which Sticks explained the reality and finality of Li's circumstance.

When Sticks had finished, Li exclaimed, "I can't be dead! There's no way."

"I'm afraid it's true," Grandma said.

"No, this is some kind of dream or delusion," he retorted.

Shaking his head, Timothy said, "It's not a dream, believe me. More like a nightmare. You're dead."

"You don't understand," he argued. "I cheated death!"

His comment brought a faint but brief smile to Grandma's distorted face. "My son, no one cheats death."

"No," he pleaded. I did. You see," he began, "I was obese and in poor health. My doctor told me I'd die soon if I didn't change my lifestyle. So I did! I did change...ate right...exercised..." his voice trailed off as he recalled May. Meeting her had been the impetus of change.

"If you made all those changes," Lauren began, "how'd you get here?"

"Yeah," Earl added.

Thinking about it for a moment, Li said, "I don't know. I had just crossed the finish line of a race, my first half-marathon."

"Give it a few minutes. You'll have your re-live soon enough," Sticks said.

Li was about to ask what Sticks meant when his eyes glazed over. As if watching a movie from afar, he saw himself crossing the finish line, arms raised in victory. Moments later, he dropped to the ground. Race officials, a medic, and May sprinted to him. But he was already gone. A vessel in his brain had burst. Like hitting a switch, his life had ended in a millisecond.

May stepped out of the way as paramedics assessed Li's vitals. An ambulance's siren squawked as it maneuvered onto the boardwalk from a side street adjacent to the finish line. Police arrived on scene to disperse the crowd. Runners, unaware of what was happening at the finish, crossed with a mixture of exuberance and concern. Li's lifeless body was strapped to a gurney and loaded into the ambulance.

"Well?" Earl asked. "What happened?"

"Brain aneurysm. Had nothing to do with my health," he said, dejected.

"Yer number was up," Earl declared.

"We all have our time," Grandma said.

"No," he said. "I don't accept that."

"There's no way to reject it," Shelinda said.

Timothy sized her up. She hadn't said much since her arrival. He was pretty sure he knew why but was unable to articulate it.

Li shot Shelinda a glance. "So I'm just supposed to accept I'm dead."

"Well, you are," Timothy said. It was a statement, not an observation.

"I was healthy, in the best shape of my life," Li implored. "I– I had a girlfriend, a wonderful woman—she helped me get in shape and lose weight. My life was good. I– I just don't understand."

"Tell me about it," Lauren agreed. "My life was good too."

Timothy noted Lauren had become more and more bitter since her arrival. She refused to accept that she belonged here. He recalled something his pastor had said once at Youth Group in response to a statement about being a good person and not believing. "There is no one righteous, not even one...there is no one who does good, not even one."

Li looked at her, finding an ally of sorts. "Why are we here?" he asked her. "I was a good person."

"So was I!" she blurted.

"So this is it?" Li asked.

"What do you mean by 'this is it'?" Grandma asked.

"I mean, this is all there is? You live your life, die, and end up here?"

"No," Sticks answered. "This is not it."

"Then what?" he demanded.

In unison, they all turned their heads toward the twin fiery doors. Scorching hot and radiating constant heat that seemed to grow ever hotter, they were the object of their attention.

"What's in there?" Li asked.

"Your fate," Grandma said.

"My what?"

"Hell," Timothy deadpanned.

"Hell? I thought this was Hell."

"No," Sticks managed a snicker. "This is the waiting area," he explained.

"What's in there?"

"You'll find out soon enough," Grandma said. "Won't be long before the Beast comes out again."

"Beast? What Beast?" Li asked.

"He's the feller that runs this place," Earl explained.

"The Devil," Shelinda clarified.

"You mean..."

"Yes," Shelinda said. "Satan himself."

Puzzled at her knowledge, they all stared at her. Timothy never realized he could speak about the Devil here. He had assumed he was unable to share his former knowledge about spiritual things. Then again, this was *his* world and abode. Speaking of him was permitted.

"Yeah," Timothy added, catching Shelinda's eye. "He's also called the Beast."

Li looked back and forth between Timothy and Shelinda. "The Devil's in there?" he asked motioning to the molten doors. "The Devil himself?"

"Yes," Grandma said. "Lucifer."

"So what happens next?" he asked.

"He comes out...whenever he feels like it...no real pattern to it...and drags souls inside," Timothy explained.

Li nodded as though he understood. He acknowledged the explanation, but he could not accept it. "I don't understand. I mean...I was happy...life was good. Why? And to die from something as rare as a brain aneurysm? It doesn't make sense," he lamented.

"Doesn't need to make sense," Sticks said. "In the end, everyone dies. The only problem is no one ever thinks about it. Everyone believes they have more time."

Li was about to ask another question when the flaming doors burst open with a thunderous crash. A searing wave of heat poured out and engulfed them as the Beast strode forward, swinging his powerful arms. Shaking his head from side to side, he emitted a shrieking roar that reverberated throughout the darkness.

Frozen with fear, Li asked, "What is that?"

"The Beast," Timothy supplied.

With each footstep, the ground, hidden by the darkness, shook. Approaching a group of souls, he looked down at them and roared. With a single swipe of each great arm, he snatched up several souls in each massive paw. Clutching them, he stared at them with his primitive red eyes. Like a monster about to devour his prey, he hissed at them. They trembled with fear and struggled to no avail for there was no escape.

Before pivoting and heading back to the incinerator that was his lair, he stood motionless and studied the waiting souls. Barely imperceptible, the faintest trace of a smile creased his odious face. Although pleasure was a foreign concept in this place, the Beast took delight in the number of souls that would belong to him for eternity.

With long, protracted strides, the Beast made his way back to his inferno. Unable to escape the Beast's formidable grip, the souls in his grasp struggled to no avail. Wailing like wounded animals, their screams were silenced as the doorway to Hell shut with a booming thud.

"That's the Beast?" Li asked.

"Yeah," Timothy said.

"He's...he's gruesome," Li observed.

"Pretty much," Lauren said.

Timothy thought back to his Sunday school days and Mrs. Shaw. He recalled her talking about the Devil, except she had called him Lucifer. Said he was a fallen angel. Had been the most beautiful of all the angels. Thinking about what she had said, he wondered, *How could an angel look so horrible?*

"Does everyone get dragged inside?" Li asked.

"Yes," Grandma affirmed. "Everyone."

"When?"

"Whenever he comes for you," Sticks answered. "Really no way to tell when that will be."

"That heat," Li said. "And the smell…what is that awful stench?"

"Death," Sticks said. "Dying souls."

"I didn't think souls could die," Li said.

"They can't," Shelinda responded.

"Then what happens in there?" Li asked, nodding in the direction of the doors. "I thought you said that was the smell of death?"

"It is," Grandma said. "It's the smell of eternal death." Turning to him, she stared. "In there, you die forever."

22

In the back of the C-130 cargo plane, Sergeant Wallace 'Wally' Lawless connected his oxygen mask to the airplane's pre-breather tube. Following a faint hissing sound, his mask filled with cold, life-giving gas. For the next forty-five minutes, he and his partner, Staff Sergeant James Robert Brennen, would saturate their bloodstream with pure oxygen in an effort to remove nitrogen prior to exiting out the back. This was done in order to mitigate altitude sickness, known as hypoxia. The two would be jumping from an altitude of 38,000 feet, where the partial pressure of oxygen was significantly less than at sea level. Fifteen seconds after exiting, they would deploy their chutes and glide for over thirty miles to the target area: Paghman, Afghanistan. Known as HAHO—high altitude, high opening—the clandestine insertion technique allowed troops to penetrate sensitive target areas undetected by gliding up to thirty miles.

Shrouded in a cocoon of pale red light, the two soldiers sat side-by-side, silent. Members of the Army's 75th Regiment Reconnaissance Brigade, they were experienced operators and spent this time mentally preparing for their mission. "Preparation is the key to mission success," Lawless always said.

In the cockpit, the pilot eased the behemoth left in a gradual bank, edging toward the Afghanistan–Pakistan border. The insertion point, as it was known, was 30 minutes out. Due to the nature of the mission, the plane would skirt the border before deployment, then return back to the air base in Saudi Arabia where they took off.

Invisible against the blanket of night sky, the military transport plane flew with its running lights off. Clandestine operations required stealth, which is why they occurred at night. The moon's absence combined with an ample amount of cloud cover ensured the aircraft would remain out of sight. Remaining undetected from radar was not possible, which is why the plane had remained in commercial airspace for the duration of the flight. It was also why Lawless and Brennen would be jumping from more than 6 miles above the earth.

Clad in an olive green flight suit and matching Nomex flight gloves, the crew chief held up both of his hands, fingers splayed. He stood in front of Lawless and Brennen, waving his hands in and out, indicating ten minutes to deployment. They nodded in unison and stood. After disconnecting from the plane's oxygen supply, they connected their hoses to the bottles mounted on the front of the parachute rig, and performed a final equipment check. Brennen verified Lawless' chute and equipment, then Lawless did the same for Brennen. Each acknowledged this with a hard tap on the shoulder.

Just as they finished, the rear cargo doors hummed to life. Like the bill of a giant pelican opening, the upper portion of the door retracted into the overhead as the lower portion dropped into the night. Had it not been for the rush of frigid air, the door's opening would not have been noticeable, obscured by the sea of pitch black. Making their way to the exit ramp, each soldier stood on either side. With a firm grasp on the nylon cargo netting that ran the length of the plane's interior, they peered out into the forbidding darkness. Greeted by a rush of bone-chilling air, the abyss of darkness awaited their arrival.

Staff Sergeant Lawless looped his right arm through the nylon strap and gripped it as he peered into the void below. Even with his oxygen mask on, he could detect the faint smell of exhausted jet fuel. *Another jump for the books,* he thought, recalling the hundreds of times he had parachuted out of the back of perfectly good aircraft.

There was nothing to see. He shifted his gaze in Brennen's direction. Standing motionless, he steadied himself against the fuselage in anticipation.

The final moment before hurling oneself out of a plane is not unlike being backstage before a performance, Lawless thought.

The red jump light extinguished, replaced by bright green. Lawless and Brennen nodded at each other and bailed out. Swallowed by the darkness, they had just reached terminal velocity when they pulled their chutes. Night vision goggles on, they used their compasses to navigate their way through the cold sea of black. As they descended, pinpoints of light became visible, an indication of life below. Unlike cities in developed areas, villages existed in the dark with only a smattering of light, a faint dot in an otherwise darkened landscape.

Their destination was the western side of a mountain ridge a few miles from Paghman, a small village area. The night vision goggles painted the world below a pale shade of luminescent green. Lights glowed like small embers in a pile of ashes. Trees and foliage loomed below in the distance as shaded variations of the landscape. A jagged line running across the horizon indicated a mountain ridge: their destination.

A downdraft began bringing the earth up to meet them faster than either of them would have liked. Landing sooner than later would mean hoofing it to the target area, which was on the far side of the ridgeline.

"Murphy's Law," Lawless said to himself. "Never fails."

Although the two had communication gear with them, they maintained radio silence. While it was unlikely that anyone below would be capable of deciphering their encrypted communication and obtaining usable intelligence, electronic transmissions emitted signals that could be detected. Knowledge of their existence would be enough to arouse suspicion and bring unwanted attention.

Flaring their canopies in an effort to create lift, they managed to gain a few hundred feet in altitude. *It won't be enough,* Lawless concluded as he calculated their distance to the target. And it wasn't. Touching down on the near side of the steep embankment that overlooked the village area, Lawless made contact with the ground. Hidden by the blanket of darkness, the gentle impact of his feet produced a small puff of dry dirt.

Brennen touched down fifty feet from him, and the two gathered their chutes, masks, and oxygen bottles and stowed them under a scant amount of brush near some shrubs.

"You good, Jimbo?" Lawless asked Brennen.

"Five by five. You?"

"Same. Let's do this."

Under the cover of night, they cinched up their rucksacks and began the trek toward the target area. The heat of the day had faded along with the sun, but the air was still humid and filled with remnants of the excessive temperatures that characterized the region. With sixty pounds of gear, they had only traveled a few hundred yards before they were covered in sweat. Dry from lack of rain and the sun's unrelenting presence, the ground was solid and crunched under their boots. The sound reminded Lawless of winters in Ohio.

The two proceeded in silence toward the target area. Utilizing a handheld GPS, they checked it every hundred meters to ensure they were on course. Lawless had estimated they'd have to cover just over five miles—an hour-long hump. Although they had landed short of their intended insertion point, they were still in good shape time-wise. With four hours until the sun turned the countryside into a frying pan, they had enough time to get in position and take cover.

Making their way through the darkness in silence, each was alone with his thoughts. As they trekked across the landscape, Lawless thought about the many missions he had been part of over the years. He thought, *Combat is something that has to be experienced to be understood. Until you're in the thick of it, combat is surreal and distant, existing only in the imagination. Once experienced, it is something that can never be forgotten.* Shifting his eyes to the left, he glanced over at Jimbo. Both had seen action numerous times in their careers, but they were fortunate, part of a small but elite group of survivors. The longer a soldier remained in service, the more funerals he attended. Looking ahead, his thoughts continued. *Combat is death. There is nothing glorious about it, nothing to envy, no reason to ever aspire to experience it. So why am I here?*

With a slight shake of his head, Lawless snapped himself back to reality. Dismissing his thoughts, he shifted his focus to the mission. Get in, get out, go home. That was it—K.I.S.S.—keep it simple, stupid.

Nearing the edge of the ridgeline, Jimbo stopped and held his left arm up, fist clenched. It was the single to halt. Lawless remained frozen, his silhouette transfixed in the darkness. Brennen's gaze remained fixed on an unseen target in the distance. After a few second, he lowered his arm.

"What?" Lawless whispered.

"I thought I heard something," he replied in a Kentucky drawl.

"Where?"

"To the right, twenty meters," he whispered.

Lawless turned his head in the direction indicated. The night vision brought to life undistinguished images of shrubs and tumbleweeds painted in green. "I don't see anything," he said. "Animal?"

"Could be, I suppose," Brennan said. His voice had an edge to it, tense due to being behind enemy lines.

"I doubt there's anybody out here at this hour," Lawless said, well aware of the paranoia that becomes second nature in combat.

"Probably not," Brennan conceded. "I just get twitchy every time I'm in country."

"I know what you mean," Lawless agreed, nodding.

The two moved forward to the target area in silence. They each surveyed the area below to determine the maximum vantage point.

Studying the village six hundred yards below, Lawless drew an imaginary line with his eyes from the compound to where he stood. "This looks good," he announced in a whisper. "Got cover with those shrubs." He nodded as he pointed.

"Yeah, I was thinkin' the same thing," Brennen agreed.

The two removed Ghillie suits from their backpacks and donned them without a sound in the darkness. Lawless un-slung his sniper rifle, an M831 that fired a .50 caliber round over a mile, and extended its tripod. The weapon had been customized with a suppressor to reduce sound and muzzle flash and had a digitized scope mounted on the stock.

Using his boot as a makeshift lawn tool, Lawless dragged its side against the dry dirt in an effort to level the ground and make it somewhat comfortable for the next twelve plus hours. Brennen followed suit and carved out a patch for himself right next to him.

Tapping Lawless on the shoulder, Brennen said, "Gonna mission prep."

"Rogo, Jimbo," Lawless replied, acknowledging Jimbo was going to relieve himself. "Right there with you."

"I figured."

Standing just a few feet apart, they urinated in silence several feet from their vantage point. Once daylight broke, they wouldn't have the opportunity to tend to bodily functions. While each had endured the misery of lying in their bodily fluids to remain hidden, it was something to avoid when possible.

Mission prep completed, the two Special Forces men took their respective positions on the ground and lay motionless in the prone position, facing the small compound in the distance. Brennen took up position behind his spotter's scope next to Lawless.

"Not long until sunup," Brennen whispered.

"It'll be like laying in gas grill," Lawless responded.

"Let's tag this target quick-like," Brennen said, "and then hightail it outta here."

"You know it."

In the spotter's scope, the compound below came to life. Lawless adjusted his scope as he scanned the confines of the compound. A simple white building covered in a layer of what appeared to be stucco surrounded by a shoulder high cinderblock wall was the current base of operations for Akheem Ahmed. Linked to bombings of U.S. bases overseas, the death of hundreds of troops, and with a litany of atrocities to his name, he was the HVT—high value target.

In many cases, HVTs were captured for interrogation. While the world would be better off without them, the information they knew was deemed valuable enough to take them alive, if possible, which wasn't always the case. Akheem, although knowledgeable and full of valuable information, had outlived his usefulness. The decision makers determined it was improbable he would provide valuable information. Therefore, he was now a sniper's target.

From their vantage point on the embankment, the two could see over the wall and into the compound. As the sun poured out of the sky, it erased the morning shadow. Transforming the black and white scene into full color, the two soldiers got their first clear look inside.

"You seein' what I'm seen', Wally?" Brennen asked in whisper.

"'Fraid so, Jimbo."

Two worn personnel trucks sat inside the compound. Resembling leftovers from a World War II movie, they were drab, dented, and worn. But they still ran. Capable of carrying a dozen men each, they sat just inside the entrance. Bearded men in uniform, each with an AK-47 slung over his shoulder, moved about the perimeter. With no threat, their movements were casual, not tactical. Except for their weapons, they resembled window shoppers, loitering about with no intended purpose.

"So much for a soft target," Jimbo sneered. After pausing for a moment to consider their situation, he asked, "What do ya wanna do, boss?"

After a long sigh, Lawless said, "We complete the mission." His voice was confident, and authoritative.

"Roger that," Jimbo replied. "Roger that." Then as an afterthought added, "We got a long way to get to the extraction point."

"Yeah, I know. Mission first, right?" Lawless said wryly.

"That's what they say. Mission first, soldiers always, or somethin' like that."

"Yeah, it's something like, alright," Lawless intoned.

From overhead, the sun's rays reached down and exposed the terrain. Peeling away the final remnants of dawn, it scorched the ground. Insulated by the camouflage suits, the two were drenched in sweat. Through plastic hoses, they drank tepid water from bladders inside their packs. Although it would keep them hydrated, it was far from refreshing.

Peering through his scope, Brennen whispered, "We've got action."

"On it," Lawless said. Squinting through his own scope, he studied the movement below.

From an archway in the rear of the compound, a rotund man emerged. With tanned skin, a chubby face, and trimmed beard, he wore a dark gray Shalmar Kameez and matching turban. He was flanked by an corpulent man dressed in a similar fashion with a longer beard, unkempt by comparison.

"There's our boy," Brennan announced almost to himself, his voice a whisper.

The two were engaged in conversation. Accompanied by hand gestures and affirming nods, each man volleyed back and forth in the verbal exchange.

"Range?" Lawless asked, his voice flat and calm.

Oblivious that they were under surveillance, the two below continued their discussion as they made their way through the compound.

"Six hundred and ten."

With a few clicks, Lawless adjusted his scope. From years of practice, he pressed the index finger of his left hand against the trigger guard. "Ready."

Below, Akheem meandered aroudn and came to a sudden stop, pointing at the other man as he spoke.

"Any idea who that other dude is?" Brennen asked.

"Not a clue, but our boy is telling him off, from what I can see," Lawless said, studying the situation through his scope.

"Seems that way," Jimbo agreed.

When Akheem stopped and turned toward the other man, Brennen said in a voice devoid of emotion, "Stand by."

Lawless's trigger finger slid inside the trigger guard. Placing it on the trigger, he took a deep breath an exhaled deliberately in preparation for Jimbo's command.

Seconds later, Jimbo said, "Send it."

After a final exhalation, Lawless depressed the trigger. The rifle recoiled into his shoulder. With a muzzle velocity of nearly three thousand feet per second, the .50 caliber projectile traveled faster than the speed of sound. Taken out by the round, Akheem dropped to the ground before the men inside the compound heard the echo of the suppressed shot. In a panic, some took cover while others peered cautiously in the direction from where the shot originated.

Lawless and Brennan did not flinch. Controlling their breathing, they pressed their bodies into the landscape. Their Ghillie suits served as camouflage and would make their presence difficult to detect, even with binoculars.

Each hoped the commotion below would subside long enough for them to make an unseen break down the ridgeline behind them and head toward the extraction point. That was not the case.

"All Hell's breaking loose," Lawless spat, remaining still.

A tall muscular man in uniform emerged from the building and began barking orders to the soldiers. Without delay they climbed into the back of the trucks, armed with machine guns and RPGs. In seconds the trucks bolted out of the compound, scrambling their way toward the sniper's nest.

"We can't take them," Brennen said. "Too many of 'em."

"You make a run for it. I'll cover you."

"What? No way. I'm not leaving without you."

"That's an order, Jimbo," Lawless said, turning to Brennen. "I've got the longer barrel. Get down that ridge and I'll be right behind you." He shifted his eye toward the two trucks. "Move," he commanded.

Breaking cover, Brennen jumped up and began sprinting toward the ridgeline. As he did, machine fire erupted behind him followed by single, powerful bursts in retaliation fire from Lawless.

Brennen covered the hundred yards in twenty seconds and was at the bottom of the ridgeline. Taking cover, he shouted to Lawless. "Go, go!"

Popping up, Lawless carried his sniper rifle in his left hand as he ran. Brennen switched on his radio, broke radio silence, and spoke into his headset. "X-ray one, x-ray one, this is Alpha two," he shouted, out of breath. "Taking fire. Heading to extraction point. Request QRF," indicating quick reaction force support.

His earwig squawked in acknowledgment. Eyes fixed on the ridge, Brennen watched as Lawless galloped over the top and headed in his direction. Then he froze at what he saw next. The lead truck sprang over the crest of the ridgeline and stopped. With the passenger door open, an insurgent stood on the side rail and leveled his rifle. Taking aim at Lawless, he fired once.

A cloud of red sprang from the back of Lawless's head. Filling the air with tiny droplets of blood, the sniper's bullet found its mark. Brennen remained in the prone position, staring at his comrade-in-arms. His eyes were wide, and his face was frozen in permanent shock. He remained suspended in time.

Staring at Brennen as he fell to his knees, Lawless slumped forward. His lifeless body thudded to the ground.

23

As the second truck continued to advance on his position, Lawless was a lifeless spectator as events unfolded. Passing by, the driver steered the vehicle toward the ridgeline. Screeching to a halt, the sudden stop on the arid ground scraped a large plume of dust that enveloped the truck and its dismounting soldiers before dissipating. Weapons poised at the ready, they scrambled down the hill, crawling along like a swarm of ants.

Following behind at a distance, Lawless gazed down the hillside into the flat of the valley. Several hundred yards away, he saw Brennen's figure running. Walking with purpose he heard several bursts of automatic gunfire aimed in Brennen's direction. The topography did not offer much in the way of cover or concealment. Spinning to left, Brennen released a short barrage of gunfire before pivoting and continuing to run.

Lawless found himself wondering if Brennen had radioed in for the QRF. He considered this as his pursuers stopped to take aim and return fire. Launching from Pakistan, the QRF would take more than thirty minutes to reach him. Brennen was a skilled Ranger, a warrior, but he was significantly out-numbered. *If they called in reinforcements, he's got no chance,* Lawless thought as he watched Brennen maneuver below.

Although the Taliban soldiers were not in as good of shape as Brennen, they were better armed and in greater number. Lawless watched, helpless, as a man took aim with an RPG and fired it in Brennen's direction. He overshot; it missed Brennen by nearly fifty yards. A second man launched another salvo that landed closer, causing Brennan to adopt a zigzag pattern. The third grenade exploded ahead and to the right of him, but it was much closer — too close for comfort.

Zagging to his left, Brennen turned around quickly and unloaded his magazine. He was too far away to do any real damage, but it would slow his pursuers down a little and allow him to catch his breath. Darting to his right, he picked up his pace. A fourth RPG flew into the air and headed right toward Brennen. Not able to assist, Lawless viewed the perils of war. Impacting less than twenty feet away, Lawless recalled what one of his instructors had said. *You never hear the one that kills ya!* He wondered if Brennen had heard the grenade as it exploded on the ground adjacent to him. Considering it for a moment, he concluded he hadn't because he never looked back or dove for cover.

Exploding just a few feet away, razor sharp metal fragments sliced through Brennen's uniform and into his body, tearing flesh, muscles, veins, and arteries. Shredding his lungs, heart, and abdomen, his body spasmed. From a distance, Lawless watched the scene in slow motion. Brennen's torso twisted violently, his legs buckled, and he spun to the ground in a distorted heap.

Turning away, Lawless observed the barren landscape had been replaced with a carpet of lush, green grass. Resonating in the distance was the faint but unmistakable harmony of a chorus. The sky had been painted a magnificent shade of blue and almost seemed to glisten. He searched for the sun, but it was absent, yet there was a brilliant light that filled the sky in front of him. As he stared at it, a man's face came into focus.

"I've come for you, my child," he said.

Lawless knelt before him and bowed his head. "My Lord."

"Arise," the voice commanded.

Standing, Lawless stared into the face of Jesus, his Lord and Savior.

"The light," Lawless began. "It was so bright."

Smiling, Jesus said, "I am the light of the world."

"And the ground," he continued, as he looked down, "it was all dirt. Now…"

Placing a hand on Lawless's shoulder, Jesus explained, "I am the way, the truth, and the life. *All* life resides in me."

"Oh, I see," Lawless replied.

"Come, let us go. I've prepared a place for you."

"For me?" Lawless asked.

"Indeed, my child. For you."

"But why? I– I've killed people. I've done terrible things. I don't belong there."

Facing him, Jesus said, "My son, you believed in me. You accepted me. Therefore, your place is with me." He paused, placing his arm around Lawless's shoulders. "Let's walk and talk, okay?"

"Sure," Lawless said as they began walking.

"My child, do not let your heart be troubled about earthly matters."

"But it is," he said. "I mean, I always knew this day would come, when I would have to give an account for the things I've done. But…" He stopped himself, realizing there was nothing he could say that would make things right. At last, he turned to Jesus and asked, "How do I account for the lives I took?"

"You were a soldier, obeying orders," Jesus placated him.

"Yeah, but still…"

Jesus stopped and faced him. His welcoming smile was gone, replaced by the face of a proven warrior. "My child, my Father, the Lord, is a man of war. There has been war since the beginning — spiritual warfare. Your battle has not been against flesh and blood, but against evil spirits. You fought in the flesh, as a soldier, with honor and integrity. There is no shame in that."

"But the people I killed…" his voice trailed off.

"That is not your matter," Jesus explained. "That is a matter for my Father." The welcoming smile returned. "And we are going to meet him soon." They continued walking.

Lawless thought about what Jesus said. He stared at the ground, his feet making fresh imprints in the grass similar to sand on the beach.

"My child," Jesus began, "war will continue until the end. Soldiers will be called upon to fight those wars just as you were."

Mulling over his words, Lawless said, "I suppose you're right, but that doesn't make it any easier."

With half a laugh, Jesus said, "Oh, most assuredly I am right."

Lawless laughed too. "Yeah, I guess you are."

Arriving outside the gates of Heaven, they stopped. The multitude of voices was audible, their refrain clear. "Glory to God in the highest," they sang. Wide-eyed, Lawless was mesmerized by the majestic grandeur.

Continuing their conversation, Jesus said, "Perhaps you can discuss your concerns with David."

"David?" Lawless asked. "You mean…"

"Indeed," Jesus smiled. "A warrior, not unlike you. He was called at an early age, from birth as a matter of fact."

Lawless was stunned for a moment. He had never considered the people he would meet in Heaven. Staring at the gates, a litany of biblical characters ran through his mind.

"Are you ready?" Jesus asked.

"Ready for what?"

"To meet my father, of course."

"I suppose so," Lawless answered.

"Right this way," Jesus said, gesturing with his arm.

Passing through the gate, Lawless was greeted by Peter. "Welcome," he said.

"Thank you, Peter," Lawless replied. Stopping inside the gate, he looked back.

"What is it, my child?" Jesus asked.

"I was just thinking. He was crucified upside down, or that's what I remember learning in church," Lawless explained.

"Indeed. He suffered and died for the Name," Jesus explained.

Turning back, Lawless was greeted by an elegant floral bouquet. Filling the air, its pleasant aroma calmed and soothed him. Standing on the golden path, he surveyed Heaven's scene. There were no words to describe it.

"Incredible," he said, at a loss for words.

"Yes," Jesus agreed. "It is."

Jesus led the way, threading a path through the many believers, all of whom greeted him. He was the host, Lawless concluded.

His head turning left and right, Lawless was amazed at all of the animals roaming about freely. "It's like a zoo."

"Animals are special to my father," Jesus said. "You'll recall he created them first. And other than man, they are the only other creatures filled with the breath of life."

Lawless stopped for a moment. "Jesus," he began. "I've always wondered something."

"Yes, I know," he smiled. "Tell me."

"Do animals go to Heaven? I mean, when they die?"

A solemn expression washed over Jesus's face. Then he smiled. "Yes."

"Really?"

"Yes. You see, sin is a uniquely human affliction. However, when man sinned, it marred creation. The harmonious relationship that was intended to exist between man and creation was distorted."

"I see. So all dogs go to Heaven?" Lawless asked by way of humor.

Smiling, Jesus said, "They do indeed, as you will soon discover."

"You mean..."

Jesus nodded. "Yes. You will be reunited after you visit my father."

For the first time, Lawless smiled. "I'll get to see Tanya again?"

"For eternity," Jesus added, as they began walking.

At the bottom of the steps to the great throne, Lawless navigated his way through the collection of crowns. Jesus followed behind and took his seat.

Kneeling before the throne, Lawless said, "My Lord, forgive me."

"Arise my child," the voice commanded.

Lawless stood.

He who sat upon the throne had a massive book on his lap. Sliding his finger down the page, he said, "Wallace Lawless, your sins have been forgiven." He slammed the book with a dull thud. "You have been granted eternal salvation, bought for you with the blood of the Lamb." He turned and glanced at Jesus, then looked back at Lawless. "Welcome to Heaven, my child."

Bowing, Lawless said, "Thank you."

Rising, Jesus said, "Come, we have a few people to meet."

They descended the marble steps together. At the bottom, Jesus took him by the arm and said, "Let's go over here," indicating a cluster of trees to the left.

"Okay," Lawless replied.

Heading toward the trees, Lawless was overwhelmed by the surrounding splendor. He had been in a rainforest once and had admired its beauty. Untouched by man, it was tranquil and serene, what he imagined Heaven would look like. Recalling that memory, he realized it paled in comparison.

"There is so much beauty here," he said, more to himself than Jesus. "The colors...they're...I I've never seen anything like them."

"I imagine not," Jesus said. "Sin marred creation in many ways. When man's eyes were opened, they were also closed. Man lost the ability to truly see beauty as it was intended be."

Lawless merely nodded.

Arriving by the cluster of trees, the group stopped talking. They turned to Jesus and smiled. They all greeted him, and he them, by name. Turning to Lawless, Jesus said, "I believe you know these two?" He motioned with his hand to a man and woman.

"Of course," he exclaimed. Overwhelmed with joy, Lawless hugged his former neighbors from his youth. Growing up, the Bakers had been a tremendous influence on him. It was Mrs. Baker who had talked his mother into sending him to the private Christian school her own son attended. That's where he was first exposed to the Bible and Christianity. The Bakers were people of tremendous faith.

"Wally, it's so good to see you," Mrs. Baker said, smiling.

"Yeah," he replied, beaming. "It's been a long time."

"Well, you'll have to tell me all about it," she said.

Jesus interrupted. "Wally, you have someone else to meet," he said. "Someone who's been waiting a long time."

Crouching down, Jesus clapped his hands and whistled. A tan German shepherd darted out from the bushes. Running in their direction, it jumped on Lawless, who immediately bent down and hugged Tanya. "Oh, I've missed you, Tanya," he said. Rolling on the ground, he scratched her tummy.

Looking down, smiling, Jesus said, "You'll never have to say goodbye again."

Lawless stood and hugged Jesus.

"Welcome, my child!" Jesus said. "Welcome to your home."

"Thank you," Lawless replied, elated. He looked over at the Bakers and down at Tanya, who was sitting beside him.

Abruptly his expression changed.

"What is it, my child?"

"I don't see Jimbo anywhere. Did he…"

"My child, you witnessed to him and shared the Gospel and lived your faith. Never did you deny my name. Many saw me and did not believe. In fact, all of creation speaks my name. Yet man is free to choose. Jimbo chose not to believe."

24

Swirling her head, Lauren looked at Timothy and said, "I'm exhausted. Are you?"

"Yeah, now that you mention it. Feels like I haven't slept in quite a while."

"I wasn't this tired after pulling an all-nighter," Lauren said.

"There is no rest here," Sticks said.

"All part of the torment," Grandma added.

"So not only do we spend eternity burning," Lauren said, "but we'll be tired forever?"

"There'll be no rest," Shelinda corrected her, recalling a conversation with Tyrone. "No break or relief."

Lauren turned to her, throwing her a quizzical glance, unsure of how to respond.

"Sounds 'bout right," Earl chimed in. "Not like you'd be able to rest anyway, bein' on fire an' all."

You're right, Timothy thought, staring at him. He shifted his gaze to the orange doors. Massive and molten, they were ominous and portended of eternal doom. They were the only thing separating them from the inferno of Hell.

"Soon, all of your energy will be gone," Grandma said. "You'll be helpless."

"We're helpless already," Lauren said.

"Indeed we are," Shelinda affirmed.

"How can we get more helpless?" Timothy asked.

"I've never felt this helpless," Li said. "How can it can get worse?"

Sticks explained. "There is no escape from this misery. It is enduring and eternal. Rest," he paused, "rest is a luxury, a temporary deliverance, from one's troubles and anxiety. This place provides no rest or deliverance." He stopped and focused his gaze on Timothy. "The torment of Hell is total and complete. It is physical, emotional, and psychological."

And spiritual, thought Timothy.

"What's that got to do with fatigue?" Lauren asked.

"The fatigue is not just physical," Sticks contributed. "What you feel now — the exhaustion, lack of energy and focus — will only get worse. When you are fully spent, you will not be able to resist the torment. Not physically or emotionally, not mentally, not in any way at all."

"This place," Grandma began, and then paused. She looked around the dark confines, over at the gateway to misery, and then back. "This place is where you die – forever."

"Forever?" Li asked, puzzled by her comment.

"Yeah, what's that s'posed to mean?" Earl wanted to know.

"It means there is no end to the suffering, no abatement of the misery or anguish. In there," Grandma said, nodding toward the doors, "you die in every way possible, over and over and over. It's a never-ending process."

It's eternal, Timothy thought.

"How do you know that?" Li asked.

A blank expression covered her face as she turned to him and said, "The screams... Every time the gates open, you can hear the screams. Their sound never fades or diminishes. If anything," she considered, glancing at the doors, "it gets louder with each new soul."

Timothy eyed the massive doors and considered her words. He had never realized how much the volume of the screams had increased since he arrived.

"And so I just die over and over?" he asked.

"Yes," Grandma said. "It's the ultimate in suffering."

"No rest for the weary," Shelinda muttered, almost to herself.

"Ya got that right," Earl concurred. "And I'm weary already."

"Me too," Li added.

As Timothy listened to their exchange, he flashed back to a snippet that, at the time, he had regarded as boring and not applicable. "They have no rest day or night," he recalled his pastor saying.

He tried to swallow, but his throat was dry, almost as if he had swallowed a mouthful of sand. The foreboding doors in the distance stood triumphant in their finality. They were a constant reminder for those crammed into the meager waiting area that their fate was sealed. Pushing those thoughts aside, Timothy said, "I'm tired too — bushed, as a matter of fact."

"There is no life in death," Grandma said. "*Rest* is for the living."

Timothy was about to say something when a new soul arrived. Adjacent to his group, he was confused and bewildered like all new arrivals.

"Where am I?" he demanded to know.

It was Earl's turn to provide the standard answer. "Waitin'."

"Waiting? Waiting for what? Tell me," Akheem Ahmed insisted. "Where am I?"

Sticks began, "You're..." and then was interrupted. Appearing next to Akheem, a soul emerged in the darkness and the process repeated itself as Sergeant Brennen asked, "Where am I?"

Timothy listened as Sticks gave them the rundown and standard explanation. Akheem spoke first in an effort to refute what he had been told. "There is no way I can be in Hell. I am a faithful servant of Allah."

"There ain't no Allah here," Earl spat. "Just the Beast."

Turning toward Akheem, Brennen stared at him and studied his grotesque features. Not able to cut through the darkness of the waiting area, the orange glow from the twin doors danced among the shadows, intermittently highlighting individual features.

"You?" Brennen blurted.

"What do you mean, 'you'?" Akheem asked.

"You. You were our target," Brennan explained.

"Your target?" Akheem retorted, anger filling his voice.

"What 're ya two talkin' 'bout?" Earl asked.

"Yeah?" Li added, caught up in their exchange.

Looking at the group, then back at Akheem, Brennen explained. "You were our target—in

Afghanistan." He focused his attention on the group again. "I was in the Army, part of a sniper team."

"Sniper?" Akheem exclaimed. "You're the one who shot me?" he demanded to know.

"Not exactly."

"What does that mean?"

"I was the spotter. My partner," Brennan paused, looking around, searching for something but not finding it.

"Yes? Your partner?" Akheem prodded.

Shifting his attention back to Akeem, Brennan said, "My partner shot you."

"And where is he?" Akheem wanted to know.

"I don't know. We split up. He must have gotten lucky and made it out," Brennen said. "I wasn't so lucky."

"Good for you!" Akheem said, with more than a tinge of satisfaction. "You got what you deserve!"

"What I deserve?" Brennen shot back. "I'm a patriot. What are you?"

"My allegiance is to Allah!"

"A lot of good that did you. Look where you are."

"Perhaps, but unlike you, I will not be here long."

"Oh? How is that?" Brennen asked.

"Followers of Allah do not remain here forever," Akheem said.

"There is no escape from this place," Grandma interjected, her words silencing them. It was a declaration.

No one said anything as her words sank in.

Shifting topics, Brennen said, "I can't believe I ended up in the same place as you." His comment was directed toward Akheem. "You're a murderer—a terrorist! You deserve to be here. I don't."

"Me? What about you? You killed me!"

"I don't kill innocent people," Brennen defended himself.

"There are no innocent people. You justify your killing because you fight for a cause. Well, so do I!"

"I fight for freedom," Brennen retorted. "I don't blow up buildings."

"You don't blow up buildings, but you bomb cities. Women and children die. What do you say to that?"

As Timothy listened to their exchange, he observed they spoke the same language. *The language of the damned,* he thought. *Here we are all the same.*

"I fight the enemies of my country — terrorists like you, who use violence to invoke change," Brennen defended himself.

"Fighting is fighting," Akheem replied. "And war is war."

"You two can bicker forever," Earl said, "but I don't reckon it'll change things."

"What do you mean?" Akheem asked.

"He means you're stuck here like the rest of us," Sticks explained. "While you may have been misled into believing this is temporary, it's not," he said locking eyes with Akheem. "No one ever leaves. Those who enter," he said, turning in the direction of the great furnace, "never return."

His voice was solemn, as though eulogizing the departed formerly among them. Everyone fell silent and shifted their attention to Hell's entrance. Ominous, its doors were magma orange, glowing red hot like giant embers. In successive waves, searing heat pulsated from them, scorching them over and over, singeing their souls.

"The great chasm," Shelinda added, almost to herself.

Timothy caught her eye. Recognition was instant and he took her meaning. He abandoned the idea of attempting to verbalize his thoughts and recollections.

Lauren was about to ask what Shelinda meant when she was interrupted by a horrendous jolt. With a booming crash that shook the waiting area, the doorway to Hell burst open. Fire spewed out, washing over those closest to the entrance. They cried out in agony, momentarily drowned in a sea of flames. From inside his repulsive fortress, the Beast wailed as he waded toward the open doorway.

"What is that?" Brennen asked.

"The Beast," Timothy explained, keeping his voice low.

"The what?" Brennen reiterated.

Almost in a shout, Earl said, "The Beast," in a tone that conveyed annoyance.

Briefly standing in the doorway, the Beast's silhouette blocked the majority of the orange and red light that provided a modicum of illumination. Plunging the waiting area into virtual complete darkness, its isolation intensified. The shadows of souls were now invisible to one another. They were indeed alone.

"What does he want?" Akheem asked, his voice quivering in the darkness.

"Souls," Grandma's voice responded.

"Whose?" he asked.

"Everyone's," she replied.

"What is that *smell*?" Brennen asked.

"Death," Grandma said.

"I've smelled death before. That's not death. It's way worse," he observed.

"It's a different kind of death," Grandma stated. "One you've never...encountered," she added, searching for the right term.

Brennen didn't know how to respond and let it go as the Beast began to move forward.

With a series of giant strides, the Beast entered the waiting area. Molten embers trailing in his wake, he strode with purpose.

Staring at him, Timothy thought he saw the faint trace of a smile on his ghoulish face.

"There is no Beast in our teaching," Akheem said.

"Figures," Brennen said, his voice snide.

Turning his massive horned head from side to side, the Beast studied the members of the waiting area. Unlike those on death row, there would be no stay of execution. Soon they would all be dragged inside and the waiting area would be empty. None would be spared.

"He seems like he's not in a hurry," Lauren muttered to Timothy.

"Yeah, something is different," Timothy agreed.

"There's no rhyme or reason to him," Sticks added.

With purposeful steps, the Beast decreased his distance to them.

"Is it just me, or is getting hotter in here?" Brennen asked.

"The Beast radiates heat," Timothy explained, as the Beast grew closer to their location.

Towering above Brennen and Akheem, they were frozen with fear. Timothy watched as the Beast leaned forward and studied them, his blood red eyes rolling over their souls. Opening his mouth, the Beast shrieked, as he spread his arms and flexed his muscular body.

With a single, deft sweep of his arm, the Beast snatched up Brennen and Akheem. Clenching their feeble souls in his massive claw, he roared and beat his chest in triumph with his other paw. Turning, he strode back to his fiery dungeon.

The doors shut with a dull thud. Temporarily abated, the consuming heat was contained within the inferno's confines, returning the waiting area to its previous, insufferable level.

"They weren't here long," Lauren observed.

"Sure weren't," Timothy agreed.

"At least the waitin's over," Earl said by way of consolation.

"What's that supposed to mean?" Lauren asked.

"I mean this waitin' is torture. I know I'm goin' in, same as you and the rest of us. But every time that Beast comes out and leaves me here...well, it's just unbearable."

"You want to go in there?" Timothy asked.

"Heck no, but like y'all been sayin' there ain't no way around it. The torment's gettin' to me, if ya know what I mean," Earl explained.

"I know what you mean," Timothy said.

"Indeed," Sticks added, "waiting for your eternal punishment is a form of torture."

25

The morning sun blossomed overhead in a clear sky that had been painted a brilliant shade of blue. Far below in the fire engine-red cab of a classic Chevrolet pickup truck, Zachary wrapped his arm around Connie Chong, his girlfriend. Pulling her close, he echoed the lyrics blaring from the radio. "Only the good die young," he serenaded her off-key.

"If that's true, you're gonna live forever, Zach," she quipped. She studied him for a moment and admired his rugged good looks.

"Hell, yeah, I am," he proclaimed with pride and laughed.

Quickly, he grabbed her head and pulled her in for a brief but passionate kiss. "Today is gonna be a great day," he exclaimed. "I'm stoked for the Cliffs, aren't you?"

"I don't know about jumping off a cliff, but I'm excited to swim. It's not even noon and it's the nineties," she said, sticking her hand out the open window and letting it dance in the wind. Excelling in style, the classic vehicle lacked the modern amenity of air conditioning.

"Cliff diving is awesome," he exclaimed. "You'll see." As an afterthought he added, "Water might be a little cold since it's only June. Takes some time to warm up. It'll be like a giant bathtub come August," he said.

"I don't know about diving. I think that will be you and Josh, not us," she replied indicating fellow high school seniors Josh Estes and his girlfriend Melanie Anderson. "Cold water doesn't bother me. I can always warm up in the sun."

"Aw, c'mon, ya gotta try it once. It's a rush and half," he explained. "You can jump from the lower cliff. Just like the high dive at school."

"We'll see," she said dismissing his comment and left it at that.

Zach returned his attention to the road. He knew Connie would do what she wanted. *There's no persuading her,* he thought. *That's for dang sure!*

Looming just ahead, Zach could see the rusted remains of milling equipment peeking above a tree line. A steel tower that once housed a limestone collection chute rose in the distance with the name Ridge Creek Quarry in faded letters.

"There she is," he announced like a tour director.

"Where?" Connie asked.

"It's just past those trees," he said, pointing to right.

Observing the dilapidated structure, Connie asked, "What did this place used to be?"

Zach explained, "It was a limestone quarry, but when a massive underground spring was accidentally discovered several years ago, it flooded."

"That sucks!"

"You're not kidding. In less than a month the quarry filled to the brim. There was no cost-effective way to pump out the water and seal the spring. It closed a short time later," he said.

He then explained Ridge Line Quarry had been abandoned for years and filled with fresh water; it soon became a local haunt for swimmers — and for teenagers who wanted a taste of daring. Its remote location offered a measure of seclusion, which was ideal for leaping from the stone face, as well as getting to know members of the opposite sex.

"But it all worked out for us," he finished with laugh as he turned right.

"I guess so," she said.

Glancing over at Connie, Zachary smiled at his good fortune. An attractive Chinese-American, she was smart, pretty, a competitive athlete, funny, and — most importantly — his! The two started dating at the end of their junior year and had been together ever since.

Catching his gaze, she asked, "What?"

"Nothing," he said, shifting his focus back to the road.

"Don't tell me nothing. What?" she demanded.

"I was just thinking how lucky I am," he paused, then added, "to have you."

"Aww," she smiled up at him. "That's so sweet." She pressed her petite athletic body against his and planted one him. "I'm lucky too," she said, rubbing his bare chest.

Clad only in board shorts, he drove barefoot, flip-flops on the floorboard. "I guess we're both lucky."

"We certainly are!" she affirmed and flashed a brilliant smile.

Arriving at the quarry, Zach pulled up next to a silver Jeep Wrangler with its doors and top removed.

"What's up?" he said to Josh, a scraggly teen with shoulder-length blonde hair who resembled a surfer even though they were a thousand miles from the ocean.

"Not much, man. Ready to hit it?" he asked.

Zach and Connie dismounted the truck. "You know it, bro," he said as they exchanged fist bumps.

"Hey, Mel," Connie said. Connie's opposite, Melanie was tall and blonde with dazzling blue eyes. He long legs darted out the bottom of a pink floral bikini.

"Hi, C, how are you?" she asked.

"Good. Great day for the water."

"Yeah, it is. Perfect way to cap off seniors' week," she said, referring to the week off they received after final exams that preceded graduation.

"You got that right, baby," Josh said as he bear-hugged her from behind and nuzzled her neck.

This produced a giggle, as she shifted her head to fend off his tickling lips. "Ah, stop it," she exclaimed.

"Love ya, baby," Josh said, releasing her and giving her bottom a playful swat.

"Right back at ya," she said.

"Give me a hand," Zach said to Josh. He lowered the tailgate, and the two unloaded an Igloo cooler. Placing it on the ground, Zach lifted the lid, proudly displaying multiple cans of beer swimming in ice.

"That's what I'm talking about," Josh exclaimed, his voice full of adolescent enthusiasm. "You da man," he proclaimed, thumping Zach on his chest with the back of his hand.

"My dad's the man," he corrected. "He hooked us up with case."

"Yeeeaaahhh, buddy!"

"Did you bring any water, Zach?" Melanie asked. "It's supposed to be a scorcher today."

"Yeah, there's water, sweet tea, and lemonade," he said.

"And Diet Coke," Connie added, ever the one preoccupied with her figure.

Cooler in tow, they made their way through the abandoned gate. Following a path along the quarry's edge, they circled around to a makeshift beach area. It was more dirt than sand, but over the years the grass had been worn away leaving a flat area that resembled a beach.

The limestone gave the shallow water the appearance of turquoise. Placing their towels and a blanket on the ground, the four settled in for the afternoon.

"Toss me a beer, Zach," Josh said, hands out as though preparing to receive a passed football.

"You got it," he said lobbing him a frosty can. Before closing the lid, he asked the girls if they wanted one.

Melanie shook her head.

"Not right now," Connie said.

"Okie dokie," he said, letting the lid fall.

Beer cans popped open, the young men delighted in their underage consumption while Melanie and Connie applied sunscreen.

"Zach, you want any?" Connie asked, raising the blue and white generic tube in her hand.

"Nah, I'm trying to get a tan," he said, gulping from the can.

"Dude, you're gonna fry like a lobster out here today," Melanie stated.

"I'll put some on in a bit," he appeased her. "Gotta get a little sun."

"Josh?" Connie asked, twisting the bottle in his direction.

"Yeah. I'm not looking to get burned like he-man over here," he said, jabbing a thumb at Zach.

Grabbing the bottle from Connie, Melanie applied a liberal amount to Josh's back. Josh finished by covering his arms, chest, neck, and face.

Downing the last of his beer, Zach crushed the can and tossed on the ground by the cooler. "Let's do this," he said as he dove into the quarry, shattering its glass surface.

Flinging the mop of dark brown hair back with a shake of his head, he announced, "Water's not too bad. Come on in," he encouraged.

"Yeah, right!" Connie said, one hand on her hip. "I bet it's freezing, you liar."

"Really," he protested. "It's not as cold as I thought it would be."

Boys being boys, and not wanting to be outdone, Josh tilted his head back and with a series of gulps, drained the rest of his beer and followed Zach's example. Tossing the crushed can, he cannonballed into the water.

Submerged briefly, he surfaced and wiped his face. Turning to Zach, he said, "You're right. It's not that cold."

"A cannonball?" Melanie asked. "Really, mister dive team?"

Josh laughed. "Hey, that's my signature move."

"Yeah, sure it is, Josh," Connie teased. "Sure."

"I'm saving my moves for the cliffs," he defended himself. "You'll see."

"You gonna a do a triple gainer?" Zach mocked, swashing a wave of water at him.

"Nah," Josh answered shaking his head. "A quadruple gainer," he jested, a smile breaking out on his face.

"You're full of it, dude," Zach said.

"Hey, I got something special planned for today," he explained.

"Well, let's see it, big boy," Zach taunted.

"Okay, okay," he said as he waded to the shoreline and exited. Stopping at the cooler, he reached deep inside and withdrew an ice-cold beer. "I need a little extra preparation," he announced, popping the top and taking a healthy quaff before heading up the slope to a waiting cliff that dangled above the water.

At the top, he peered out at the surface below and gave a wave.

Looking up, Melanie shouted, "C'mon, Josh. Let's see what ya got."

"I'm coming," he said. Taking a few steps backward, he ran toward the edge and leapt. As he bragged, he executed a series of twists and turns before plunging into the depths of the cool, fresh water.

When he emerged on the surface, he swam to where the three were waiting. Zach said, "That was about an eight."

"Are you kidding me?" Josh said, splashing water at him. "That was at least a nine."

"No way, dude. You made too big of a splash."

"Let's see what you've got," Josh challenged him. Swinging his arm across the water's surface forcefully, he splashed him in protest.

"No problem," he replied and turned toward the shoreline. As he did, Connie grabbed him by the arm and gave him a long, youthful kiss that was passionate and sensual before he headed to a narrow dirt path that lead up to the outcrop overlooking the quarry.

Zach made his way to the top in no time. Walking forward, he looked over the edge, stared at his friends, and then shifted his eyes upward, taking in the expanse of the quarry. Other than the intrusion of birds chirping and squawking in the distance, the quarry was silent and peaceful

"We don't have all day," Josh shouted with his hand over his eyes to block the sun's intrusive glare.

"Okay. I'll be right down," he shouted back.

Backing up as far as he could, he began sprinting toward the edge, bent on outdoing Josh. A foot from edge, he slipped and left the knife edge sideways. Cascading toward the bottom, he flailed about wildly.

As they watched him fall like a circus clown, Melanie, Connie, and Josh laughed, believing his actions to be a joke.

"And he thought my dive was bad," Josh jabbed.

Landing precariously close to the shoreline, Zach's body splatted in just a few feet of water.

"Oh, my God!" Connie screamed, as they all raced to where he landed.

Normally the laws of physics would cause a falling body to plunge well beneath the surface of the water. That's what should have happened in Zach's case. But it didn't. Not gaining enough momentum to propel him away from the rock face and shoreline, he landed head first in the shallow water. A vertical stone four feet beneath the water broke his fall. Shaped like a shark's fin, it split his head and face like a melon. Zach's body collapsed in the water and floated unconscious in a pool of blood.

26

"I wonder why the Beast took both of them. I mean, they just got here," Timothy said.

"Well, from their conversation, one was a terrorist," Lauren noted. "A pretty bad guy."

"Yeah, but...the other one, he was a soldier, one of the good guys."

Grandma sneered at his comment, drawing his attention and Lauren's. "There are no good guys," she explained. "Not here. Here everyone is equally bad."

"I'm not bad!" Lauren retorted. "I'm a good person. At least I was," she added.

"So you like to think," Grandma said. "But as good as you claim to have been, you still ended up here."

"I don't know why I'm here," she responded, "but I know I'm not bad—not bad enough to end up here."

"Good people don't end up here," Grandma explained.

"Perhaps," Lauren responded, "but don't you think are variations of bad?"

"Not here, dear," Grandma replied.

"So you think a murderer is just as bad as someone who, I don't know, drinks too much and gambles?"

"Apparently that's true," Grandma said. "Let me ask you, what did you do to end up here?"

"Nothing!" Lauren shouted for emphasis. "Nothing at all. I was at the wrong place at the wrong time."

"Weren't we all," Grandma retorted.

Timothy listened to their exchange and wanted to comment, but he knew his voice would be silenced. There was no truth here except that which existed in his mind. And that was a truth that could not be spoken. Instead, he asked, "You weren't at the wrong place at the wrong time, right? Died of old age?"

"Yes, that's true," she answered.

"It doesn't make any sense," Lauren protested. "Why we ended up here or why the Beast only takes certain people."

"There's a madness to his method," Sticks pointed out. "A madness we cannot understand. In the end, it doesn't matter because we will all receive our due."

"That's not my due," Lauren said. "I deserve better than this!"

"Mine either," Li agreed. "I don't belong here either."

"All are deserving," Shelinda said.

Lauren stared at her, as did the others. Not outspoken, Shelinda said little, injecting comments here and there.

"Do you think you deserve to be here?" Lauren asked with caution, not wanting to draw attention to her admission of suicide.

"Yes," Shelinda deadpanned. "And it has nothing to do with taking my own life."

"Then why?" Lauren wanted to know.

"I made poor during my life," Shelinda replied.

"Me too," Timothy added, catching her eye. They exchanged a brief look of recognition and understanding.

"You?" Lauren asked Timothy, her voice raising an octave. "How did you choose poorly? You aren't old enough to make poor choices."

"It's not a matter of age," Shelinda said. "It has to do with accountability." Turning to Timothy, she said, "I imagine you were old enough to be held accountable."

Timothy nodded. "I was."

Lauren pondered his answer for a moment. As she did, Earl decided to add his opinion to the conversation. "I'll be the first to 'mit I made poor choices. Made 'em all my life, as a matter o' fact." He paused for a moment, thinking. "'Bout the only good choice I ever made was not selling my daddy's farm."

"You were a farmer?" Timothy asked.

Earl snickered. "For a time. But farmin's hard work. Makin' shine's much easier!"

"Oh, yeah," Timothy acknowledged, recalling his story.

"What's accountability got to do with any of this?" Lauren blurted. "And how can you not seem to care?" she hurled at Earl.

"Listen, missy, it ain't like I don't care," Earl explained. "There ain't nothin' I can do 'bout it. Neither can you."

"There's nothing any of us can do," Sticks declared. "Except wait."

As they all contemplated Sticks' words, a shadow arrived in the midst, next to Timothy. For a moment, he thought he was seeing things. Although they were all uniquely distorted and disfigured, the soul next to him resembled something from a horror movie.

With his head and face split down the middle, Zach Cooper's mouth moved on each side of his face as he asked, "Where am I?"

The term *freak show* immediately popped into Timothy's head. As he studied Freak Show, Sticks delivered what had become the standard explanation.

When he finished, Timothy asked, "What do you remember?"

"I was cliff diving with my girlfriend, best friend, and his girl," Freak Show said. "That's all I can remember."

"It'll come back to you once you have your re-live," Timothy said as he explained the impending process.

Moments later, Zachary's facial expression went blank as he relived the final moments of his life.

Zachary watched as he stumbled off the cliff and landed face first in the shallow water, splitting his head and face down the center. He watched as his friends raced to his side and called for help. Shortly thereafter fire trucks, police cars, and an ambulance arrived on scene.

Zach watched the scene unfold. Connie sobbed as the ambulance sped away. Moments later he was watching his body, strapped to a gurney, being wheeled into a trauma room. Standing over him, a nurse stood at the head of the operating table and held the two sides of his head together.

Momentarily letting go, his face separated all the way down to his chin. Remarkably his jawbone was still intact.

Like an invisible participant in a movie, Zachary stood at a distance and observed as a nurse said in a flat voice, "BP is 90 over 50 and falling." Another nurse grabbed a syringe from a stainless steel tray and inserted it into an IV tube, then plunged it. "Pushing," she said, her eyes focused on his arm.

"Still falling," the first nurse said.

Before she could reach for a second syringe, the all too familiar single tone of death permeated the operating room. Immediately the team reacted, well versed in resuscitation procedures. Adrenaline was administered via the IV. Reaching for the paddles, a physician shouted, "Clear," before zapping Zachary. They all looked at the monitor. The flat line had not changed; the tone continued to resonate. The trauma doctor tried several times to restart Zachary's heart. It was no use. With massive internal bleeding, his young body had given out.

The image in Zach's mind went blank and he returned to confines of the waiting area. He blinked his new reality into focus. "So, this is Hell?" he asked in disbelief.

"No," Grandma answered. *"That* is." She indicated the massive twin doors that glowed ominously in the distance.

"This can't be real," Zachary objected. "It just can't!"

"Oh, it's real, alright," Earl spat.

Li nodded his agreement.

"You don't understand. I graduate from high school next week," Zachary protested.

"Not anymore," Grandma said.

"Tell me about it," Lauren sympathized. "I just started college."

"But- I- I can't be dead. This has got to be some kind twisted dream."

"It's not a dream," Timothy said in a consoling tone, as though such a thing were possible.

"I had my whole life ahead of me..." Zachary's voice trailed off.

"Yeah, me too," Timothy said.

"Same here," Lauren added.

"What happened to you?" Timothy asked, curiosity getting the better of him.

"I was cliff diving. Slipped and landed on my head."

Timothy nodded. "That makes sense."

"What do you mean?" Zachary asked.

"I mean your face and head," Timothy explained. "It's split down the middle."

Zachary looked around, as though trying to get a sense of his disfigurement, but it was no use. "I can't tell what you mean." He tried to lift his arms and feel his face, but he found the effort beyond taxing. "Why is it so difficult to move?"

"This place will drain away all of your remaining energy," Sticks said. "In time, you will have no energy at all."

Zachary was still in a state of disbelief. "There's no way this is real. I refuse to believe it."

"It will sink in," Timothy said. "Doesn't take long."

"When that there Beast comes out, you'll see," Earl added.

"Beast? What Beast?" Zachary asked.

"You'll find out soon enough," Grandma said.

"He comes out of those doors," Timothy explained, shifting his eyes toward the glowing entrance to Hell, "and drags people inside."

Zachary stared at the doors. "When does he come out?"

"Whenever he wants," Grandma chimed in. "No pattern to it."

Timothy studied Zachary. Even amid his grotesqueness, he could tell Zachary was beginning to accept his fate.

A piercing shriek emanated from behind the molten doors. Like nails on a chalkboard, its shrill pitch reverberated within the souls of those awaiting their fate. Resonating, its tone was unsettling and invoked fear.

"What's that?" Zachary asked in a panicked voice.

"The Beast," Timothy said.

Bursting open, a deluge of heat poured from the inferno within. Caught in the wave, they all cried out as the searing heat engulfed them. The Beast strode through the doorway, full of defiance, and plodded in their direction.

"Wha– what– is– *that*?" Zachary stammered.

"The Beast," Timothy said.

"He's coming this way," Zachary said.

"I know," Timothy said. *Probably coming for me*, he thought.

All eyes were fixed on the Beast as he moved toward them. Timothy studied him, staring into his red eyes. They were lifeless yet at the same time were all-seeing. His arms were massive and strong, unlike anything Timothy had ever seen, and swung with each step.

As he approached them, the blistering heat intensified. Feeling like he had been set on fire, Timothy shuddered. He heard Lauren scream behind him. Stopping in front of them, the Beast studied them. Bending forward he roared like a savage animal about to attack. Then in a swift motion, his arm shot out and grabbed Grandma from their midst. Squeezing her soul like a vise, her eyes bulged.

"Aaaaaaaaaaaaaaahhhh," she blared in pain. He studied her momentarily, taking satisfaction in her strife. His grip was firm and unyielding. Her fate was sealed.

The Beast turned and retreated to his private inferno. Scanning the waiting souls as he turned, they all felt his beady eyes roll over them.

He's studying us to see who will be next, Timothy thought.

Grandma screamed at the top of her lungs in his mighty grasp. It wasn't a scream released by fear. Grandma's scream had the familiar and distinct tone of intense pain and suffering as she smoldered in the Beast's claw.

They were all helpless spectators looking and listening. Crying out in total, unabated agony, Grandma's plea was silenced only when the great doors slammed shut. The blast of heat subsided but provided little comfort.

"I'm still burning," Lauren said, her charred skin smoldering and emitting the smell of death.

"Me too," Li said.

"I feel like a pig on a spit," Earl said.

"Yeah," Timothy replied, throwing Earl a glance.

"I still can't believe this," Zachary said. "One slip on a rock, and this..." he paused, "this is my future?"

"This is not your future," Sticks corrected. "It is your past, present, and future." He stopped for a moment, letting his words sink in, then added, "In other words, this is your eternity."

My eternity too, Timothy thought.

27

"Dad, what time will Uncle Ned be here?" Jeremy asked.

Exchanging glances with his wife, Veronica, Jim replied, "Sometime this afternoon. His flight gets in at one."

"You're not picking him up at the airport?" Jeremy's younger sister of two years, Kelly, inquired.

"Not this time," her father said. "He wants to rent a car. Said it was free with all of his points."

"Is he going to the water park with us tomorrow?" Jeremy wanted to know.

"Yes," Veronica supplied.

"Awesome!" Jeremy exclaimed. Having just turned thirteen, he was growing up quickly. "The last time I saw him, I was as tall as he was. I bet I'm taller now."

Laughing, Jim said, "I don't know about that. How much do you think grew in a year?"

He caught the transient, but sad, expression that washed over Veronica's face at the reference to time. Ned was Jim's older brother. Five years apart, they had never been close. The loss of their parents within eighteen months brought them together several years ago. With their parents gone and age representing less of a difference, they were the only family each other had.

"I grew almost four inches, dad," Jeremy announced.

"Well, we'll find out if you're as tall as Ned in a little while," Jim said, glancing at his watch. "His flight from Arizona should be on the ground in a bit. He'll text me when he lands."

"What does Uncle Ned do again, Dad?" Kelly asked.

"He's a sales rep for a pharmaceutical company. Spends most of his time traveling, which is how he earns all the points for free airfare and rental cars."

"Does he like traveling so much?" Kelly asked. At eleven, she was quite precocious and inquisitive.

"He does," Jim said. "Ned has always enjoyed his freedom, what some call wanderlust."

"Wanderlust?" she asked, knitting her freckled brow.

Laughing, Jim said, "That means he doesn't like staying in one place too long."

"That's probably why he isn't married," she observed.

It was Veronica's turn to laugh. Jim turned toward her as a smile smeared across his face.

Returning his attention to Kelly, he affirmed, "I think you're right." Considering Kelly's question, Jim wanted to explain her uncle wasn't against marriage. It just wasn't something for him. Autonomy mattered most to him. Having the freedom to do what he wanted when he wanted was something he refused to sacrifice. "Why don't you and Jeremy go and make sure the guest bedroom is straightened before Uncle Ned gets here, okay?" he prompted.

"Okay," she said, full of enthusiasm. "C'mon, Jeremy." Shaking his head, Jeremy followed his sister at a discreet distance.

An hour after the guest room was prepared, Ned parked his rental car in the driveway. Before he could open the door, Jeremy and Kelly ran out the front door to greet him.

"Uncle Ned!" Kelly exclaimed.

"Hey, Uncle Ned," Jeremy said.

Hauling his hefty mass out of the car, he bear-hugged Kelly and Jeremy.

"You two have gotten so big," he said.

"Ned," Jim said as he gave him a hearty hug and slapped his back several times.

"It's good to see you, bro," he said, still hugging him.

"How are you?" Veronica asked as she gave him a brief hug. She was tall and lean and still shapely despite having given birth to two children. A daily exercise regimen combined with a vegan diet kept her looking young.

"I'm good, I'm good. So happy to be here with y'all," he said, using the back of his forearm to mop his face. Ned was the exact opposite of Jim. Ned was rotund, whereas Jim had the physique of a runner — because he was a runner and vegan like Veronica and the kids.

"Let's get out of this heat," Veronica said.

"Sounds good to me," he agreed. "After traveling all day and with this heat, I could use a cold brewski."

Jim and Veronica exchanged a quick glance as they all headed inside. Ned enjoyed his beer to say the least. While Jim and Veronica weren't exactly teetotalers, they didn't keep alcohol in the house. It wasn't part of their lifestyle, and they didn't want it to be the norm for their children.

They settled into the living room. Jim said, by way of placation and compromise, "Hey, Ned, I didn't get a chance to hit the store. How about a glass of cold iced tea or lemonade?"

"Sure. Lemonade sounds great. I can grab a brew with dinner," Ned answered, as Jim headed into the kitchen.

"Oh?" Veronica asked, intrigued.

Leaning back in the overstuffed arm chair, Ned said, "I thought I'd treat to dinner."

"Well..." Veronica began.

"Listen, I know y'all eat healthy, and I get it. We can go someplace that has vegan food. Lots of places have vegan items on their menus now. C'mon, I haven't seen you people in over a year. Let me at least treat to dinner."

Although Jim was in the kitchen, he was not out of earshot. Returning, he handed Ned a frosty glass of lemonade. With raised brows and a single, upward nod of his head, he smiled at his wife.

"Sure," Veronica said much to the delight of Jeremy and Kelly.

"Great," Ned said, taking a healthy gulp of the cold beverage. "Then it's settled."

They spent the afternoon catching up and listening to Ned detail his travels. Every time he told a story about a different city, he always talked about the food and where he ate. As Jim listened to his brother, he studied him. Recalling an image from his youth, Ned was fit and trim. Although he was never an athlete, he had been in pretty good shape. But despite his excessive weight, which teetered on the border of obesity, he was happy.

At the children's urging, they had dinner at Olive Garden. Ned pigged out on scampi and pasta, and washed it all down with several cold beers. Jim and Veronica ate plain spaghetti and salad. Kelly and Jeremy had raviolis and breadsticks.

After dinner, Jeremy and Kelly watched a movie in the family room, just off the kitchen, while the three adults sat around the kitchen table and talked.

"Thanks again for dinner," Jim said.

"Hey, you're welcome. I was happy to do it. Been too long since I saw you—and them," he added, turning his attention to his niece and nephew.

"What do y'all have planned for summer?" he asked.

"We have vacation Bible school coming up in a few weeks," Veronica said.

"Oh, well, that will be nice," Ned said, politely sidestepping the mention of religion.

"The kids are really involved in the church," Jim said.

Shifting uneasily in his chair, Ned replied, "That's, a, that's great. Keeps 'em busy, right?"

"Ned," Jim began, "it's okay to discuss the Bible and talk about church. You know where we stand. We've never hidden about who we are."

"And we don't judge you," Veronica added, patting his arm. "You're family, and we love you."

"That's right," Jim affirmed.

"I know," Ned relented. "It's just...well, the Bible and church was never my thing. I mean, if it helps y'all, I'm all for it. It's good to have something to believe in. But me?" he asked, point to his chest with a chubby finger, "I'm just not a believing kind of person."

"You can be, Ned," Veronica reassured him.

"Ned," Jim said, "give me just a few minutes to share a few things with you. If you're not interested, I'll drop it, okay? I'll never bring it up again. But," he said, leaning over the table, "I've been praying for you."

"We all have," Veronica corrected him.

"Right," Jim acknowledged turning to his wife, "we all have. Kids too."

Ned swiveled his head into the family room and back. "They've been praying for me?" he asked.

"Yes," Jim said, rising from the table. Retrieving his Bible from the kitchen desk, returned to the table, and opened it. He then shared the Gospel with his brother. "Ned," he began, "the basic message of the Bible is salvation." He paused for a moment. In John's Gospel, he read from the third chapter, sixteenth verse.

"Even I know that one," Ned said.

With a smile, Jim said, "Many do. What they don't know, though, is the simplicity of salvation of just believing and asking for forgiveness."

As Jim and Ned conversed, Kelly came over and sat on her uncle's leg. "Are you learning about Jesus?" she asked.

Her face was innocent and sweet. "Yeah, darlin', I guess I am," Ned said.

His voice lacked sincerity, which she picked up on. "Uncle Ned, don't you want to go to heaven when you die?"

It was a simple question. But the answer was more complicated than he could explain. "Sure, I do," he answered. "It's just that..."

"All you have to do is ask Jesus into your heart," she explained, "and he'll come and live there forever. Right, Dad?" she asked, looking across the table at her dad.

With a shocked expression, Jim said, "Exactly. I couldn't have said it any better."

"Just fold your hands like this," she said, interlocking her fingers as he followed suit, "close your eyes," she closed her eyes and then peeked through the corner of her right eye. "Your eyes aren't closed," she admonished.

"Okay. Sorry," Ned said in compliance and closed his eyes.

"Now repeat after me. Dear Jesus..." she waited. "You say that," she urged.

"Uh, okay. Dear Jesus," Ned repeated.

"Please forgive me..."

"Please forgive me."

"...come live in my heart..."

"Come live in my heart."

"...and make me your faithful servant."

"And make me your faithful servant."

"Amen!"

"Amen."

Jumping off his knee, she jumped up and hugged him. "See how easy that was?" she asked. "Now you'll be in heaven with all of us one day."

*   *   *   *   *   *

The next day was a scorcher and a perfect day for the water park. At 10 a.m. they arrived at the Watertown Water Park en masse. The cloudless sky provided the sun with an unobstructed line of sight to blaze over the entire park. By the time they reached the pass office, the t-shirt draped over Ned's massive frame clung to his skin. The extra weight that hung from his frame insulated him and turned his body into a self-contained sweat machine. It also put considerable strain on his heart and respiratory systems. Ned paid for his pass and entered the park.

"C'mon, Uncle Ned," Kelly led him by the hand.

"Alright, lead the way," Ned relented as they headed toward a long wooden set of steps. Although the park had just opened, the line zigzagged at the top and snaked down the steps and multiple platforms.

"This is my favorite ride, Uncle Ned. You'll love it," Kelly beamed.

Inching his way up the steps, sweat poured down Ned's face. "Feels like an oven," he observed.

Fortunately, the line moved pretty fast.

"Are you excited?" Kelly asked.

With half a laugh, Ned replied, "I'm excited to get into the water and cool off."

"The water probably isn't that cold," Kelly said.

"Well, it will still feel good," he said as they continued their climb up the wooden steps.

Once at the top, Ned and Kelly were given a large, inflated tube that fit two people. Plopping in the back, Ned's mass expanded the blue rubber of the tube. With Kelly in front of him, he asked, "You ready?"

Gripping the sides, she turned back and said, "Sure am."

"Okay," he said and pushed off, and the two headed down a steep, green ramp. As they descended, they gained speed like an airplane heading down a runway before sliding upward to the right in the half-pipe as the tube turned suddenly to the left.

"Woo!" Kelly screamed.

Heading into a series of corkscrew turns, water poured over them. Ned breathed a sigh of relief as the water washed over him. It wasn't cool by any stretch, but it was refreshing. Heading out of the last turn, they descended a short distance before being deposited in a waiting pool, where their sudden deceleration ejected them from the tube.

"That was a blast, wasn't it, Uncle Ned?"

"Sure was," he agreed.

Tube in tow, they waded to edge of the pool and waited for Jeremy, who arrived seconds later.

"My turn to ride with you, uncle Ned," Jeremy said as Ned climbed out of the pool and sloshed water on the concrete.

"Sure thing, buddy," Ned said. The two meandered their way to line, which seemed to have doubled in length.

"After this, we need to hit the wave pool," Jeremy said.

"Now that sounds refreshing." Ned smiled at the thought.

There was little to no shade at the bottom of the line, and the sun was blistering.

"I feel like an ant under a magnifying glass," Ned stated, "and I can't escape its tortuous rays."

Luckily for him, he was wet from being in the water, but that was evaporating, replaced by sweat.

"We're almost to the top," Jeremy announced.

"Thank God!" Ned said, catching his breath.

Ned wasn't used to this level of activity, or any level of activity for that matter. His life consisted mostly of sitting—sitting on planes, sitting in cars, sitting at airports, sitting in meetings, and sitting in restaurants. Traversing up the levels of steps was the most exercise he'd had in a long time.

By the time he reached the top, his heart was pounding and he was out of breath. He knew he'd have to take a break after this one. Taking the proffered inner tube, he sat in the back and Jeremy climbed aboard on the front. Grabbing the sides, Ned said, "Here we go," and pushed off as hard as he could.

As he did, he felt a sharp pain shoot down his left arm and across his chest. The pain became tightness and he struggled to breathe. Sitting in front of him, Jeremy was unaware of what was happening. As they meandered the twists and curves of the slide, he shouted, "Yeaaahhh!"

When the slide spit them out into the pool, Ned plunged to the bottom of the water before slowly bobbing to the surface. Jeremy didn't notice. Not looking back he swam to the side of the pool to wait for his uncle.

Reaching the side, he looked back and saw his uncle face down in the pool. Immediately two lifeguards jumped into the water.

"Uncle Ned!" Jeremy shouted.

The lifeguards were well trained. In seconds they had Ned on his back and were maneuvering him to the side of the pool where more lifeguards and park officials were waiting. Rolling Ned's mammoth frame out of the pool, the closest lifeguard began CPR.

Hearing Jeremy's shout, Jim, Veronica, and Kelly raced over.

"Ned!" Jim yelled.

"I called 911," a park official said. "Is he with you?" he asked Jim.

"Yeah, yeah, he's my brother," Jim said. Lifeguards bent over his brother, but all Jim could do was watch.

Veronica held her husband's arm tight and fought to hold back tears. With a blank expression, Kelly stood and watched as though nothing were wrong.

"He'll be okay, Dad," she said, looking up at him. "God will watch over him."

Jim just stared at her, not sure what to say, and stood by helplessly.

In the distance a siren blared. The rescue squad was less than a mile from the water park. They were no strangers to incidents. Every year the sun and heat won victories, some minor, some severe, and a few fatal.

Jim studied Ned. He was pale. Not the kind of pale from abstaining from sunlight. He was covered in the paleness of death. Jim stood frozen in shock and stared at his brother. His eyes were open and fixed. Jim prayed in silence, but in his heart he knew it was too late. Moments later, paramedics arrived. Assessing the situation, they administered adrenaline and started an IV. This was more out of habit and procedure than it was to stave off death.

In a matter of minutes, Ned's body was strapped to the gurney. They made their way to the waiting vehicle and slowly pushed the collapsible bed inside. Jim asked, "Where you taking him?"

"Beach General, sir," he said before climbing in the back and pulling the door shut.

Jim, Veronica, Jeremy, and Kelly watched as the ambulance sped off with Ned.

28

Ned watched as his brother, sister-in-law, niece, and nephew huddled together in prayer after the ambulance departed. He wanted tell them he was fine and not to worry, but he couldn't.

"Let's get to the car," Jim said, corralling everyone, eager to get to the hospital.

"Sure," Veronica said. "C'mon, kids," she prodded.

Ned walked with them as they made their way to the parking lot. In single file, they crossed a wooden bridge and looked both ways before crossing the main road in and out of the park.

Funny, Ned thought, *I'm not hot anymore.*

As they approached a car, a man surrounded by a bright light was waiting for them. *Looks familiar*, Ned mused.

"Ned?" the voice said.

"Yeah," he responded as he watched his family get in their vehicle.

"I've been waiting for you."

"You have? Why?" Ned inquired.

"To take you home."

"Home?" Ned asked as he stared at the huddled mass inside the car. "That's my family," he explained. "My home is with them."

Smiling, the man said, "Well, it most certainly was with them. That is, until a few moments ago."

Ned's face screwed into a contorted expression, as he recalled the events. Gradually putting the pieces together, a wave of recognition washed over his face. As he began to drop to his knees, Jesus stopped him.

"Please, my child. Stand," he said in a gentle tone.

Ned stared at him for a moment. As he took in Jesus' features, he stopped and turned around. Looking back at his brother's car, he saw Kelly sitting in the backseat. She was calm and unmoved by her uncle's loss. At perfect peace, she stared out the window almost as though she could see them.

Shifting his attention back to Jesus, Ned said, "I don't understand."

"What's to understand?" Jesus asked. "Salvation is a simple process. She understands," he said, smiling as he motioned to Kelly.

Perplexed, Ned remained silent for a moment. "What I mean is, I never did anything for you. This all just happened last night."

"Yes, I know. I was there." Jesus smiled a laugh.

"You were?"

"Of course, my child. Whenever anyone receives me, I am there. And from that moment on, I am with them—always, unto the end of the age."

"I see," Ned said. "But still..."

"Come," Jesus urged, "we'll talk about it on our way."

"On our way? Where?"

"Heaven, of course," Jesus responded.

With a blink of his eyes, Ned was no longer in the parking lot. Standing in a field of green, he detected the fain aroma of flowers as it danced on a soft breeze. Somewhere in the distance he heard singing. "Is this Heaven?" he asked.

With a brief smile, Jesus said, "No, but we're close. Let's walk and talk, shall we?" he gestured.

As they walked through the lush green carpet of grass, Ned said, "Like I was saying, this all just happened last night. And now I'm here. I didn't have a chance to do anything."

"What do you mean?" Jesus asked.

"My brother, Jim—I guess you know his name," Ned interrupted himself as Jesus allowed himself a small laugh, "he's active in his church. Teaches Sunday school, volunteers, and works with the summer camp. His wife is schoolteacher in a private Christian school. But me?" He said, turning toward Jesus, "I haven't done anything. All I did was wake up this morning...and die."

"I see what you mean," Jesus replied. "Well, let me see if I can explain, okay?"

"That would be terrific," Ned said.

"When someone accepts me as their Lord and Savior, Ned, I enter his life, his heart. I'm with that person for the rest of his life. People who believe in me are mine," Jesus pointed toward himself. "They are my sheep, and I am their shepherd. Each has a unique purpose. Therefore, they cannot die without my permission."

Ned studied him for a moment. "So you're saying you let me die?"

"In a manner of speaking, yes."

Ned's face sagged a bit.

"Don't look so downtrodden," Jesus encouraged.

"But why?" Ned wanted to know.

"Why did I let you die?"

Ned nodded.

"So you could serve your purpose, of course," Jesus answered.

"My purpose?" Ned asked.

"Yes. You see, every believer has a purpose. Young, old, male, female, rich, poor—it doesn't matter. When someone believes, that person becomes part of my kingdom. And everyone in my kingdom has a job to do, a role to serve. You had a very special purpose, Ned."

Ned considered this as they walked. Looking up, he saw a pearlescent gate just ahead. "So you're saying that even though I was only a believer for a short while—a matter of hours actually—I had a purpose?"

"Yes. Of course, you did."

Ned nodded, pursing his lips. "Okay, I'll bite. What purpose did I serve?"

"Ah, I thought you'd never ask," Jesus said, exuberance filling his voice. "Please," he motioned to his left, "observe."

The resplendent foliage vanished, replaced by the image of Jim, Veronica, Jeremy, and Kelly. Outside their house, a news van was parked in the driveway. A young, African American, female reporter stood with a microphone poised and spoke into the camera.

"I'm Shawndrika Wright, and I'm with the family of Ned Gerrard, who suffered a fatal heart attack today at Watertown Water Park."

Turning to Jim and Veronica, she said, "This is such a terrible tragedy. I'm so sorry for your loss. Was your brother in poor health?"

"He was overweight," Jim said. "In his younger days he had been an athlete, but of late…" Jim took a moment to recover. "The heat index was over a hundred today, which didn't help him any." Veronica squeezed his hand for support.

"I see," Shawndrika said, nodding, adding a generous dose of artificial sympathy for the viewers.

"We miss him," Veronica added through a choked voice.

"Yes, I'm sure you do," Shawndrika said with practiced sincerity. Bending down, she adopted the affected tone adults use when speaking with children. "What about you, sweetheart?" she asked Kelly. "Are you doing okay?"

"I'm doing just fine," Kelly beamed, not one to be bashful.

Ned couldn't help but smile at her response. "Good for her," he said, as he continued to watch.

"Oh?" Shawndrika said. "And why is that?"

"Because last night Uncle Ned prayed with me and accepted Jesus into his heart. So I know he's in Heaven with Jesus."

Kelly's response left Shawndrika speechless. "Ah…" was all she could manage before Kelly interrupted.

"Jesus lives in Heaven with God and the angels. It's where I'm going when I die, where Uncle Ned is now.

"Do you know Jesus? Because I do. I can introduce you, if you want," Kelly said. "And anyone watching. He's wonderful."

The image disappeared and the lush foliage was back. Turning to Ned, Jesus said, "You see, my child, no one, *not one*, of my children ever dies in vain. Although it may not be understood at the time, everyone has a purpose."

It was Ned's turn to be speechless for a moment. "Will anyone ever piece all that together like you showed me?" he asked at last.

"No," Jesus said with a smile. "But that's okay. You see, all that matters is you served your purpose so that someone else could serve theirs." He smiled again. "That's how it works," he added as a twinkle momentary glistened in his eye. "Christianity is...a process of sorts. Individuals believe and serve in ways unique to them. You see, all are given gifts that serve the collective, the body, that is. Each complements the other."

Ned nodded his acceptance. "Makes sense, I suppose." After considering things, he stated, "So my purpose was to allow Kelly to say what she said on the news and spread the word."

"Exactly!" Jesus exclaimed.

"And I guess her words will impact someone who was watching and so on, right?"

"Ah, now you've got it," Jesus said.

Ned nodded. "Complicated process, but it makes sense."

"We're almost there," Jesus announced. "The gate is there." With a wave of his hand, they began walking. "There's someone I want you meet," Jesus said. "You have a common experience."

Arriving outside Heaven's gate, Ned turned to Jesus and gripped his arm. With a look of concern, he said in low voice, "I can't go in there."

"Why not?"

With a gesture of his head, he said, "Those are good people in there, people who did things, lived good lives."

Jesus laughed. "Oh, I assure you, Heaven is full of sinners." Shifting his attention toward the gate and Peter, who stood at the ready, he explained, "There aren't any good people. They're all believers, like you, the only difference is all have been forgiven."

"Are you sure?" Ned asked with trepidation.

"Absolutely," Jesus said. "Absolutely. Come, let's go and meet my Father."

Peter greeted them as they passed through the gate. The bouquet of flowers washed over Ned.

"There are so many flowers," he observed.

"Yes," Jesus commented.

"What is that singing?" Ned asked as they made their way through the garden.

"Those are angels," Jesus explained. "They sing praises to my Father without ceasing."

Cocking his head to the side, Ned asked, "Are those chimes I hear?" referring to the intermittent tinkling of bells in the distance.

Smiling, Jesus said, "Yes. They ring every time a sinner repents."

Ned nodded at the explanation and wondered if they had rung when he repented as they threaded their way through groups of believers. Small groups of people engaged in conversation, but they all stopped and smiled at him as he passed by. Several threw him a wave. Tending to the enormous garden that was Heaven, people gathered fruit and vegetables that were free from blemish.

In the distance, Ned saw a field full of zebras, horses, giraffes, and lions galloping in unison. Foxes roamed about, wolves zigzagged over the landscape. With no sense of fear, they played without fear, companions for eternity.

"Place is like a zoo," Ned said.

"Something like that," Jesus replied. "All the animals are here, as you will see."

"I'm sure I will," Ned replied as they approached the great throne.

Ned's gaze was drawn up the marble steps to a golden throne surrounded by more angels than he could count. With smiles stretched across their faces, they sang in perfect harmony. Their beauty was beyond description. Ned was at a loss for words.

"They're magnificent," Ned managed, still in awe.

"Indeed," Jesus said climbing the steps.

Ned followed suit. At the top, he knelt before the throne and bowed his head.

"Arise, my son," the great voice commanded.

Staring into the face of his Creator, Ned was overwhelmed by his glory. "My Lord," he acknowledged.

A massive tome upon his lap, and Ned studied him as he turned the pages. Scrolling down the page, the Lord looked up and said, "Edward Gerrard, you have been granted salvation, sealed by the blood of the Lamb." He motioned his head to the right where Jesus was seated and looked back.

"Your sins are forgiven. Welcome to paradise, my child."

Dipping his head for a moment, Ned replied, "Thank you, my Lord."

Jesus rose and escorted Ned down the steps. At the bottom, he said, "Come with me. I want you to meet someone."

"Okay," Ned said and walked with him.

Heading toward a group of people, Jesus led the way. Patting people on the arm, he greeted everyone with enthusiasm, and they greeted him back. Arriving at the small group, he called out, "Dismas?"

A man with his back toward them turned around. "Hello, Jesus," he said. Rugged-looking with dark hair and strong features, he was an imposing figure with a gentle manner.

"Greetings. This is Ned," he said, motioning with his hand.

"Hi, Ned," he said revealing a brilliant smile.

"Dismas," Jesus began, "I thought you might recount your story to Ned. You see, he felt a little like you did when you first arrived."

"Sure. My pleasure," he replied. "Be happy to oblige."

"I'll leave you two to talk," Jesus said as he excused himself.

"So," Dismas began as they stepped away from the group, "you must have died just after repenting."

"As a matter of fact, I did," Ned confirmed.

"Me too. You see, I was crucified next to Jesus, on his right side," Dismas explained.

"Really? I don't know much about the Bible," Ned explained.

"That's okay, even if you did, you might not know much about me. I'm only in a few verses, and I'm not even mentioned by name."

"So, what's your story?"

"Well, I was a criminal—a slave, actually. Tried to escape and got caught. The Romans didn't play games. I was found guilty and sentenced. Just so happened to be on the same day Jesus was crucified, lucky for me." He paused. "I'd heard of him. Most people had, but I didn't know much. Not enough to believe."

"You never met him until that day?" Ned asked.

"No, not at all."

"What made you believe?" Ned inquired.

"Well, I'd heard about his message, the miracles he performed, healing, and so on. Romans were savages. They didn't tolerate instigators. When I saw him—Jesus, that is—carrying his cross, I just knew he was who he said he was. Hard to explain really, but I just knew it. So when Gestas, the guy on the other cross, made fun of him, I rebuked him. He didn't get it. And," he gestured to the expanse of Heaven, "a short while later I was here."

"Wow, that's pretty amazing," Ned said with bewildered expression on his face.

"When I got here and saw Jesus, I was like you. Felt like I didn't belong because I hadn't done anything. But," he said, raising his index finger, "Jesus set me straight."

"I bet he did," Ned laughed.

Dismas laughed too. "Oh, he did. He told me that what I had done would be talked about by scholars, theologians, Sunday school teachers, and ministers for a very, very long time."

"What did you do?" Ned asked.

"I believed. Just like you. You see," he said, turning toward Ned, "like Jesus explained to me, salvation is pretty simple when you get right down to it. All you have to do is believe. That's it. It's that simple."

"And that's what I did," Ned said.

"Yep. All it took was someone to show you the way. So simple, even a child could do it."

Ned thought of Kelly and smiled. "It sure is!"

29

With the departure of Grandma, Timothy's group fell silent. In many respects, she had been their leader, the one who seemed to understand the dysfunction of this place. Although there was little rhyme or reason to be found, she provided explanation. In her absence, they all fell silent. The only sound was the faint metallic hum of agonizing screams emanating from behind the fiery doors in the distance. They were an ever-present reminder that their fate—eternal damnation—was inescapable.

"I can't believe she's gone," Lauren said, verbalizing his thoughts.

"Yeah. I know. Seemed like she was here a while."

"She was here when I got here," Sticks said. "But we all have our time."

Timothy nodded. "We'll all be gone at some point," Timothy said.

"Indeed," Sticks agreed. "No one will be spared."

"Indeed, no one will," Shelinda agreed.

Li had accepted his reality and shook his head. "This is all so horrible."

For the first time since arriving in the waiting area, Timothy felt opeless and alone. Thinking back over his short life, he realized the foolishness of his decision to abandon God and drop out of church.

"This is the ultimate abandonment," he stated.

"What do you mean?" Lauren asked.

"I mean," he began, choosing his words deliberately so they could be spoken, "we're all alone. We don't have anyone. Not here, especially not in there," he said with a slight indication of his head toward Hell's doorway.

"Those who abandon become abandoned," Shelinda said.

Timothy nodded his recognition of her deeper meaning. Although his father had abandoned him and his sister at a young age, Timothy never fully understood what that meant. Not until now. Being abandoned meant more than being left behind. Abandonment removed all hope and negated love of any kind. It meant turning one's back and no longer caring.

"We turned our backs," he responded, "and ignored what we shouldn't have."

Shelinda nodded her agreement.

Mulling it over, he realized something. *You can't abandon something or someone you never cared about*, he thought. *That's what this is. God had cared about me but because I had no time for him, God turned his back on me.*

Turning to Lauren, he said, "We don't matter. We don't have any value or meaning...or significance. It's like..."

"We don't exist?" Lauren supplied.

"More like we never existed." Timothy locked eyes with Shelinda as he made his observation. Although he didn't know her background, he knew enough from her comments to know she understood the deeper meaning behind his words. He couldn't recall the verse, but he remembered the general idea about Jesus not knowing those who did not believe.

He shook his head.

"What?" Lauren asked, sensing his frustration.

"Nothing," he said, knowing he couldn't speak of such things. "It's just...this whole thing, being here, knowing I'm going in there," he nodded in the direction of the Devil's dungeon. "It's agonizing."

"Yeah," she said. "It sure is."

"This...this is Hell," Li said. "In its own way, it is Hell."

"This," Sticks announced, "is where the agony begins, in the mind, and conscience."

Timothy thought about his words. "Yeah," he said at last. "It sure does." *This is what it must be like to be on death row. The only difference is there won't be a stay of execution. No one will be making a last minute call. They had no advocates, no representation.*

As he contemplated this, he was reminded of a quote. "The greatest trick the devil ever pulled was convincing the world he didn't exist." *But he does exist,* Timothy thought. *Does he ever!*

He studied those around him. Sticks, Lauren, Earl, Shelinda, Li, and Zachary. They were all like him. *We denied God's existence and refused to believe what was so readily obvious,* he berated himself. *We were all deceived.* Refusing to believe the Devil's existence had guaranteed their admission to Hell. To reject Christ is to accept the Devil whether one realizes it or not.

Zachary listened to their comments. The newest member of their group, he had not grasped the full weight of his situation and begun to accept it. "How often does the Beast come of there?" he asked, his eyes darting to the glowing doors.

"There's no pattern," Lauren said.

Timothy nodded his agreement.

"Plus, there ain't no way to keep track from what I can figure," Early chimed in.

Timothy mused over Earl's words. *Time doesn't exist here,* he considered. The absence of time was foreign to them. Time was a unique quality that pertained to the flesh, not the spirit.

"How does the Beast decide who to take?" Zachary wanted to know.

"We don't know," Timothy answered. "Sometimes he's angry, grabs those closest to the doors. Others it seems like he's looking for certain people."

"The ways of the Beast are not understood," Sticks said.

"Just seems to take people at random," Li interjected.

"I've never seen anything like it...not in a movie...not anywhere," Zachary said.

"None of us ever have—until here," Sticks said. "The Beast is not of the earthly realm."

"What realm is he from then?" Zachary wanted to know.

"The spiritual," Shelinda supplied.

Her words hit Timothy like a thunderbolt, and he recalled something his mother had lectured him on repeatedly. "We're in a battle," she used to say, "spiritual warfare—the battle for your soul!"

Why didn't I listen? he asked himself. *I was in a battle, and I lost. I never even fought!* Fixating on the twin white-hot doors in the distance, he concluded, *I lost my soul — forever!*

"This heat is incredible," Zachary said, changing subjects. "I feel like I'm standing in a frying pan. And that smell? I can taste it." His divided head resembled a split log whose sides moved in unison as his mouth opened and closed. Gone were the recognizable facial features. "What is that?"

"The smell of death," Sticks said.

"Smells like...decay. Reminds me of infection," Zachary commented.

"In a way it is," Shelinda said.

Timothy knew she was referring to spiritual decay, the rotting of the soul. There was no life in Hell, no life of any kind. Only death. Timothy understood that all too well.

"Yeah," Timothy agreed.

"Smells worse than pig manure on a hot day," Earl interjected.

"I wouldn't know," Timothy said.

"I would," Lauren said. "He's right. It's way worse than that. Way, way worse."

"I don't smell it anymore," Timothy said. "Not much anyway."

"You get used to it for a bit," Sticks said. "But then it gets worse and starts all over. It never fades. All part of the torment."

Considering his words, Timothy said, "I guess. The heat's worse than the smell."

"Agreed," Earl said. "But not by much."

Hell had it all, Timothy thought. *Heat, smell, fear, overwhelming fatigue without rest, loneliness, and hopelessness. It's the perfect prison*

"I grew up in the heat," Earl said. "Never got used to it. Ev'ry day, in the summer on the farm, under the sun, felt like an oven. There weren't no shade, neither." He paused. "One partic'lar summer, when I a teenager, hottest summer on record, matter o' fact, I 'member my daddy sayin' it was hotter than Hell." He shook his head. "Boy, was he wrong!"

"The heat out here is nothing compared to the fire that awaits us," Sticks said.

"What fire?" Zachary asked.

"In there," Sticks motioned with his head. "The Lake of Fire."

Lauren was about to say something, when a muffled roar that shook the ground stopped her. They all stared at the glowing doors.

"Again?" Timothy asked, more to himself than the others.

"Wasn't he just out here?" Lauren commented.

"Maybe he's just angry," Timothy said.

"He's always angry," Lauren stated. "That's all he is."

"What's happening?" Zachary wanted to know.

"Don't know," Timothy said.

"Is the Beast coming back out?" he asked.

"I hope not," Timothy answered.

An eerie silence filled the waiting area. For a moment, even the resonating screams of agony seemed to be squelched.

"I don't hear anything," Lauren whispered. "I mean nothing. Why is it so quiet?"

Timothy just shook his head.

As the one who had been there the longest, they all looked at Sticks for an explanation. He remained silent and did not offer any information.

Timothy was about to ask him what he thought, when the Beast's roar caused the chamber of darkness to rumble like an earthquake. From behind the great doors, a blood-curdling shriek pierced their souls. *Is the Beast in pain?*

There was no time to consider the question. With a resounding boom, the blazing doors burst open. A tsunami of fire spilled out of the inferno.

Searing heat filled the waiting area, engulfing the waiting souls in smoldering agony.

Their screams were indistinct, an involuntary, homogenous blend of pain and suffering. Like a gruesome chorus, they wailed uncontrollably. Timothy stared at the doorway, waiting for the Beast to appear.

As the initial wave of singeing heat dissipated, Lauren said, "That's never happened before."

"It happened to me once," Sticks announced. "Before you arrived."

"Why?" Lauren asked.

"No idea," he said. "The only thing in there is burning souls."

"And the Beast," Timothy added.

"And the Beast," Sticks corrected himself.

"Speaking of…"Timothy said, eyes glued to the doorway.

Exhaling a mighty roar, the silhouette of the Beast appeared in the open entrance. A wall of fire danced behind him like a curtain upon a stage. With a giant stride, he entered the waiting area, towering over its inhabitants.

Emitting a low rumbling growl like a wild animal stalking its prey, he moved with purpose. His arms were massive, covered in scales, and flexed as he moved. Wielding enormous strength, he strode deliberately. Confident in the supremacy of his evil, he moved toward them.

Timothy locked eyes with the Beast. Immediately he knew. "This is it," he said in a low voice to himself.

Hearing him, Lauren said, "No! Don't say that."

"He's staring right at me," he said.

"Look away," she urged.

"I can't," Timothy said. Like a tractor beam, he was caught in his gaze.

Staring into the face of the Beast, fear covered Timothy. Emerging from within, it consumed him. Although the Beast's eyes were solid blood red without pupils and no sclera, Timothy felt his gaze. In a swift motion, he extended his massive paw, and the Beast snatched Timothy. Timothy was unable to look away.

Burning in the Beast's iron grasp, Timothy howled in anguish. More than the pain from the heat, the totality of fear shook him to his core. Face to face with the Beast, Timothy stared at the presence of pure evil. The full import of his situation was now upon him, and he cried out in sheer agony. Caught in the Beast's mighty grip, Timothy wailed violently. In addition to radiating heat, the Beast's paws were covered with pointed barbs. Like thorns on a rose bush, they pierced Timothy's soul as the Beast clenched his vise of a hand.

The Beast loomed over Timothy. Frozen with fear, he stared up at the primitive creature who reigned over Hell. Up close, the Beast resembled a Tyrannosaurus, except it had massive arms and no tail. His teeth were jagged, pointed, and savage. Massive horns protruded from his head.

Pivoting, the Beast about-faced. With each step toward the bottomless pit, the scorching heat increased. Unable to struggle or move, all Timothy could do was scream. As the Beast swung his arm backward, Timothy could make out the countless shadows of unbelievers that filled the waiting area.

Crossing the threshold of Hell, the massive doors slammed shut. Their dull thud was the sound of finality and an eternity of misery. Inside, Timothy looked out at the Lake of Fire. *This is more like an ocean of fire,* he thought. As far as he could he see, flames shot up from molten pit.

Bobbing in the flames were countless souls, all screaming in agony. *Noooo!* Timothy thought. *No!* Just then he felt himself flying, then falling. Plunging into the fiery depths, he tried to no avail to reach the surface. Drowning in sulfur and brimstone, his scream was stifled as he swallowed the liquid fire. Consumed, he rose to the surface for a brief instant. Other damned souls flailed about desperately around him, plunging him under the fire in order to remain on its surface.

Joining the other condemned souls, he wailed and bellowed. The fire tore away at his soul without devouring it. In the distance he saw the Beast standing on the shore. With a look of satisfaction, he delighted in the suffering. Timothy wanted to call out, to invoke God, but the molten fire filled his throat and drowned his voice.

Bouncing in the fire, Timothy looked up and saw the great chasm that separated Heaven and Hell, which could never be crossed. A scrambling hand found its way to Timothy's head and plunged him under the fire. When he bobbed back to the surface, the chasm was gone.

30

Lifting her black veil, Thelma placed the worn baseball glove inside the coffin under Timothy's left arm. Sporting a red and white jersey with matching solid white polyester pants, he was dressed in his school's baseball uniform and looked like he was ready to take the field.

"I can't believe he's gone," Janel said, standing by her side, clinging to her mother's arm. Also dressed in black, tears streamed down her face.

"I know," Thelma wept.

Surrounded by a garden of flowers, Timothy's casket was positioned in front of the church's altar. A table had been set up to the side that was lined with pictures of Timothy — sitting on Santa's lap as a young boy, Little League baseball, team photos, and yearly school portraits. They captured the images of youthful energy and of life — a life that had been cut far too short.

Entering from behind the pulpit, Pastor Stanley placed his Bible and notes on the pulpit and descended the platform. A tall, thin, African American man, graying at the temples, he possessed a gentle confidence. Lithe, he glided with refined grace.

"Good morning," he said in a deep baritone as he gave each of them a hug.

"Morning, Pastor," Thelma said, as she wiped her cheeks with a handkerchief.

Janel forced a half smile at him.

"Is it time?" Thelma asked.

Checking his watch, he replied, "We still have a few minutes. I'll go and check the vestibule." He patted her on the arm and strode down the center aisle of the modest sanctuary. With its windows open on either side, the morning sun broke through the shutters and gathered on the maroon carpet in a sea of gold.

Although empty now, in a just little while the sanctuary would be filled with family members, friends, and neighbors. A pastor for over thirty years, Stanley knew death was difficult in any circumstance, but it was particularly difficult when it was the death of a child. In his career, funerals were something he never got used to, which he considered a good thing.

"Oh, Timmy," Thelma said, looking down at her son. "You were such a joy." Unable to control the tears, she wept.

Leaning into her, Janel sobbed. "I miss him so much, Mom."

"So do I," her mother said, hugging her tightly.

"I miss you, baby brother," Janel said as a river of tears poured down her face.

Clinging to each other, mother and daughter embraced and cried together. With Timothy's demise, they were a family of two now.

The clicking of the sanctuary's door latch disrupted Thelma and Janel, who both turned toward the rear of the church. Hands clasped in front of him, Pastor Stanley stood in front of the twin doors and gave a single nod.

"Are you ready?" Thelma asked her daughter.

"No. Are you?"

Thelma shook her head and wiped her eyes a final time before shifting her attention to her pastor. At her nod of assent, Pastor Stanley opened the double doors, revealing a vestibule full of mourners. Entering single file, they walked somberly into the sanctuary. There was no hurry, no race to share a moment of joy; only sadness and grief awaited them.

Approaching the grieving mother and daughter, men and women, young and old, offered condolences, exchanged hugs, cried, and filled the empty pews. Remaining as collected as possible, Thelma and Janel hugged everyone in turn and thanked them for coming.

"I'm so sorry for your loss," some said.

Others offered words of encouragement: "I'm praying for you both."

Making his way through the line, Thelma saw her neighbor, Daryl Cavanaugh, approaching. A seasoned veteran and retired soldier, he was a rugged man with a chiseled jaw who was no stranger to confrontation. Today, though, his countenance appeared feeble and frail. He was a beaten warrior.

Taking Thelma's hands in his, he avoided her eyes and focused on the carpet. Tears streamed down his face and fought with himself not to sob as he spoke. "I'm..." he began. "I'm...so sorry, Thelma," he managed to get out before bursting into tears.

Taking him in her arms, Thelma pulled him toward her in a hug. "It's okay, Daryl. It's okay. It's not your fault," she said, rubbing his back. "It's not your fault." She held him and they wept together.

*   *   *   *   *   *

Sitting in the front row, Thelma held Janel's hand while Pastor Stanley delivered the eulogy.

Manning the pulpit, he began. "What can we say about death? We shun it, try to avoid it, even tell ourselves it won't happen to us. Yet it comes for all of us. Sometimes," he paused, glancing down at Timothy, "it comes too soon."

Thelma tried to stifle her tears with no success.

Continuing, Pastor Stanley said, "Death presents a challenge for the living—a challenge to find a new normal, a challenge to go forward, to continue on with our lives, and a challenge to fill the void another's absence has left."

Stopping, he opened his Bible and recounted the familiar story of Lazarus' death. Coming to John 11:35 he read, "'Jesus wept.'" Looking out over the congregation, he repeated the verse, his voice soft and consoling. "'Jesus wept.'" He paused for a moment. In a louder voice, he proclaimed, "This is the shortest verse in the Bible. 'Jesus wept,'" he said it again. "Why did he weep? Surely, he knew he was going to raise Lazarus from the dead. Surely, he knew he had the power to raise him. There was no doubt in Jesus' mind about what he was about to do. Yet," he motioned to his open Bible on the pulpit, "we read, 'Jesus wept.'"

The church was filled with silence. All eyes were on the man of God as he delivered his message. "'Jesus wept,'" he blared. "He wept because man was not created to die. Today, today we weep with Jesus; we mourn together at the passing of one of our own."

Janel buried her face into her mother's chest and sobbed. A neighbor sitting behind them rubbed her shoulder.

"Death is permanent, unyielding, and inescapable. It is final and unwavering," Pastor Stanley continued. "But for those who believe, it is not permanent, for Jesus said, 'I am the resurrection and the life. The one who believes in me will live even though he dies.'"

Pastor Stanley paused. He was no stranger to death. Presiding over more funerals than he cared to remember, it never got any easier. It particularly difficult when it was a child.

Stepping down from the pulpit, he stood on the platform behind Timothy. He stared at him for a long minute, and then raised his eyes to the congregation. "My friends, today we weep as remember Timothy. We mourn his passing. In the days and weeks to come, we will miss his presence. Yet at the same time, we celebrate his life. An energetic young man, he was full of enthusiasm, especially when it came to baseball. And even though he was a Yankees fan, we still let him into church."

He smiled as the congregation emitted a slight laugh in unison, thankful for the brief levity.

"Timothy's passing is a reminder to us all that life, this transient time in the flesh, is fleeting. While it may seem to pass slowly in youth, its days slip by all too quickly in old age. Like changing seasons, the spring of youth rapidly becomes the winter of old age."

Pausing, Pastor Stanley surveyed the congregation, practically making eye contact with everyone. Motioning to Timothy, he said, "Recall his memory with love and fondness, laugh, and smile. For death is not the victor. Death has been swallowed up in victory." In a triumphant boom, he said, "'Where, oh death is thy victory? Where, oh, death is thy sting?'" he quoted 1 Corinthians 15:53-55 from memory. "Our victory is in Christ, who alone bore the sins of the world. In him is eternal life for all those who believe. Let us pray."

With heads bowed, Pastor Stanley prayed, "Father, we thank you for Timothy, for his life, for those who knew him, for those whose lives he touched. We ask that you comfort all those who grieve and mourn. Provide your peace, the peace that passeth all understanding, until that day when there will be no more death, no more sadness, and no more tears. Father, I ask that you put your special blessing on Thelma and Janel. Let them feel your presence during this time. Fill them with your spirit.

And now, Father, bind our hearts together as we recite the prayer you taught us...'Our father, who art in heaven...'" he began as the congregation joined.

When they had finished their recitation, Pastor Stanley announced, "This concludes the memorial service for Timothy Jones. Everyone is invited to participate in the graveside service following."

*   *   *   *   *   *

Entering the cemetery, the driver of the hearse navigated the vehicle along the circuitous road that ran around the facility's perimeter. Right behind, Thelma and Janel sat in the back of the limousine. They rode in silence. Cemeteries were a reminder of finality and mortality that demanded quiet reverence. Coming to a stop, they waited for the driver to open the door for them before exiting.

Pastor Stanley, having ridden in the vehicle behind the limousine, arrived with them.

"How are you holding up?" he asked Thelma.

"I'm okay," she replied.

"You?" he shifted his eyes to Janel.

"Hanging in there," she said.

"Okay. We'll wait for the pallbearers and follow to the grave," he explained.

They waited as the line of vehicles came to a stop. Making their way to where they stood, a straggle of teenage boys clad in matching baseball uniforms approached the hearse.

Meeting them there, the funeral director, who had driven the hearse, opened the door and gave them similar instructions as he had at the church.

A nondescript man, he said, "Just go slow because we have a long walk, okay? I'll be at the front. Everyone ready?" he asked.

The boys all nodded in unison.

"Okay, let's go," he said.

As they slid Timothy's casket from the rear of the vehicle, the members of his middle school baseball team lined either side. Once turned toward the waiting grave, a man clad in a kilt, standing adjacent to the site, began playing "Amazing Grace" on the bagpipes.

Thelma, Janel, and Pastor Stanley fell in behind the processional with the others in tow. The morning grass was soft and damp as they walked. Flanking their pastor, Thelma and Janel each clung to his arms. The finality of the moment washed over them, and they cried and sobbed.

Entering the canopied area, the pallbearers lowered the casket onto the waiting straps that would lower the Timothy into the grave. Moving off to the side, they took their place opposite the area designated for family.

Stopping, Thelma and Janel released Pastor Stanley's arms and took their seats. Friends and family members filed in behind them and around the corners. Holding his Bible in front of him with both hands, the pastor waited with practiced patience for everyone to gather around. Turning toward the bagpiper, the clergyman gave a brief nod. A moment later the air was still and silent.

"Friends, let us pray," Pastor Stanley said. Heads bowed, he said, "Father, we thank you for your love, for loving us in our fallen state, for the salvation you offer through your son, and for providing family and friends to aid in our comfort. Be with us now as we say goodbye to Timothy. Provide your comfort. Bless all of those here and reveal your presence to them so that all may know you. Amen."

"Amen," everyone replied.

Opening his Bible, he read, "'There is a time for everything, and a season for activity under the heavens, a time to be born and a time to die.'" He closed he book and held it at his side. "Many things compete for our time today. Unless we're waiting, time is something we never seem to have enough of. We use watches and calendars to manage our time and keep track of it, but we cannot control it. God has given each of us a finite amount of time," he said as he addressed the crowd. "What we do with that time defines our lives. Make no mistake about it, friends, that time is ours. However, we must use it wisely." He paused. "The prophet Isaiah wrote, 'Seek the Lord while he may be found; call on him while he is near.'"

He stopped for a moment and focused on Thelma and Janel. With a river of tears streaming down their faces, they held each other for support.

"Friends," he continued, "we rejoice in Timothy's life, and we take comfort knowing that God is our refuge and our strength, an ever-present help in trouble. His Son, Jesus, overcame the grave and conquered death and reigns in Heaven," he proclaimed, arms raised. "Hallelujah!"

Opening his Bible, Pastor Stanley concluded the service with a reading. "'Enter through the narrow gate. For wide is the gate and broad is the road that leads to destruction, and many enter through it.'"

The full weight and import of his words struck Thelma like a thunderbolt. A panicked expression covered her face as she considered Timothy's resentment of the church and the Bible, his admitted lack of faith and disregard for eternal matters. He believed the church and thoughts about death and eternal life were for older people, not young people who had their whole lives ahead of them. It was then, in that single moment, that Thelma realized there was no hope; there was no mercy for Timothy. He had taken the Road to Hell!

Epilogue

Most of us don't like to consider our own mortality, and in our younger years, we want to think that death is too far off to think about too much. But the truth is that none of us is guaranteed tomorrow. We've all been shocked and saddened by losing a friend or family member who has tragically passed away years before their time (as happens throughout the stories in this book). As uncomfortable as the thought is, we should all pause to consider our mortality. Yet, even though life will slip from our mortal bodies, each possesses an eternal soul.

Most people believe in an afterlife (though a smaller percentage believe in something like Heaven than something like Hell). As Dr. Bishop has rightly stated, the Bible never gives us a highly detailed description of the joy awaiting redeemed humanity in Heaven. Likewise, Scripture does not graphically depict all the horrors ahead for the condemned in Hell. The bliss of Heaven and the terror of Hell both likely defy human language and imagination. Yet Jesus was clear that both Heaven and Hell are real places. His teachings on the afterlife — and the writings of the biblical authors — show us that Bishop's depictions of Heaven and Hell are certainly not beyond the pale. Heaven is a paradise, a place of eternal beauty and love in the presence of God. Hell, by contrast, is a place of continuous torment, sorrow, and eternal separation from God.

Ask the average person who says he believes in Heaven whether he's going there. If not a majority, a plurality responds with a wishy-washy, "I hope so," or an anxious "I don't know." Continue asking the same person what they think it takes to get to Heaven, and that person typically responds with, "You have to be a good person." This answer begs the next question, "Do you think you've been good enough?" The respondent often quickly returns to the original, "I hope so."

The Bible is God's word, penned by divinely inspired human authors. It definitively answers who is worthy of Heaven. Scripture tells us that "No one is righteous, no not even one" (Romans 3:10, New Living Translation). Further, the Bible says that "everyone has sinned; we all fall short of God's glorious standard." (Romans 3:23, NLT). We may find ourselves tempted to think of God as a kindly old grandfather who winks at sin as if our evil deeds and wrongdoing were nothing more than a child's mischief. But the Bible says in Romans 6:23, "For the wages of sin is death...." A wage is something earned. Sin earns us death, not just the physical death that will someday befall each of us, but spiritual death in Hell. No exceptions.

Thankfully, Romans 6:23 shifts from the worst news ("the wages of sin is death") to good news—the best news ever for fallen and sinful humanity—"but the free gift of God is eternal life through Jesus Christ our Lord." Jesus of Nazareth, the Son of God—the very God in human flesh—left His glory in Heaven and lived a perfect and sinless life among sinful humanity. Human beings would ultimately execute Him by crucifixion—perhaps the bloodiest, most painful, and overwhelmingly humiliating form of death devised by men. But the story doesn't end there. Praise God, three days after his seeming defeat at the cross, Jesus rose again from the grave, victorious against sin, death, and Hell! Jesus is alive today!

The Bible tells us in John 3:16 (NLT), "For this is how God loved the world: He gave His one and only Son, so that everyone who believes in Him will not perish but have eternal life." Fully God and fully human at once, only Jesus Christ could bear God's wrath against sin. You're not good enough or religious enough to get into Heaven. And, thank God, you don't have to be. Instead, Scripture tells us, "He is so rich in kindness and grace that he purchased our freedom with the blood of his Son and forgave our sins." (Ephesians 1:7, NLT).

The Bible tells us that God freely gives eternal salvation by His grace through faith in Jesus Christ (Ephesians 2:8-9). You can't work your way into Heaven, and again, you don't have to. What's the catch? If Jesus died for your sins and my sins — and if salvation is God's gift — then we're forgiven, and we're all going to Heaven...right? Yes, there is a catch. God's forgiveness and salvation in Christ are not automatic. The Bible calls us to repent — to turn away from our sins and selves — and turn in faith and trust to Jesus Christ. The Scriptures put it this way in Romans 10:9 (NLT), "If you openly declare that Jesus is Lord and believe in your heart that God raised him from the dead, you will be saved."

Jesus calls us not to agree with a set of facts about Him. Jesus never asks us to "accept Christ," but to put our full faith and trust in Him. But Jesus doesn't call on us to take our eternal salvation and tuck it away like some "fire insurance card." You see, eternal life doesn't begin in the hereafter — it starts in the here and now. Jesus calls us to follow Him wholeheartedly, to become His disciples. Jesus promises His followers an abundant life (John 10:10). No, Jesus doesn't promise a life free of pain, sorrow, and suffering. Indeed, He says that to follow Him in this world is an invitation to trouble (John 16:33). Instead, He assures us that He has overcome and that He is always with us (Matthew 28:20). He promises to walk with us through our trials, giving us peace that defies understanding even as life's storms howl around us (Philippians 4:6).

There's no special sinner's prayer, no formula you need to say. Just call out to God in your own words. You might say something like this: "Father in Heaven, I know I'm a sinner, and I know I'm bound for an eternity separated from You in Hell. But, I believe that you sent your Son, Jesus Christ, God in the flesh, to die for my sins. I put my faith and trust in Him—I decide to follow Christ, both here and now and in eternity. Father God, I want to see Heaven. Forgive my sins, Lord. Give me the salvation you offer in your Son, Jesus Christ, in whose name I pray. Amen."

If you have decided to follow Jesus Christ as your Lord and Savior, I encourage you to find a good Bible-teaching church. No, you don't need to go to church for Jesus to save you—and no church or denomination can save you. And yes, probably like you, most Christians have "issues." Still, the church will help you to grow. It will be a source of encouragement, accountability, and learning as you grow in a personal relationship with God, His Son, Jesus Christ, and His Holy Spirit.

Blessings in Christ,

Bart L. Denny

Th.M. and Ed.D. Candidate

ABOUT THE AUTHOR

William Bishop currently serves as the Production Manager for the Admissions Department at Regent University. Formerly, he was the Faculty Lead for the Business Department at Stratford University as well as a distinguished professor. He is a veteran of the United States Navy, where heat attained the rank of Chief Petty Officer. In support of national tasking, he deployed to the Mediterranean, Arabian Gulf, and South America. Additionally, he served as a leadership facilitator and program manager at the Center for Naval Leadership. He is the author of *The Currency of Leadership, Leadership in a Box: Developing a Networking Organization*, and *Going Home: A Networking Survival Guide*. He holds degrees from Excelsior College (BS), Regent University (MBA, DSL), and is a graduate of the Executive Education Program at Harvard Business School (Authentic Leadership Development). Bill is an avid runner, SCUBA diver, and rides his longboard for hours every week. He resides in Virginia with his wife, twin daughters, and two dogs.

—